DEAD RISING

THE TEMPLAR - BOOK I

DEBRA DUNBAR

Dead Rising
By
Debra Dunbar

PREFACE

Give thy servant an understanding heart to judge thy people, that I may discern between good and evil.
1 Kings 3: 9

CHAPTER 1

The sun had set by the time I made my way out of the theater. Mist, heavy in the muggy summer air, made the streetlights seem as if they had halos of gold. Music thumped from a club down the block, and the faint aroma of steamy garbage hit my nose.

Baltimore. My new home. A city where it seemed the streetlights were the only things with halos.

The play had sucked. What had possessed me to go see an artistic rendering of the 1793 yellow fever outbreak in Philadelphia, set to Bernstein-style music no less? Ugh. Just, ugh.

I *know* what had possessed me. Boredom. It was Wednesday night. What else was I supposed to do? Certainly not hang out with friends or go on a date like normal people. No, I was watching people die in three acts. The actors, their careers, the audience. I think a little bit of my soul died in that theater.

And now I faced the prospect of driving through the less-desirable portions of the city, thinking about jaundiced, feverish people coughing up blood clots. Driving back to my tiny, ratty apartment, where I'd sit the rest of the evening alone, sleeping and counting down the hours until I put on a scratchy polyester shirt and khaki pants, and went to my minimum wage job.

Why did I think this was a good idea? The whole thing, not just the crappy play. My days were one mind-numbing hour following the other. It was minimally better than the life I'd left back home. No wonder normal people turned to drink and drugs.

It was a sad commentary on my life that I felt a jolt of excitement to see a man standing beside my car, obviously waiting for me. He wore leather several shades darker than his skin with a chain belt. Kinky. Weird. If he'd have been a human, I would have pulled the mace out of my purse in preparation to defend myself. Since he was a vampire, I instead got out my car keys.

Yep, they were very useful when it came to gouging and scraping skin, but it was the heavy, 14-carat gold Celtic cross that hung from the keychain that would serve me best in a fight. Not that I *wanted* to fight a vampire. The gold cross and a few quick spells were all I had to combat his superior strength, speed, charisma, and those darned pointy teeth.

I could sense vampires who were within a reasonable proximity to me. By sight, definitely, although there was nothing particular about them that should have made them stand out from the other humans. No, it was something else, some kind of sixth sense, some weird feeling that crawled up my back every time one was near.

He turned and I recognized the broad cheekbones and the dark eyes. Dario.

Vampires liked to hang out around the Inner Harbor and Fells Point. I'd seen this one in a lot of the pubs where friendless women like me passed the time, no doubt trolling for tourists to eat. I'd seen him enough during the last six months that I'd started sending over Bloody Marys and leaving notes at his table with "type O Negative" and the phone number of the local blood bank.

My harassment wasn't one-sided. He liked to respond by sending me drinks loaded with those little plastic swords, or napkins with drawings of demons dragging off nuns and stick-figure knights chopping the heads off dragons. Lately he'd begun signing his artwork, which was how I knew his name. That was pretty much *all* I knew. In spite of the drinks and notes, we'd never spoken. Dario kept to his side of the pub, picking up a different woman each night. I stayed to my side, drinking cheap beer and eating happy-hour food.

Dario usually wore jeans and T-shirts, or the occasional khakis and button-downs—whatever helped him blend in best with the humans. I had no idea why the sudden Village People homage.

I snickered. "On your way to a bondage club?"

Even with his sudden lack of fashion sense, I had a weird fascination with this vampire. He didn't try to bite me, and I didn't try to cut his head off, which shouldn't have been enough to give me a thrill every time I saw him. Yes, he was always picking up women right in front of me, but that didn't dull the joy I felt every evening that I ran into him. Better them than me. The dude was total eye candy, but I wasn't desperate enough for male companionship to allow someone to chomp on my neck.

And it's not like we really had much in common, what with him being a creature of the night and me liking to be in bed by two a.m. at the latest.

He ignored my jibe regarding his outfit. "Leonora needs to see you."

"Who?" Was Leonora one of his dreamy-eyed blood

donors? Because I was not up for a threesome, tonight or any other night.

"The Mistress? The leader of the Baltimore *Balaj*?"

Balaj. The vampire equivalent of a werewolf pack or a witch coven. I hadn't known the local leader's name, which was a dumb move on my part, especially since I'd been sending one of her family alcoholic beverages pretty much since I arrived.

And yes, the thought that a vampire Mistress wanted to see me sent a cold chill up my back—one I tried to hide with a show of false bravado. "What, she wants me to make her a chai latte with an extra shot of plasma?"

Dario's face remained expressionless, as usual. In spite of my attempts, I could never get him to crack a smile. Or even scowl. "No. She needs to consult a Templar."

My hand went instinctively to my right wrist, covering the red cross tattoo symbolic to our Order. We all got one once we started Knight training. After a few weeks of covering it with wide leather bracelets I finally gave up, figuring no one would recognize the mark for what it was. Apparently I was wrong.

"I'm not a Knight."

"Obviously." His lips twitched.

Oooo, a less than subtle smack-down. It wasn't quite a smile on the vampire's face, but I'd take it. And I figured if he was smiling, then this request for my presence wasn't likely to end in my death. Although with vampires, one never knew.

Templars and vampires didn't have good history. Nine hundred years ago we'd slaughtered them by the thousands. I'm sure many of them remembered that, and the ones young enough to not have lived through the massacres would have heard the tales. We'd come to a truce back in the nineteenth century, but we weren't what you'd call friendly by any definition of the word. Metaphorically speaking, they stayed on their side of the bar and we stayed on ours.

Yeah. And I'd been sending one of them drinks for months. Clearly I liked to live dangerously.

"So what does Leonora want with a non-Knight Templar?"

"That is not for me to say." He gestured toward the black SUV parked next to my ancient Toyota Camry.

I could refuse. If he tried to force me I could poke him with my gold cross keychain, run as fast as I could and scream for help. Of course, even if I got away I'd be facing an evening sitting alone in my shitty apartment staring at the walls, thinking about yellow fever and waiting for a bunch of bloodsuckers to sniff me out. That truce should guarantee my safety, but in reality there were no guarantees. I couldn't think of anyone in my Order who had any sort of business with vampires—nothing to give me an indication of what to expect at this "meeting."

"I need some promise as to my safety." I might like to live dangerously, but walking into a house full of vampires without at least a pinky promise was beyond even *my* reckless impulses.

He sighed dramatically. "Have I attacked you in any dark alleys to date? In spite of your provocative advances I've kept my distance. I promise you'll be safe—from me, from Leonora, and from the other vampires at the house. There. Feel better?"

Advances? Provocative advances? I felt my face heat up. Friendly teasing, maybe. Provocative advances, no. In spite of his reassurances, I hesitated.

"Look, you're a Templar. As tasty as you look, dining on you carries a price that none of us are willing to pay. Now get in the car."

By price he meant the wrath of my family and Order if I

was attacked in violation of the treaty, although I got a weird feeling he was also alluding to something quite different. Either way, I'd run out of arguments, so I walked over to the passenger side of the SUV and climbed in.

Dario slid into the driver's seat and started the car. As we headed to the north end of town, I debated texting someone to let them know where I was going. Who, though? *Going to see the vampire Mistress. Call in a Knight if I'm not back by morning* wasn't the type of message that would be received well by any of my coworkers at the coffee shop. And my family… No, I was flying solo on this one.

"Templar or not, one more word about my attire and I rip your throat out." There was a sort of dry humor to Dario's voice not mirrored in his expression. I was perversely thrilled to be eliciting *some* kind of emotion from the vampire, no matter how violent his threat.

"So I can't sing YMCA?" Baiting this vampire had become my new hobby. Hopefully Dario wouldn't take my teasing as additional provocative advances.

"Not if you want to survive the night."

"Joking." I was going for some sort of dark vampire humor. I was trapped in his car. He'd already threatened my life. I figured I might as well keep going and see the extent of a vampire's funny bone.

"I gotta ask, do you guys ever turn into bats and fly around?" Once the Halloween decorations came out, I wanted to stock up on some rubber bats to send his way with the Bloody Marys.

He looked offended. "No. Do you?"

"I'm working on it. Flying, that is. It would save me a ton in gas costs, not to mention auto insurance. Although if I was going to choose an animal, I'd pick something better than a bat. A raven would be a good choice since I'm living in Baltimore."

It wasn't a total lie. Transmogrification *was* on my bucket list. Not that I was likely to reach that level of magical power in this lifetime.

The vampire shot me an appraising glance. Go ahead. Let him think I was some kind of Gandalf with boobs. Hmm, what else could I pester him about? I'd seen him consume food occasionally as well as normal human beverages. Dario turned his eyes back to the road and it was my turn to stare at him. I could make some crack about holy water, or ask if last Sunday's sermon had touched his soul in the same way it had mine. Or if he ever found himself stepping carefully around picket fencing, just in case he tripped and impaled himself through the heart.

"Why are you staring at me?"

"I was wondering if you like garlic. Like garlic bread, or white pizza, or spicy marinara because no one actually just sits down and eats garlic. I don't think anyone could do that, vampire or not."

"Are you asking me out to dinner?"

"Ghak." That, I did not expect. The idea of me asking a man out, let alone one who had, for all intents and purposes, probably been dead for hundreds of years, was inconceivable.

Unsurprisingly, Dario misinterpreted my mangled protest.

"I like Italian food." He turned to face the road, his voice bland, expressionless. "Is tomorrow night good?"

Was he joking? Oh wait, this was Dario, the vampire whose face seemed permanently botoxed into a rigid state. "Ummm…" I tried to think of an excuse, but nothing came to mind. All I did every evening was watch television and cook up Ramen noodles, or sit alone at some bar drinking the cheapest beer they had. Tonight's theatrical production had been a rare adventure.

"Sesarios? Their *granchio ancona* is quite nice, and they have a chianti I particularly like."

I opened my mouth only to snap it shut. Holy shit. I had a date with a vampire. Centuries of us slaughtering them, and them occasionally killing a few of us, and I had a date with one. I didn't think the truce meant we were free to date. Hmm. I wasn't confident enough in Dario's ability to accept rejection to correct his mistake and the prospect of some decent food *did* sway things in favor of this date.

A date. With a vampire. Dad would kill me if he found out. No, actually Dad would give me a list of questions to ask Dario, as if I were Barbara Walters on an exclusive interview. Mom was the one who would kill me. I did the side-eye thing and wondered if Dario had any intention of having *me* for dessert? That expression of satisfaction on his face…it was making me more than a bit uneasy.

Oh well. At least I had additional reassurances of getting out of this meeting with Mistress Leonora alive. Dario would want me to remain alive at least until date night.

"I'll pick you up at your place at nine."

Nine. After sunset. I'm guessing this restaurant kept late hours in the summer. Did they have vampire investors? Were they aware of the peculiar dietary inclinations of their guests? Vampires weren't truly "out" when it came to the human world, but they did trust some with the knowledge of their existence.

I wasn't sure how I felt about going to a possible vampire-friendly establishment. I'd need to make sure I slapped the leather bracelet back on to cover my tattoo, just in case someone thought I was there on official business, or decided to retaliate against me for my Order's pre-truce activities.

"Okay. Nine it is."

Certifiably insane, that's what this was. Although Templars did take the pursuit of knowledge seriously. Dad was always on my case about being well informed. How better to find out about vampires than go out to dinner with one.

You could read a book, dummy. Well, that was true and I certainly had a lot of books at my house. But nothing beat field experience when it came to research.

I gave up baiting Dario to check out my surroundings. After six months of living in this city I was ashamed to admit I wasn't familiar with anything north of Hopkins. Baltimore was an odd mix of blue and white collar, of tourists and residents, of crushing poverty and waterfront wealth. We were far from the harbor, but the houses going by outside my window definitely belonged to the well off. I'd have to GPS this later and find out exactly where we were in relation to my house.

Fancy brownstones gave way to a collection of Victorian and Queen Anne style homes with balconies and wraparound porches festooned with lush Boston Ferns. We pulled into one driveway and up to a three-story home nearly hidden behind massive oaks and maples. The dim golden light from the windows made me think of candles. Romantic, but all I could imagine was drapes catching fire and the whole house going up in flames—which wouldn't be a good thing for a house presumably full of vampires.

Dario parked the SUV alongside two others and the moment I got out I felt them—dozens of vampires. Maybe more. My skin prickled and I rubbed my arms. I couldn't see any of them, but I could feel them nearby. For a fleeting moment I wished I had my sword, but it wasn't like I could ask Dario to swing by my apartment on the way to this meeting. I didn't usually carry it around. Sitting through a play with a huge sword in hand, even a play about yellow fever, wasn't socially acceptable.

The vampire took my arm with a motion that seemed

more protective than forceful and led me across the brick courtyard to the entrance. Once inside I was relieved to find the golden light was from shaded lamps and not open flame, although why I was worried about a bunch of vampires burning to death, I don't know.

Three vampires met us in the foyer—a big bald guy and two steely-eyed women. They all wore black leather, and I forced myself to not comment. I might feel reasonably comfortable teasing Dario, whom I'd seen out and about for months and had a sort-of minimal friendship with, but not these vampires who looked like they had even less of a funny bone than Dario did.

"New blood slave, Dario?" one of the women commented. A slow smile curved her lips but never reached her eyes. "She's pretty sweet. If you don't want her, I might be interested."

Dario's hand tightened on my arm. "This one's off limits, Rosa. She's the Templar."

The woman sidled up her smile widening enough to show her fangs. I reached in my pocket and wrapped my fingers around the keychain, but Dario edged in front of me before I could pull the crucifix out. He hissed, and the woman backed off.

There was one of those significant moments of silence. I forced my fingers to relax on the crucifix.

"Leonora is waiting."

The woman tensed, then lowered her eyes, backing up and stepping to the side. This whole thing was a bad idea, but I was in it to win it at this point. Might as well soldier through this meeting. As dicey as it might get, it had to be better than yet another boring evening alone in my apartment.

My four vamp honor guard led me into a living room converted into a throne room. A carved wooden chair sat facing the door, big enough for two to sit with minimal intimacy. The windows were covered with heavy drapes, the lighting barely enough to make out the shadows. Dario halted, and since he was still holding my arm, I did, too.

And we waited. For once I kept my mouth shut. The house was eerily silent, the only sounds were the crickets outside and the brush of tree limbs against the windows. The vampires were like statues beside me. Finally I heard the soft whoosh of a door swinging on well-oiled hinges and three more vampires entered the room. The air crackled with their energy, prickling my skin and making me feel slightly claustrophobic.

So. Much. Leather. I bit my tongue and watched as one woman made her way to the seat of honor. She was tall and generously proportioned with a pale oval of a face. Her black hair was curled and arranged in a complicated updo, her eyes dramatically made up. Impressive cleavage squeezed northward from the riveted corset. The woman had a serious rack. I swear she could put a tray on her boobs and serve hors d'oeuvres.

Leonora sat. I held my breath, waiting for the tight leather pants to give way, but they held. She leaned back and crossed her legs, further testing the limits of modern tailoring.

"Solaria Angelique Ainsworth to see you, Mistress," the bald vampire beside me announced.

I cringed at the God-awful name my parents had saddled me with. Aria. Aria Ainsworth was what was on everything except my birth certificate and the family Bible. Even the shortened version was weird. I would have changed it years ago, but names had power when given in ceremony and I wasn't willing to leave that power behind—even if I had the worst name in the history of our Order.

Dario jabbed an elbow into my side. Suddenly I realized

the vampires were staring at me expectantly, and had been doing so for a while. I made a hasty bow. "Pleased to meet you Mistress Leonora."

The vampire Mistress got right to the point. "We have been told you are a Templar."

I glared at Dario who didn't even have the grace to flush. I guess this was payback for those Bloody Marys and snarky napkin messages.

"Yes, ma'am. I haven't taken my Oath, though."

She blinked. "Not taken…but you must be at least thirty years old."

"Twenty-six." Guess I needed to start moisturizing. Maybe a little Botox of my own would be a good idea.

Leonora exchanged an unreadably blank glance with Dario. "But you are an Ainsworth? Tarquin Ailpean Ainsworth's great-granddaughter?"

Okay, maybe I wasn't the only person in the history of the Templar Order who had been given a truly horrible name.

"I am."

I could feel her confusion. My great-grandfather was a legend among the Templars. His descendants had been… disappointing. Still, children of Templar families took the Oath at twenty-two and began their lifetime of service. They didn't shirk their duties for four years then skip off to make espresso in Baltimore.

"We request the gift of knowledge," Leonora announced. The former confidence in her voice was now edged with doubt.

Knights of the Temple had three guiding principles that served as the focal points of their lives. One of those involved the pursuit and recordation of knowledge, which included ensuring that knowledge was openly available to all—and that did mean all. If the Prince of Darkness himself flagged one of us down on the street corner to ask directions, we'd be duty bound to provide him with such. Good and evil were subjective concepts, and we were not in a position to judge. Only God held that right. In the normal course of things, a Knight would have smiled and told her they would be honored to do so.

But I wasn't a Knight. And I was on the verge of being evicted from my crappy apartment if I didn't find something that paid more than making lattes.

"Do you now? Well, if I decide this job is a good fit for my talents, I'll be requesting the gift of U.S. currency."

Her eyes narrowed. It was forbidden for Knights to take payment, but I had rent to pay. Overdue rent. And I was sick and tired of my Ramen noodle diet.

"How do I know you can perform this task? If you have not yet taken your Oath, then how will you guarantee your silence concerning what we are requesting of you?"

I shrugged. "I understand if you don't trust my abilities or discretion. You could always make your request to another Templar, one who actually is a Knight."

Again, there was an uneasy wordless exchange between Leonora and Dario. There were only a few thousand of us Templars left in the world, and less than one hundred on this continent. Knights don't respond to supplications for aid over e-mail or via phone, requests must always be made in person—which meant Leonora would need to travel to Virginia, New York, or California. All of those were outside the safety of her *Balaj's* territory. A Templar in the hand, no matter how untested, was definitely worth two in the bush in this instance.

After a long moment, the Mistress nodded and pulled forth a paper. She handed it to another vampire who couriered it the five steps to me. "We need you to identify this mark, and tell us everything you know about it."

I looked down at the paper. This was a *bit* embarrassing.

Everything I knew about this mark was a big fat zero. It wasn't any of the more common angel or demon sigils. Although it bore a slight resemblance to Mars, it wasn't planetary in nature. Maybe if I'd stuck around and become a Knight, I'd actually know what the heck this thing was.

I pursed my lips and pinched my chin in an imitation of my college professor. When you don't know squat about something, it's best to bullshit. "Small details make all the difference when it comes to sigils and magical marks. I'd like to consult some of my texts to confirm my suspicions, and give you a definitive answer rather than conjecturing."

All those years in boring elder meetings, and the only benefit was that I could say "I don't know" in a way that made me sound like I truly *did* know. Nobody could talk their way around a situation like the Knights Templar. Legends abounded of how we rid a holy site of the devil by talking the poor guy into a painful state of boredom.

I took a steadying breath and made my outrageous demand, ready to negotiate. "Five thousand dollars, flat fee for this job. Half up front, half upon completion."

"You have seven days." Leonora got up and walked out, flanked by her bodyguards and the three vampires who had escorted me into the room.

No negotiation? Really? Earning five thousand dollars in one week was exciting, but her easy acceptance of that amount made my stomach roll over. I looked down at the symbol on the paper again, worried that this job wasn't going to be as simple as I had originally thought.

Dario tightened his hand on my arm, almost to the point of pain, and steered me to the exit. "Hey," I protested, trying in vain to pull free from his grasp. The former protective feeling I'd had from him was gone. This seemed more like he was marching me out to rough me up in the driveway.

"I will give you your payment in the car," he told me. Was it my imagination, or did I detect an edge of disappointment to his voice?

15

The money was indeed in the car. I stuffed the wad of bills into my purse, but not before counting it first. Twenty-five hundred dollars. I'd be caught up on rent. I could stop stealing rolls of toilet paper from the library bathroom. I could actually add some protein back into my diet.

And if I didn't find out what this symbol meant in seven days, Leonora would have me at the bottom of the Chesapeake Bay, weighted down with cinder blocks, Templar or not. No, she'd probably lock me somewhere in her home for vampires to feed from until I passed out from anemia. I glanced over at Dario. He was pretty hot, and necks *were* an erogenous zone. I could see how women everywhere thought the idea of tall, dark, and handsome sinking his fangs into your neck would be orgasmic. I don't know, maybe it was, but puncture wounds hurt, blood loss was no fun, and orgasms didn't last forever. I'm quite sure they didn't last long enough to make it worth the dizzy hangover feel, throbbing neck wounds, and weeks of withdrawal symptoms.

I glanced over at the vampire in question. Maybe, with

the right vampire, it *would* be worth it. Before I could continue on with that suicidal train of thought, Dario's phone rang. He shot me a quick glance and began speaking in an unfamiliar language.

Okay. Vampire business. Not for my ears. Got it.

My hand touched the folded paper in my pocket. Where to begin my research? I had thirty or so reference books back at my apartment, not counting the occult ones I'd picked up over the years. I'd start with the basic symbols then see what was left if I removed them from the equation. With any luck, I'd be in bed in a few hours.

"I need to get back, so I'll drop you off here." Dario put his phone down and pulled the SUV to the curb, setting the emergency brake.

I looked up, surprised. "But my car is back at the theater." And we were nowhere near my house. I glanced around at the boarded up buildings, the convenience store with a healthy number of loiterers outside indulging in their own sort of commerce, at the street lights, half of which were not working.

Dario didn't answer and before I could dig in my heels and refuse to leave the vehicle, he'd unbuckled my seatbelt and was leaning across me to open the door.

No way. If he got that door open, he'd have me out with a quick shove. I thought of my gold keychain, but that was more for temporarily stalling a vampire while fleeing. I didn't want to flee, I wanted to stay safely in the car while Dario drove me home. Or to *my* car. Either one.

Since my seatbelt was off, I shifted, blocking the door handle with my body. "You can't just leave me here! Can't someone else handle it?"

"No. You need to get out. Now."

I didn't like the tone of his voice, or his fingers digging into my arms as he tried to move me aside. I wedged myself in place and braced my feet against the middle console, not bothered by the rather intimate position that put us both in. He pulled, I pushed, but ultimately his strength was greater than mine, even with the force of my weight in play. I felt the handle jab between my shoulder blades. The door flew open, and I fell backward onto the curb.

It wasn't an easy landing. The SUV was up higher than a regular car would have been, and I was launched backward from the way I'd had myself braced against the door. My tailbone hit and I rolled, not wanting to bounce the back of my head against the broken concrete of the sidewalk.

It gave Dario just enough time to slam the door, lock it, and take off. Asshole. He'd dumped me in a less-than-desirable neighborhood with twenty-five hundred dollars in my purse and nothing to defend myself with besides a can of mace and a gold keychain. Yes, I was a Templar. Yes, I'd been trained to fight, but the majority of that had been with a sword—a big hand-and-a-half sword. It's not a modern weapon. People don't go walking around cities with huge swords strapped to their backs. People don't even go walking around the countryside with huge swords strapped to their backs. Why couldn't the Templar weapon of choice be a Glock? We weren't in the Middle Ages anymore.

I had a sword, one I'd named Trusty, back in my apartment hidden under the mattress and secured by several magical spells. Why I'd bothered to bring it to Baltimore, I'll never know. It's not like I could use the thing for more than a Halloween accessory. The sword was too big to lug around. I might not have a concealed carry permit for a pistol, but I could at least stash a knife in my purse. It would come in handy the next time I got shoved out of a car in a bad area.

I was wishing I'd had a knife now. Even the ones I used to chop vegetables or cut steak would have been welcome. Dario's and my little scuffle hadn't gone unnoticed, and the group on the corner was eyeing me with amusement. Trying to preserve my dignity, I stood and brushed off my ass, giving the small crowd a quick nod as I turned to leave.

I started walking with false confidence while getting my bearings. It was important to at least look like I knew where I was going. My car was in Mount Vernon. My apartment was in Fells Point. Leonora's place had been somewhere in north Baltimore. I listened for the sound of traffic as I walked and checked the street signs, hoping to find a major intersection. I'd been here six months, but I hadn't spent my time roaming the far reaches of the city.

There were some side streets that looked like residential neighborhoods, but I decided I should stay to the main roads. Sketchy as they might be, streets with loiterers and some traffic were better than quiet neighborhoods where residents were probably used to sleeping through gunshots and fights. I paused at an intersection and made a quick decision, feeling a mixture of relief and anxiety as I saw a sign for Johns Hopkins University—ahead five miles. At least I knew roughly where I was. And I *wasn't* in the best neighborhood for after midnight on a Wednesday.

I headed south, trying for the quickest route south and east. Row houses gave way to shops and stores, small pockets of gentrification nestled among distressed properties and abandoned homes. I turned a corner and saw a church, barely indistinguishable from the shops and houses beside it. The sign above the doorway was worn, but clearly proclaimed that services at Saint Mark's Evangelical were held Sundays at eight and eleven.

Pilgrims on the path. One of our three founding principles was to safeguard the journey of pilgrims on the path. Traditionally that had meant Christian pilgrims on their way to Jerusalem or other holy sites. For the last century our elders had debated what this meant in a modern era. What defined a pilgrim? And should we expand the definition of "path" beyond one of Christianity?

Whatever the elders might eventually agree on, I doubted it included that guy beating the shit out of a hooker in the narrow space between the church and the building next to it.

I shouldn't care. I wasn't a Knight, and even if I was, I doubted any Templar would consider a hooker to be a "pilgrim on the path." Highway to hell maybe, but not on the path.

She might not be a pilgrim, and she might not be on a righteous path, but I just couldn't turn my back and walk away from someone getting the crap beat out of them, especially against the wall of a church. I dug in my purse, thinking that if I was going to be a hero, I wasn't going to be a stupid one.

It was times like this I could use that really big sword—the one I'd left home under my mattress. Luckily I'd spent the last five years pursuing non Templar-sanctioned extracurricular activities.

"Lume creo." Blue fire launched from my fingertips, speeding in a line toward the pair grappling against the wall. Before either could react, the flames licked up their pants and consumed them.

Illusion. No one was harmed in the making of this rescue, but unfortunately my little spell didn't allow me to differentiate between victim and attacker. Instead of running, the woman did the stop-drop-and-roll right beside the guy. I was hoping to keep this whole thing impersonal, but clearly that wasn't the way it was going to go down.

I ran into the alley and grabbed the woman, pulling her away from the man. *"Foi."*

The fire vanished. It took the man about two seconds longer than the woman to realize that he had no physical injury. By that point I had her out into the street. Thank you

Mom for insisting I spend all that time in the gym lifting weights.

"Run," I told her. She took off one way, her skirt still up around her waist, shoes left behind. I hesitated a second too long and felt the impact of a body tackling me from the side. My shoulder hit the ground with a sharp stab of pain, and in my sideways vision, I saw the hooker still running. *Go, baby, go.*

I rolled, feeling the gravel digging into my skin and catching my breath at the horrible stench of old sweat and garlic. Man, this guy stunk. His smell was the least of my worries as his fist punched my already bruised shoulder with the force of a Mack truck.

The woman was home free as long as she hauled ass. And the longer the guy who had knocked me to the ground kept his attention on me, the better her chances of getting away. I took a few blows to the stomach, curling in to lessen the impact and struggling to keep my dinner on the inside of my stomach.

"Bitch. What the fuck was that? I'll make you pay, bitch."

I caught my breath at the amount of garlic in the man's words, then let it out in a whoosh as his fist hit my stomach once again. I couldn't take much more of this. Out of the corner of my eye, I saw the hooker round the corner, far enough away for me to finally defend myself. I rolled, unloading the can of expired mace in the guy's face.

He screamed with the pitch and volume of a pissed-off banshee and jumped away from me. Evidently that expiration date was just a marketing ploy to convince consumers to buy more frequently, because that stuff was far from ineffective.

I scrambled to my feet, running in the opposite direction from the woman, of course. Making sure that the guy was more likely to follow me, I stumbled on purpose a few times, slowing down to look back and double check that he was after me as opposed to her. It would really suck if this asshole managed to go back for the prostitute after all I'd done to free her.

His breathing sounded like a tornado as he narrowed the distance between us. Block after block of row houses ended and I ran beside a brick fence line surrounding a park. I heard the footsteps behind me. My lungs burned along with the muscles in my legs as I hauled ass as fast as I could alongside the fence. My poor diet the past month had taken its toll, as had the lack of regular, regimented exercise I'd done up until I'd left my Templar training. And the shoes. Yes, I was blaming the shoes, too. Either way, I was one sorry Templar if I couldn't outrun a John on the straight.

Maybe that mace wasn't full strength after all. He was gaining and I could practically feel his garlic-laden breath on my neck. I was fast, but out of shape compared to him. There was no way I could outrun a guy with longer legs and some serious adrenaline. I needed to use my agility to an advantage. Reaching out my right hand I jumped, grabbing the top edge of the brick fence as I vaulted over it.

The ground was soft on the other side. I tucked and rolled, springing to my feet in what looked to be a park. Glancing around quickly to orient myself, I saw the shadows of tall trees and geometrically shaped bushes, all vague lumps of gray sheltered by the wall from the streetlights. Behind me my pursuer grunted and scrabbled as he tried to get over the brick fence. With any luck he'd give up.

Nope. I ran and heard the thud of the man's body against the ground the same moment my foot stubbed against something hard and solid, pitching me onto my face. Luckily the ground was soft and velvety grass cushioned the impact of my body against the sod. Stupid sandals. I was never wearing heels again. Only hiking shoes and joggers, just in case a vampire ditched me north of town and I needed to run from some dude who'd been assaulting a prostitute. I wasted a precious second to cradle my bruised toes and saw what I'd tripped over. It wasn't a rock, it was a grave stone.

The moon came out from behind a cloud, illuminating the "park" around me in a rolling ocean of white. Neatly placed rows of green were bisected by rectangles of marble. Ahead the markers rose several feet tall, headstones gleaming in the silvery moonlight.

The call of the moon wasn't the only thing I felt. Magic bit sharply through the air, tingling along my skin like an electric pulse. There were a lot of spells that required a full moon and a graveyard, but none smelled like rotted flesh and mothballs, none felt like a thousand maggots moving along the ground. Shit. The ground really was moving, and it *was* maggots. Grass vanished, dirt shifted like sand parting around me. I rolled, desperately trying to find some portion of the ground that wasn't turning into a silt-like form of quicksand.

Solid ground. I panted, my hair spilling around my face as I struggled to my feet, no longer worried about the man who'd been chasing me. Flesh and blood I could deal with, this I couldn't—at least not without some serious preparation.

Brushing the hair from my eyes I saw them. White smoke rolled up from five graves, swirling in columns. Limbs extended, features formed, and before me were five specters.

I heard a gasp from behind me. "Holy shit. What…who are you?"

Correction, five specters and one bulky man. He was smeared with dirt, his clothing torn from rolling in an alley and falling over a brick fence, but he still was intimidating. Well, he would have been intimidating if I hadn't been pretty sure he was pissing his pants right now.

"Magic fire. Ghosts." The man took a few steps back, his eyes huge as they darted between me and the shadowy ghosts. "You're a fucking witch. A fucking witch." He barely got the last word out before running and nearly throwing himself back over the fence. I should have been glad. That was one last threat I needed to face. Instead I was feeling a spike of fear at being left alone with five newly risen spirits.

Templar instruction on ghostly spirits was only geared to clearing a path for pilgrims and Knights to pass safely, and my extracurricular magical studies didn't lean toward the necromantic. I didn't know *anyone* who delved into that sort of thing. Evidently someone did, and that someone was nearby.

I touched my heart, and went down on one knee. The specters were fully coalesced and beginning to gather their power. My skin prickled with the chill of their presence. My heartbeat jumped, but I didn't have time for a panic attack or an adrenaline freak-out. I was trained for this. I may have spent my life in privilege, my only experience academic, but these rites had been drilled into me from the moment my Knight training began.

My heart rate normalized. I made the sign of the cross. *"Jesu, luys im chanaparhy."*

A tunnel of light appeared, reaching from my feet to the end of the cemetery. The specters shrieked, floating backward to give the glowing path a wide berth. I rose and walked carefully forward, aware that the light closed behind me as I passed. The spirits didn't give up, following me at a safe distance, howling. I still felt the chill of their presence, the malevolence of their intent. Who had brought them from the grave? And for what purpose?

A thousand years ago a necromancer would summon hundreds of spirits to march before an army, to strike fear into the hearts of the opposing forces. Many fled. If the necromancer was highly skilled, the specters could even kill. But that was history. In modern times, spirits were only called for the purpose of communing with loved ones—séances and that sort of thing.

Someone's surviving relative had a lot of money, and some pretty pissed off dead family judging from the specters following me.

The locked gates of the cemetery were in sight. Darn, I'd need to climb over them, too. I wasn't dressed for this sort of thing, and my shoes sure as heck weren't ideal either. I paused, gritting my teeth at the wave of cold that surrounded me from the spirits. I took off my cute sandals, looping the straps over my wrist. Then I began to climb.

The protective tunnel of light held until I was over the fence, then it vanished plunging me into a world of darkness. I jumped back a few steps from the gate, my heart pounding until I realized that the spirits weren't rushing to attack. As my eyes adjusted I saw the specters safely inside the grave-yard. Interesting. I paced the gates a few moments, watching them as they bounced against invisible barriers. Were they unable to leave the cemetery boundaries? Could they only go a certain distance from the resting place of their physical bodies? Or could they only wander so far from their summoner?

Either way, they were on one side of a set of iron gates and I was on the other. I smiled, waved, and headed south-east, leaving them behind.

CHAPTER 3

*E*very wall space of my tiny one bedroom apartment was covered with books. They were on my little café table, across the kitchen counters, on the floors, couch, bed. Normally they were three-deep in the cheap book-shelves and stacked in precarious columns on the floor. Now the bookshelves stood empty.

I was exhausted. I'd been up all night researching this symbol and I needed to be to work in an hour. Well, I hadn't spent *all* of my time on the symbol. I'd been acutely aware of carrying a large sum of money on me as I made my way through the city, and my apartment wasn't in the best neigh-borhood. I figured most robberies were committed by guys, so I hid the cash in a box of tampons. Then I spent about an hour on a yucky-face spell to deter anyone who might decide to check the feminine hygiene products for money. After work I'd give the cash to the landlord, but until then I wanted to take every precaution to make sure it stayed right here. Paranoid, but as Guardians of the Temple with all of its magical artifacts, we Templars tended to take the possibility of theft very seriously.

Money secure. Still no idea on the symbol. And I was going to be dead on my feet for my shift. Hopefully I wouldn't screw up too many coffee orders. That wasn't the only worry on my mind this morning, though. Those specters in the cemetery haunted me in a metaphorical sense. I hadn't seen any signs of a pending zombie apocalypse outside my window this morning, so I was assuming whatever purpose the spirits were summoned for was benign. Still...

I grabbed the quickest shower in the history of mankind and ran down the stairs in my work attire with a mess of wet hair and no makeup. I needed to pick up my car anyway. If I hustled, I'd have time for a quick stop before my shift.

Splurging on a taxi with a twenty from the tampon box, I retrieved my car and was parked in front of the cemetery in record time. Funny how different things look during the daylight hours. The neighborhood which had seemed so dark and menacing last night now just appeared battered and sad. The garbage bags in the alleyway had spilled open where rodents had chewed through, their contents beginning to ferment in the morning heat. The dealer and hooker clientele at the little corner convenience store had given way to two elderly men sipping coffee and a handful of children counting their pocket change. Even the cemetery was transformed by sunlight. The grave stones and markers were still in neat rows, but the grass showed signs of a careless mowing and the gates I'd climbed the night before were rusted. And unlocked. I pushed one and it gave way with a squawk.

Had they even been locked last night? I'd not bothered to check, assuming they were. I was just glad I didn't have to repeat my climbing again today, especially in my work clothes.

Five graves stood out among the rest, the sod tossed

about in huge clumps, the dirt looking as if someone had taken a giant mixer to it. Two men stood beside one of the disturbed plots—one with a ring of iron-gray wooly hair around a bald pate, the other younger and shaved bald. The younger shook his head in disgust as he smoothed the dirt back over the grave.

"Family of yours?" the elder man asked, watching me approach. "I'm so sorry this happened. We'll have it back to rights in just a few."

I glanced at the headstones. Robertson. Five graves right next to each other, same last name, same date of death forty years ago. I did some quick calculations on the ages. Forty and thirty-eight on the adults. Children aged sixteen, ten, and eight.

Oh my. A whole family lost in one day. Fire? Car accident? Plane crash? Whatever had happened, this certainly *was* incentive for someone to disturb spirits at rest. An aunt or a cousin, perhaps. Or even a child. By the dates on his grave, Lincoln Junior was certainly old enough to have fathered a son or daughter. I winced at the thought of being a parent at sixteen, but had seen enough of the world to know it wasn't an unusual occurrence.

"Friend of the family," I told the older man. I had no idea how well he'd known the Robertsons and didn't want to find myself caught in a lie.

He scowled down at the bare dirt. "Some people have no respect for the dead. Luckily there wasn't too much damage. Just even these up, put some sod and seed on them, and they'll be looking back to normal in a few months. I'm pretty sure I can even sand that mark off the stone, too."

Mark? I bent down and swept the dirt from the headstone, tracing the edging and words with a finger. There. It was tiny, barely noticeable. If the old man hadn't been so thorough about searching for damage, he would have missed it. It was likely any visitors would have missed the faint scratching at the corner of the stone, too. I wetted a finger and cleaned the rest of the dirt off to see it better.

And for the second time in twenty-four hours my heart raced. The graffiti that had been scraped lightly on the stone wasn't a tag or rude word, it was a symbol. It was the same symbol as was on the piece of paper I carried in my pocket, the symbol Leonora had paid me to research.

What in the world could the Robertson family, deceased forty years ago, have to do with the vampires? And what was this mark? Obviously it had something to do with the raising of the specters last night. Like the elder man had said, just a few swipes with some fine grit sandpaper would erase them. If they'd been done weeks ago, had nothing to do with the spirits I saw last night, then the symbols would have been dulled by rain by now. Just in case, I checked the other stones and saw the same mark.

"Do any of the other markers or headstones have this graffiti?"

The man shook his head. "I didn't check them all, but none of the other ones in this section do. Terrible, that someone would target this one family for such disrespect."

I didn't necessarily see raising the dead as disrespect, being a non-judgmental Templar and all, but necromancy wasn't something we got within a hundred miles of. Artifacts and grimoires dealing with the subject were mostly locked away at the Temple. Even our Librarians, who prided themselves on the pursuit of all knowledge, thought carefully before cracking one of those books open. It wasn't forbidden, but necromancy had a sort of ick factor that made a Templar want to head for a hot shower.

Suddenly it made sense why I had come up with a big fat zero in my research so far. I didn't have the right texts. Nor the right knowledge. Neither my Templar education nor my side hobby had delved into this specific branch of magic. I'd need to go elsewhere than my own library to find the answer to what the symbol meant. I had three sources I could explore, and unfortunately all three options sucked.

And I was going to be late to work if I didn't hustle up. I stood, brushing the dirt from my formerly clean khaki pants. "Thank you… uh, for taking care of them." I gestured toward the markers, not sure how to take my leave of the two men without seeming rude.

"It's my job, Miss." The elder man held out a hand. I took it and noted the warm grittiness of his skin, the solid feel of bones beneath muscle and skin, the firm grasp that went with the quick pump up and down.

Nice guy. Sucky job. Although right now I would have traded him in a heartbeat, and I didn't mean my part-time job at the coffee shop either.

* * *

THE COFFEE SHOP was busy for a Thursday. The usual lunch crowd gave way to a handful of people who made the little tables and couches into mini-offices, typing away on their laptops. Tourists wandered in, cooling down with frappe creams. I surveyed them all from behind the stainless steel of the espresso machine, feeling like a queen among her people.

They *were* my people. I'd only been living here six months —hardly a resident, let alone someone who could claim any sort of attachment to this city. Even still, I felt like I belonged here, as though I'd spent every moment of my life among the streets and waterways. I cared about this city in a way I'd never cared about a place before. And I was as enchanted by, as protective of, the residents and visitors as I would have been a schoolyard full of children.

Yeah, how sad was my life that watching random strangers like a benevolent goddess of caffeine in a coffee shop was the highlight of my day? I'd grown up so close to my tight-knit family that I'd never realized what a challenge it would be to made friends as a stranger in a new city. Templars had a bond of purpose that brought them together—the same bond that tended to exclude other humans. What was I supposed to say to these people? How could I turn random observances about weather and sports teams into a friendship? I could chop a gjenganger to pieces with a sweep of my sword, but I had the worst social skills in the world. No doubt that was the reason the closest thing I had to a friend was a sexy vampire that I hadn't even spoken to until last night.

I put a swirl in the crema of a cappuccino and smiled as I handed it to the hipster dude on the other side of the counter. I'd only been in Baltimore six months. Maybe friends in that short of time were too much to ask.

One of my coworkers sidled up to me, bumping my fist with an empty cup. "Hey, Aria. What are you doing tonight? Wanna hit the Powerplant?"

It took me a second to realize that Brandi was speaking to me. Yeah, the other employees spoke to me, as did the customers, but nobody had invited me anywhere. Loneliness vanished in a rush of excited hope. I'd never been much for going to dance clubs, but I would have attended a sewing circle if it meant I might possibly have a friend.

But there was a roll of money in my bathroom cabinet, and the potential for more. I hated to blow off the only friend offer I'd had in…well, in six months, but I had to get back to work researching. And maybe take a nap.

"Uhh, maybe next week?" What excuse could I give Brandi? I'm not really good at making things up on the fly, so I just blurted out the truth. "I'm researching a magical symbol, and I've only got a week to do it or the vampires might kill me."

I expected her to run screaming. I didn't expected a bouncy hand clap and a huge smile. "Seriously? Let me guess, you're an elf."

Huh? Whatever gave her the idea that I was an elf? "No, I'm a Templar. Not a Knight though. I left the Order before I took my oath." Honesty seemed to be working so far so I figured I'd just keep on with it.

"A Paladin! I'm *so* psyched to find out that you are into RPGs. We've got an Anderon game on Wednesdays. I'll totally see if I can invite you. Do you LARP, too?"

I was fluent in four languages, but she'd lost me. "I love to LARP." I had no idea what that was, but if it got me out of the apartment and gave me the chance to make friends I was going to LARP.

"Oh. My. God. Next Saturday is the LARP in the Park. We could use a Paladin. Meet us there at noon and wear your armor. Oh, and bring a dish for the potluck."

Brandi skipped off, shouting, "Can you believe it? Aria is a Paladin."

I didn't have the heart to correct her. Paladins were Templar wannabes, do-gooder vigilantes who ran around fighting evil. Their average life expectancy upon taking their own version of the Oath was about six months. Not that it mattered. I was more worried about where I was going to find armor by next Saturday. And figure out what the heck a LARP was.

* * *

I'D SCORED a three hour power nap after my shift that had left me feeling more groggy than refreshed. I powered onward with quick hits off an energy drink chased by a pot of coffee, sorting through books and putting ninety percent of them back on the shelves.

Three people might be able to help me. Well, two people and one... other thing.

Dad was a Librarian class Knight, which meant his specialty was cataloging and researching the vast sources of information inside and outside of the Temple. He was one of the few Templars who were entrusted with sacred texts and written-word artifacts outside of the Temple. If he didn't have what I needed in the vault at home, then he'd know where to find it. Of course, that meant I'd need to return home—supplications always must be made in person, and that rule went for us Templars as well as the humans we were supposed to help. I hadn't been back home since I left six months ago. This wouldn't be a quick in-and-out research trip. I'd be expected to stay for dinner, to catch up on family news, and to face the mess I'd made of things when I left. Eventually I'd do that, but I wasn't quite ready yet.

I'd briefly been a member of the magical society *Haul Du*. Like eight months briefly. My departure hadn't been my idea. Some jerk had discovered I was a Templar and leaked the information. Racist pigs. Although I understood their reluctance to have someone as a member who was sworn and duty bound to reclaim any item of magical significance and stash it away in what amounted to Fort Knox. Still, I felt a combination of resentment and hurt every time I thought of my dismissal from *Haul Du*. I'd made friends there—the first non-Templar friends I'd ever had. And I'd felt at home—more at home than I did even with my family. They understood the excitement of magic, the need to do more with it than lock it away in the Temple. They felt there were secrets in this world and the next, puzzles that could be unlocked through study and partnership with those above and below.

Which was my third option. There wasn't anyone at *Haul*

Du who would speak to me anymore, even Raven, who had been my closest friend. I hadn't had time to find other connections in Baltimore who might be legitimate practitioners. And I was understandably reluctant to seek them out anyway. I really didn't want to get close to a group of people, to feel a sense of belonging only to be thrown out once again. Still, I hadn't spent my eight months with *Haul Du* learning to make coins disappear or pulling rabbits from my hat. Mages weren't reluctant to go to the source when they wanted to know something. My Dad was an amazing Librarian, but there were beings that made him seem like a rank amateur.

Demons.

Yeah, I know. With proper precautions, dealing with demons—or angels, although that was a whole other situation entirely—didn't have to be a life-threatening activity. It's not like Templars weren't accustomed to dealing with celestial or infernal beings. We had a long history of communing with the messengers of God, and there were numerous times we'd defended the Temple against the minions of Satan, or beaten back the forces of darkness to clear a path for those righteous souls on pilgrimage. This was sort of the same, only different. Mages called forth these beings, containing them safely while they made their request.

Okay, actually they were demands. I'll admit that made me a little uneasy. These weren't nice postmen and waitresses we were trapping, they were beings of evil, although some of them were less evil than others. The Goetic demons who got summoned were relatively harmless. The mage asked for information and the demon was bound to provide it. Bound. As in they could not return to hell or escape the confines of the circle until they coughed up whatever the mage wanted.

Normally I never would have considered doing such a

thing, but I'd seen the ceremony performed several times. I had the ritual, and the demon's sigil that I'd seen safely summoned before. Outside of some initial bluster, the demon had seemed rather eager to provide the information, and easy to both contain and banish back to hell. Not a big deal. I'd spent my life doing lesser magics, the sort of things a Templar should know how to do. Eight months as a ceremonial magician might not sound like much, but I'd been studying their methods for nearly a decade and had quite the advantage over most of the initiates. Which was probably why someone had gotten to digging around and discovered my heritage.

I could do this. As stupid as it sounded, this was an easier and quicker option than crawling back home to ask a favor from the family who thought I'd turned my back on twenty generations of Knights. I could do this.

Yeah. And that's why my palms were so sweaty. I wiped them on my pants and picked up a copy of the leather-bound notebook I'd used as a personal grimoire while with *Haul Du*, and the three reliable books I owned on sigils and summoning. This was going to be a long night. I'd better make some more coffee.

Two cups later I was sprawled across my couch, notebook on the pillow beside me, nose-deep in one of my reference books, when I heard the knock at the door. It opened, even though I knew I'd locked it, and standing in the doorway was Dario. He wasn't wearing his bondage club attire tonight. Instead he looked like a sexy prime-time lawyer in a charcoal-gray suit with the jacket tossed over his shoulder. I stared at him over the back of my couch, stunned into silence both by his incredibly hot appearance and his nifty door opening trick. Was that a vampire thing?

"Can I come in?"

Now *that* was a vampire thing. Thresholds held power—

some more than others. Vampires weren't the only beings who needed permission to cross one, but they suffered the most in trying to force an entry.

I opened my mouth to invite him in, then snapped it shut once I remembered him ditching me in a bad section of Baltimore to walk home. He couldn't come in if I didn't invite him. All I had to do was get up and slam the door in his face. Although he could keep opening it and pestering me from outside the threshold. In all honesty, I did want to invite him in so I could chew him out for last night without all my neighbors hearing.

But not without a bit of groveling on his part first. I flung out a hand. *"Pechar."* The door swung shut, the bolt latching. I loved that trick.

Then I heard the bolt slid free and the handle turn. The door squawked as it opened. "I asked to come in."

"Pechar."

The cycle repeated itself. This was getting old. Time to drop the passive-aggressive magic and yell at him to his face.

"Please come in." I made the welcome as frosty as I could, but the vampire didn't seem to care. He strolled in as if he owned the place and I jumped off the couch, stomping around it to confront him. He blinked in astonishment as he saw me, his eyes dropping then traveling up my body. I'll admit, I didn't look my best. My hair was a massive snarl of dark-brown that I'd tied on top of my head. I'm sure it looked like some sort of personal atomic bomb blast. My clothes were wrinkled, sweat and coffee stained from work. I had on no makeup, and I probably had bags under my eyes from lack of sleep as well as indentations on my face from the couch cushions.

Dario, on the other hand, was standing there like some dapper GQ model. Screw him. I might look like a homeless waif, but he'd left me by the side of the road over an hour's walk from my house. I could have been robbed. I could have been raped or beaten up. I could have been poltergeisted by those cemetery spirits. He was in a whole lot of shit right now, and that sweet suit wasn't going to help him one bit.

"You're not going in *that*, are you?" he asked.

Huh? "Going where?"

"Sesarios. It's nine o'clock."

My brain did a one-eighty and I stared at him with my mouth open. I'm sure it added to my stunning good looks at the moment. "You don't seriously think I'm going out to dinner with you after that stunt you pulled last night? And how the hell did you know where I live?"

He smiled. It was one of those slow, panty-melting smiles, like the ones I'd seen him give his victims in pubs and clubs. I'm ashamed to admit it kinda worked on me, too. Everything south of my waistband tingled and my brain stuttered.

Hey, it had been a long time since a guy had given me that kind of look. And I did need to eat. Someone else paying for dinner was a huge incentive. I might have a bunch of money in a tampon box, but after I paid the rent, there wouldn't be much left for fancy Italian dinners.

"You must be starving." His voice was deep and smooth. It was the kind of voice that opens bedroom doors. "It looks like you've been working all day. I'll bet you've barely had anything to eat."

I hadn't. And I *was* going to give in and let him buy me an expensive dinner, complete with wine, appetizers, and dessert. But I wasn't going to give in easily even when he looked and sounded like sex on a stick right now.

"You dumped me miles from both my apartment and my car with drug deals going on less than twenty feet away, and a hooker getting beaten up in an alley a few blocks down. You've got some nerve showing up here tonight and thinking I'm going to go anywhere with you, let alone dinner."

"There was an urgent situation requiring my immediate presence." He gave me a charming smile. "Surely you understand the nature of duty and responsibility?"

I wasn't an idiot. I got the dig that I was a Templar who was past the time when I should have taken my vow. And that smile? Dario was the king of the expressionless face. If he was smiling, it was because he wanted something. I doubted it was just that red stuff flowing through my veins.

My stomach growled. I did want to pump him for more on why the vampires needed information on this symbol—a symbol connected with calling dead spirits—so much that they were willing to pay a prodigal Templar, a non-Knight, five grand to research it. And I was really, really hungry.

"Lobster, and expensive wine, and cannoli," I told him. "Actually, I want an extra box of cannoli to go." I really liked those things. Normally I'd practice some temperance to keep my lithe figure, but a month of Ramen noodles had left me with a pastry craving that would make a heroin junkie cringe.

The smile vanished with my capitulation, replaced with a critical eye. He glanced over my scruffy appearance once again. "How long will it take you to get ready?"

Are you kidding? There was a cannoli calling my name. "Give me ten."

I left him and dashed into my bedroom, stripping as I hit the doorway. A quick sponge down, a versatile black dress with heels, a quick brush of mascara, and I was almost ready —except for my hair. I hadn't combed it this morning, and it truly did look like a nuclear power plant meltdown. I ripped the elastic out, staring with dismay at the dark tangles that adored my head and cascaded down past my shoulders. Shit. Without an hour of product and flat irons there wasn't much I could do but scrape it back into a bun and hope for the best.

I managed to wrestle the knotted mess back to the nape

of my neck, pulling a couple strands out to drape along my face. There. Almost as an afterthought, I grabbed a tube of lipstick and slapped it on, noticing with amusement that it was blood red.

"Ready."

There was no double-take, no hot sultry glances. Dario looked at his watch then nodded approvingly. "Nine minutes. I'm impressed."

Great. I should have just gone in my grungy work clothes. Hopefully there'd be someone at Sesarios who appreciated my effort. Maybe I'd flirt with the waiter. In the meantime, all I had was this vampire who looked like electroshock therapy wouldn't get a rise out of him. Again I thought of last night with a bit of resentment, which reminded me that I needed to take precautions.

"Hang on a second. I need to grab something." I dashed back into my bedroom, not to get a condom but to grab a fifty out of my money stash. If Dario was going to ditch me in Little Italy after I'd had half a bottle of expensive Chianti, then I was taking a cab.

"You keep your money in a tampon box?"

I whirled around at his astonished question, shocked that he'd followed me into the bathroom and that I hadn't heard one footstep. And yes, I was still holding the box in one hand and the fifty in the other.

He tilted his head. "A tampon box that is far more repulsive and off-putting than a container for feminine hygiene products should be."

I knew my face was red. I hastily closed the lid of said box and stuffed it back under the bathroom sink, pocketing the cash. "It's a spell to deter theft. I don't always have time to run to the bank, and my rent is due."

Dario nodded and raised an eyebrow. "Nice job. I know the money is there and I wouldn't think of touching that container. Of course, I'm not particularly motivated by money."

I bit my tongue before I could ask him what he was motivated by. Not my business, and I was pretty sure I didn't want to know the answer anyway.

Sesarios was in a narrow brick building on the corner of two equally narrow streets. After slowly bouncing our way over the potholes, Dario parked his SUV at the rear of the building where the dim lights barely penetrated the shadows. I clutched my purse, resisting the urge to get out my keychain. It seemed like the perfect place for a vampire to get his blood fix for the evening, out of sight and hearing of pretty much everyone in the city.

Around front, the lighting was much stronger, as well the smell of garlic and pasta. Inside, Sesarios seemed a typical dressy Italian restaurant. Well, except for the vampires. They were everywhere, dining with others of their kind and/or human companions. I looked around, my eyes big as I tried to calculate just how many of them there must be in the city if over twenty were in this tiny place.

The hostess, a red-blooded human, took us down a set of stairs to a cozy section with even more vampire diners. Thankfully fresh baked bread and the instantly-appearing bottle of wine took my mind off being surrounded by so many undead.

I took a sip of the wine. It was good, really good. Just like the wines I'd grown up drinking. We'd pretty much remained silent since we left my apartment and I realized that unless I came up with some small talk, I was going to wind up really drunk. What topic should I introduce at dinner with a vampire? It seemed rather rude to jump right in and ask him about the Robertson family and the necromantic nature of the symbol I was researching for them. Maybe discuss the weather, or sports? I didn't know much about baseball. Did he LARP?

"So how does a Templar reach the age of twenty-six and not take her oath?"

Wow. I'd just learned that vampires had no manners whatsoever, and small talk was clearly not one of their skills.

"I didn't make the cut." I wasn't about to answer his question with the truth. It was better to have him think I was inept.

He gave me a sideways look. "You *all* make the cut. If you were a half-wit with no limbs, they'd still make you a first level Knight. There'd you stay, with the minimal pension, for the rest of your life." He took a sip of wine, and I swear I saw a faint smile. "You have fully functioning arms and legs, and although I have my doubts about your wisdom, I'm sure you're quite intelligent."

I ignored the dig about my lack of wisdom. Given that I was having dinner with a vampire, he was probably right on that score.

"Thank you." I had to change the topic of conversation and quick. "So... how about those Orioles? Think they'll make it to the World Series this year, or what?"

"They're already out of the playoffs. So why are you not a Knight? Why are you living in a cheap apartment in Fells Point and not off playing polo or guarding the Temple?"

That stung. I suddenly saw us through his eyes, wealthy and entitled people who held themselves apart from the masses and kept to themselves. If I was honest though, that was what *I* saw when I looked at my Order. We'd fallen so far from the Knights we'd been hundreds of years ago. But none of that meant I was going to side with a vampire against my own family. "I'm on an extended course of study. Super-duper top secret. I'd tell you about it, but then I'd have to kill you."

"So secret that you go around flirting with vampires in pubs, that you walk around with your Templar tattoo openly displayed? Come on, Aria, any extended course of study could be taken *after* your Oath. Why are you not a Knight?"

Flirting? I hadn't been flirting! "I think that you misread my intentions. I'm not interested in you that way. You aren't going to ever drink my blood, or do anything else with me, so get over the idea that I've been flirting with you."

I knew my face was as red as the marinara on the guy's plate at the table next to us. Oh sheesh, Dario *was* hot and I *was* tempted… but he was a vampire.

And I was a Templar.

"This hot and cold routine of yours sorely tests my willpower, Aria. I've never met a Templar before, and I'll admit I'm intrigued. Forbidden fruit is always tempting. But you know that, don't you?"

His voice had that soft note in its depths again. My eyes went to his lips and I suddenly felt like I couldn't breathe. He was accusing me of teasing. Was I? Had I been? No. The Bloody Marys and notes might have been construed as flirtatious, but I hadn't meant that. I'd never done anything to let him think I was remotely interested in having him in my bed —or his fangs in my neck.

Liar. My pulse raced and Dario's gaze went to my throat. He was good-looking, sexy, and he was right—something in me loved to play with the forbidden. Play. Not have. I *had* been teasing.

"Sorry. I didn't meant to lead you on like that." My voice sounded as though I'd not had a drink of water in days. His eyes darkened.

"If you were human, I would have taken you months ago and locked you in my house to be my blood slave. Every night I'd arise to claim you as mine. I'd leave you in the morning so weak you could hardly stand."

Why did that sound so hot? Oh. My. God.

"But I *am* human." Why did I say *that*? It was as if I *wanted* him to carry me off. I knew what happened to blood slaves. It wasn't pretty, and it was a life usually measured in weeks. Or months if your master had a decent measure of restraint.

"Yes, but unlike most humans *you* are a Templar. We vampires might outnumber you thousands to one, but Templars have access to a storehouse of weapons. I don't ever wish to be on the business end of any of those weapons."

The Temple. We were forbidden from using any of the artifacts. We were only to catalog them, to keep them safe. But...yes, we did have access to magical items that could level the world and destroy pretty much any being alive or dead. Still, if the threat of weapons in the Temple was the only thing that held him back, those tethers were gossamer thin. No Templar would break their vow and remove *anything* from the Temple.

Dario gave me a wry smile and reached out a finger to trace the column of my neck. "I remember enough of my lost humanity to know how a parent feels when their daughter is threatened. Truce or not, your father would unleash the hounds of hell if he thought I harmed one hair on your head."

Not true. It was my mother he needed to fear. Dad would tell her which hounds to use, and she'd come to my rescue like a Valkyrie on the warpath. Lately our relationship had been rocky at best. She never missed an opportunity to remind me of what a disappointment I'd been, but if the shit hit the fan, she'd not hesitate to give her life in my defense. Or in vengeance.

"Even so." Dario stroked the pulse that beat in my neck, his voice husky. "Even so, I might find death by some ancient weapon worth the risk. Immortality is but a punishment if one does not take the very things which make one feel alive. So be careful, Aria. I have lost control in the past, and that was nothing compared to the very primal urges I feel right now."

I couldn't breathe. Even after he took his hand from my neck and turned his gaze from mine, I still couldn't breathe. At that moment, nothing seemed to appeal more than throwing my life aside for a brief existence of servitude to a vampire—*this* vampire.

His eyes locked on mine once again as he sipped from the wine glass. The red Chianti reminded me of blood and I curled my fingers against the table.

"Why didn't you take your Oath, Aria?"

The words didn't sway me as much as his dark eyes and seductive tone. I was in trouble, serious trouble, with this vampire. *Snap out of it, Aria.* "I didn't want to. I may never want to. And that makes living with my family or with other Templars kind of uncomfortable."

So much for not answering his question. Dario looked oddly pleased with himself. I wasn't pleased—either with him or with myself. Some shitty Templar I was, giving in with a few sips of wine and sexy-vampire talk. Lord forbid I ever face serious interrogation. I'd fold like wet cardboard, especially if I had a decent glass of wine in my hand and a hot guy within half a mile.

"What was it like, growing up a Templar?"

I gulped down half of my wine. Might as well have something to blame all this on besides my hormones and lack of willpower. "It was pretty much like any other childhood. Well, except for training in swordplay and practicing protective blessings since the age of six."

"So ...soccer, birthday parties with bounce houses, and summer vacations at Disney World?"

I snorted and drained the rest of my wine. "Uh, no. No birthday parties, vacations were in France and Italy studying art history, and our sporting events were equestrian activities. It's critical that we be skilled in riding, just in case we needed to throw on some plate mail and thunder across the fields of battle on our charger."

He smiled. I actually got a vampire to smile—*this* vampire. Score one for me.

"So what was *your* childhood like?" The moment I asked I could have kicked myself. He was a vampire. His childhood was probably in the eleventh century.

The smile faded. "I don't really remember my childhood. I'm fairly sure it didn't include art history or equestrian activities, though."

Where was that wine? I grabbed the bottle and filled my glass, taking another gulp.

He toyed with his glass, long fingers caressing the edge. "I *can* tell you what it's like to be a vampire. Since you've been so forthcoming about your life."

I set down the wine. "I'd like that."

"Okay." Dario set his wine aside and leaned forward, both arms on the table. "I was turned in Haiti and brought to what is now Florida. I remained there with my Master and *Balaj* until a rival clan forced us out. We made our way north until we found a territory we felt we could take."

"Baltimore?"

He nodded. "We've been here ever since, about two hundred years, give or take a few decades."

"But you mentioned a Master. Leonora didn't turn you?"

"Thirty years ago my Master and Maker was killed. Leonora took over the *Balaj* as Mistress at that point."

Holy cow. "Who killed him?"

I wasn't aware of any Templar sanctioned purges in this century, and vampires didn't like to leave their territory. I felt somewhat guilty about my prying but I was dying of curiosity. Yeah, I know, I had no problem asking a vampire about his resistance to garlic and his legendary ability to turn into a bat and fly, but I was uncomfortable that I'd asked him who killed his Master.

He shifted in his seat, rolling the stem of the wineglass with his long fingers. "That is not something I will share with you. I've told you enough already about us. It's time to change the subject."

Really? I think not after his seduction routine earlier. If he could dig for info on me, then I could do the same. "Leonora is your sister?"

He scowled. "Blood sister. She was turned long before I was. Have you made any progress on identifying the symbol? I saw that you were researching tonight."

I ignored the question and concentrated on the information. Haiti. Dario had probably been a slave before he was turned, but Leonora was white. Had their Master been a plantation owner, or a vampire immigrant from one of the European families, coming to a new world in search of territory and the opportunity to begin a family of his own? It wouldn't have been an easy journey, crossing the Atlantic with a severe sensitivity toward sunlight. Modern nonstop airline travel made things so much easier for vampires than a lengthy journey via boat.

Did vampires swim? Or sink? And if they didn't need to breathe, what happened if they sank?

But another question took priority. "You've told me your timeline. You still haven't told me what it's like to be a vampire."

The waiter arrived with our salads, and by the time he'd offered us cracked pepper and freshly shaved parmesan, I figured the moment had passed and we'd be off to another topic of conversation. I ate a few bites of the salad, reveling in the taste of fresh vegetables. I was probably on the verge of malnutrition from my cheap-food diet the last few months. This was heaven.

"Hunger."

I halted the fork halfway to my mouth, thinking for a second about my own hunger before I realized Dario was referring to a very specific vampire hunger.

"It never ends. Never." His voice was dark and husky as his eyes met mine. "You learn to push it to the back of your mind, to control your response so you don't turn into a feral killing machine, but it's always there. Every waking moment. Sometimes when sunrise comes, you welcome the oblivion of sleep because it's the only time you don't feel the hunger."

The fork still hovered midway between the table and my mouth. That…that didn't sound fun. I wasn't sure what to say. What *do* you say to that sort of revelation? No wonder he didn't smile.

"Everything else is secondary. Families are bonded together due to our maker, but it's the hunger that truly ties us." His eyes darkened. Before I could take another breath, his hand was gripping my wrist, the fork bouncing into my salad bowl. "There are things I want, things I remember, but the hunger overtakes all other desires."

Total appetite killer. Now instead of crispy vegetables I was thinking of death by exsanguination and Dario's fingers digging into the skin of my wrist. I felt a warmth, a burning heat. The vampire grimaced but held on for a few seconds before letting go. I saw the blisters on his fingers, watched them heal before my eyes.

"It's spelled," I explained, fingering my cross tattoo. "Adrenaline activated." Which didn't normally do anything but make my wrist hot while in traffic or base jumping. What idiot thought this was a good idea I didn't know, but I was rather appreciative for the spell at this particular moment.

He grimaced, shaking his fingers as if the healed wounds still pained him. "I'll remember to grab your left wrist next time."

"Or some other part of me," I joked, picking up my fork again. Sheesh, even after our conversation I couldn't help but tease this guy. I must truly have a death wish.

We ate in silence for a while. By the time our entrees had arrived I'd worked up the nerve to continue my interrogation.

"So, as you noticed, I've started my research on the symbol and it appears to be related to summoning dead spirits."

That didn't elicit any particular response from Dario, but given his normal lack of facial expressions, I wasn't surprised.

He toyed with his ravioli before speaking. "Have you determined exactly what it does?"

I scarfed down a few bites of my Lobster Alfredo. It smelled amazing, and tasted even better. If only I could eat this every night. "No. But I'm curious to know why your Mistress is wanting information on a symbol used in necromantic magic."

"Consider it a precautionary measure."

I waited, taking the opportunity to eat more of my pasta, but Dario didn't elaborate. "Why? Surely you guys don't run around checking graffiti all over the city just in case it's magical in nature. What happened for Leonora to think this symbol was so important that she needed to bring in a Templar?"

There was a moment of frosty silence before he replied. "You don't need to know that. Tell us about the symbol and you get paid. That's our deal."

Suddenly my food tasted like sawdust. "But the background will help me in finding out the rest of the details on the symbol. If you want a thorough report, I really need to know."

"It's not your business."

Stupid, stubborn vampire. "It *is* my business, and not just because I'm doing this job for you. If there's something going down in my city involving necromancy, I need to know about it. How the heck did Leonora come across this symbol and why does she need to know about it?"

His fingers tightened on the fork. "Those would be a question for Leonora, not me."

"She's not here. You are. This is important and I need to know."

His eyes darkened. Suddenly he wasn't that cute vampire I'd been pestering with drinks and annoying questions anymore. He was a powerful being who could end me right here, or in the parking lot behind the restaurant.

"You will drop this line of questioning right now."

I felt like all the blood had dropped right out of my body. I'd seen Dario emotionless. I'd seen him intense and sexy. I'd never seen him like this. What was this "date" about? I knew he wanted me, or at least my blood. Right now, he didn't even seem interested in that.

"Why are we here?" I waved a hand to the side. "Here. In the restaurant together eating pasta and drinking wine?"

The vampire set down his fork and leaned back, his expression becoming distant once more. "I've been assigned to keep an eye on you, to report back on your progress. I figured that dining with you was the best way to do that. Now you can either make this a pleasant experience or an unpleasant one. Your choice."

The Lobster Alfredo turned into a lead weight inside my stomach. We weren't here because he found me attractive, or my O-Negative Templar blood irresistible. We weren't here because he thought I was a cool person to hang out and have dinner with. We were here because he was supposed to keep an eye on me and report back to his Mistress. All those Bloody Marys and drinks with plastic swords had meant nothing. Yes, he wanted me, but I was off limits. This meant nothing but business to him.

And that shouldn't bother me as much as it did.

Fine. Screw him. If Dario wanted business, he'd get business. I'd hit up the internet when I got back to my place and figure out what the connection was between the Robertsons and the vampires. Then I'd finish up the job and have the joy of never dealing with these soulless blood-suckers again.

I ate my pasta in silence, not worrying about small talk anymore. Let the vampires foot the bill for a decent meal. It's not like I needed to impress my companion with my quick wit or anything. Eat. Go home. Get to work.

My plate was nearly half empty by the time Dario broke the silence. "I'll give your information to Leonora about the spell being necromantic in nature."

It wasn't anything close to an apology. Business. This was all about business. "Please let me know what she says."

I interpreted his expression as "when pigs fly". "If Leonora wants you to know, then I will convey the information."

My temper flared. I blamed it on the wine and my bruised ego. "You ask me to do a job, a job that I have a seven day deadline to complete or presumably I will cease to live, a job that, judging by all this, is important to the vampires here in Baltimore, but you won't clarify details or communicate information I need to do the job?"

I completely couldn't read the expression on his face, although I got the feeling I was supposed to. "You don't need that information. Research the symbol. Tell us what it is, what it does, and do that in the next six days."

I was beginning to hate vampires. No wonder my ancestors had killed them on sight. "All you do is repeat the party line to me. Can you tell me nothing without your Mistress's approval? Do you ask her permission to feed? Does she prescreen all of your prey? Isn't there anything you can do without her authorization?"

The stem of the wineglass snapped in his hands. "Watch your tone."

What I'd said was out of line, but there was no need to snarl at me as if I were a bad dog. He'd grilled me about my life choices, turning on the seduction to pry information out of me. He'd arrogantly informed me that I wasn't going to get any information from him that might help me do my job. Yeah, the vampires were paying me, but a business arrangement like this had an unspoken agreement for a good-faith exchange of information. And I'd had more of this vampire tonight than I could stand.

He'd abandoned me last night in a shitty neighborhood miles from home and never even apologized. But I guess as my minder, my parole-officer for this job, he didn't need to apologize.

"Fuck you." I slapped my napkin on the table and without even a glance in his direction, got up and stomped out the door. I had money for a cab. Heck, I could walk home if I didn't have these heels on. I wasn't one of his vampire groupies, I wasn't about to have him tell me to "watch my tone", like I was his needy, desperate, blood-slave.

CHAPTER 4

Taxis weren't always the easiest to find in Little Italy, especially on a Thursday night, so I headed toward the Inner Harbor, knowing I'd encounter one there with all the clubs and tourists. Three blocks later I had to lean against a street sign and take off my heels. The sidewalk was cool against my feet, and kind of sticky. I tried not to think of all the disgusting stuff I was probably stepping in. Barf, urine, pizza grease, spilled beer—no, I wasn't going to think of that, but the moment I got home I was scrubbing my feet with that anti-bacterial stuff.

It was a long walk before I hailed down a ride, and the taxi from the Inner Harbor to my apartment was stupidly expensive. My feet were filthy. I was angry at Dario, and angrier at his Mistress. I was also worrying about my looming deadline.

But first things first. After scrubbing my feet practically raw, I curled up on the sofa and opened my laptop. I typed in "Lincoln Robertson", his date of death, and "Baltimore".

God bless those Google people. I was well aware that there were still things that would require my journeying into the dark recesses of a records room with miles of microfiche, but computers made preliminary research so easy. Even the Templar Librarians had begun cataloging electronically and scanning manuscripts. They'd never be available over the internet, but it was nice to know there were back-up records and a speedier way of searching than sitting at a table, paging through papyrus with gloved hands.

The obit came up first. Funeral service details and place of eternal rest were given for the family. No "in lieu of flowers" request to hint at cause of death. The pre-deceased by list was short, and one name stuck out—a daughter, Shay Robertson. I made a note of the name. There hadn't been a marker for Shay Robertson at the cemetery that I could remember. She could have been buried elsewhere, especially if she'd died as an infant. Still, it was worth checking.

The survived-by list was much longer. Aunts, uncles, cousins. Lincoln's mother had still been alive as well as his wife's parents. They'd come from large families, both with multiple brothers and sisters with their spouses and children. I was going to need another piece of paper if this continued. Finally I paused at the last name. Russell Robertson, a son.

I frowned. The whole family had died on the same day, minus a daughter that had died before them...and this Russell. The eldest child's grave had been Lincoln Junior, so I assumed Russell was a younger child. Where had he been? What had happened that shielded him from whatever killed the rest of his family?

I closed out the tab with the obituary and pulled up the next one. *Parents and Three Children Found Murdered.* I winced at the pictures of the family smiling at the camera in their Sunday finest, at school photos of the children. They'd been found by the surviving child and his aunt, who had been bringing him home from a sleep-over. There was some conjecture that the murders were gang related.

I didn't know much about gangs, but I couldn't see them just randomly killing a family of five. It seemed a bit excessive to be an initiation rite. Could Lincoln Junior have been involved in a gang, and this was revenge by a rival group? I made a quick note to check, even though juvenile crimes weren't public record.

Follow-up articles to the murder were scant on information. Police asked the public to come forward with any information. There was a suspect questioned, but released. That was it. No charges made. It seemed as if this remained an unsolved case. And the only way for me to dig further would be to get off my butt and check police records. Tomorrow. When it was daylight and normal people were up and working.

Which left me staring at the books I'd been perusing prior to Dario's arrival. This was the other end of the project, the one that got me paid and kept me from dying an early death. I fingered my personal grimoire. Why not? It was almost midnight on a Thursday, I was wide awake thanks to caffeine that even a few glasses of wine couldn't negate. I might as well summon myself up a demon and put this project to rest.

My cheap apartment had carpet, which is far from ideal when trying to delineate a magical space. It's downright deadly when drawing a summoning circle meant to hold a demon. I couldn't exactly do this out in the parking lot without drawing a crowd and possibly finding myself in the loony bin. That left my kitchen or bathroom vinyl, neither of which were large enough. Technically you could summon a demon into any size circle, but I didn't want to risk trying it with one three feet in diameter.

So much for my security deposit. I dug through the junk drawer and grabbed up a utility knife that I used to cut up boxes for recycling. Then I proceeded to remove my carpet. Thankfully it wasn't the glue-down type, and it came loose easily from the tack strip around the edges. I rolled it against a wall and surveyed the multi-colored padding that lay underneath. It was… disgusting, although at least it didn't smell of anything beyond dust and old carpet glue. I was going to pretend those stains were from some long ago party where lots of beer had hit the floor. Yeah.

I removed a few sections of padding, prying the staples up with my utility knife. Luckily the subfloor underneath was plywood and not chipboard. I sat back and eyed the four-by-eight piece. I could do a four-foot diameter circle within one sheet of plywood, or deal with the joints and create a larger circle across two sheets. I ran a finger along the seam and grimaced. No one cared if one section was a bit higher than the others, or if there was a gap. The foam and the carpet evened it all out.

This was risky enough without trying to contain energy across two gaps. Four feet it was. Better than the three feet it would have been in my kitchen or bathroom, but I wasn't sure the extra foot was worth all the demolition work I'd just done. Hopefully the demon would appreciate the extra space.

I cleaned my piece of plywood as best as I could, then got out my paint set. In a pinch, chalk worked, but it often left gaps and smudges that allowed energy leaks—or room for a demon to escape. I painted until my wrists ached. By the time I was done it was ten minutes until midnight. Perfect.

I had a four foot circle, binding runes on the inside reinforced by another circle. I'd thought about adding a triangle, just in case, but that would have made the summoning area really tiny. Besides, this was a low level demon, commonly summoned for information. I'd never seen him need more than one circle.

I double checked the sigil in the center, took another look at my incantation, and thought of what offering I could make to the demon as I lit the four black candles, and then the incense.

Yes, my landlord was gonna kill me. Whatever had caused those stains on the carpet padding probably wasn't as bad as defacing the carpeting, having dangerous open flame, *and* bringing a being from hell into the apartment building. The last was probably an event worthy of immediate eviction, even if the lease didn't specify any prohibition against demon summoning. I'd just need to be careful and make sure none of the other residents knew. Luckily this should be a fast ritual.

"I invoke, conjure, and command thee spirit to appear before me in this circle. Come into this circle and give answers, faithful and true, to all my questions. Come peaceably without delay into my presence."

Kneeling, I drew the demon's sigil on parchment and touched it to the flame of the candle in the southern quarter. It caught so fast I barely had time to toss the burning paper into the metal bowl.

"Vine, I request your presence. Appear before me and hear my appeal."

I opened the bottle of wine, pouring some into a crystal glass and setting both bottle and glass at the edge of the circle. Then I sat down to meditate. Centering, balancing, I let go of this world and called out, "Vine, I respectfully ask you to appear. I need your knowledge, and would like to share an offering with you"

A surge of energy hit the room, rocking me backward. The candle flames went sideways, incense smoke flattened on the ground in a spiral around the outer edge of the circle. This wasn't typical. My breath caught in my throat before I managed to push the anxiety away and focus, pouring my energies into strengthening the perimeter. I shouldn't have needed to do it, but something was wrong about the energy flowing into the circle.

I felt it, pressing against me, compressing my lungs to the point that I could barely breathe. One by one, the flames atop the black candles went out. The runes glowed bright white—the only light in the room. Dark as it was, I saw it. Smoke blacker than the darkness around me rose in a column from the floor, flowing outward only to be halted by the line of runes.

The pressure…it was as if an anvil were on my chest, as if the building had collapsed on top of me. I took tiny breaths, tried not to panic, and kept the circle intact. What was up with Vine? I'd seen him summoned twice before, witnessed three other demons being summoned, none of them ever appeared like this. And none of them ever put forth this amount of energy.

The black smoke coalesced into a bipedal shape. Eyes glowed like coals, blue flames around the edges. In the dim light of the apartment I could see the impressive horns rising from his head, the gnash of sharp, white teeth in a black snout. This wasn't Vine. I'd copied the sigil accurately, summoned according to the most formal of methods. What in hell had responded to my summons?

"I respectfully request the presence of Vine. Any other demon is not welcome."

That was a bit confrontational, especially given the type of runes and circle I'd cast, but I was getting scared. Where was Vine? Who was this demon and why had he responded? There were very specific rules concerning evocation and invocation and the dealing with celestial and infernal beings, and this flew in the face of all of them.

Vine is otherwise occupied, so I am here in his stead.

I fought back a wave of terror. Vine had never spoken.

He'd always communicated his information either through dream or divination. Who was this?

Who is this Templar Knight who summons demons? Clearly your Order's manifesto has taken an interesting turn.

Shit, shit, shit. I'd used an invocation, not an evocation because the Goetic demons were somewhat friendly and helpful. They responded best to polite respect, to offerings and requests. And they expected an open channel of energy with the mage. The circle I'd drawn was meant for balancing energies, not forcibly holding malignant spirits.

My mind was screaming a warning, but all I could do was focus every bit of my mental capabilities toward containing this being. I had an instinctive feeling *this* wasn't a friendly or helpful demon.

"Thank you for attending, but your presence is not required. Depart to hell forthwith, not to return unless summoned anew."

That was kind of the equivalent of saying "get the fuck out of here, please". The response was a roar of power that knocked me backward. I lost focus. The runes dimmed, then darkened, plunging the entire apartment into blackness. Something cold brushed my side—icy cold, sharp pain, and then numbness.

"*T'voghnel anmijapes,*" I screamed, throwing all of my power into the banishment every Templar learned before they could walk.

The sound of small explosions all over my apartment had me curled in a ball, shielding my face. I felt the demon's power like a vise on my head… and then nothing. I counted my breaths, waiting in case that metaphorical other shoe was about to drop. When I finally opened my eyes and rolled upright, the golden glow of a street light was streaming through a broken window into my apartment. Candle fragments, broken glass and wine were all over the floor. I got up and made my way to the light switch, careful to not step on any of the broken glass.

It was just as horrible with the lights on. In fact, I was tempted to turn them off and go to bed, hopefully to awaken to a miraculously repaired apartment, but I knew better. Slipping on my flip-flops, I grabbed a roll of paper towels and a broom, and got to work.

Cleaning wasn't easy when your hands were shaking. Wine and broken glass wouldn't be a problem, especially since the carpet was nicely rolled up against the wall and still relatively clean. It was the lack of window that was going to cause me some serious trouble. It was past midnight on a Thursday, and I didn't have a sheet of plywood to nail over the thing. Would someone try to rob me up on the third floor? I thought about the money in the tampon box, about my need to sleep without worrying if someone would climb in and assault me. Tired as I was, I'd need to do one more spell—an illusion this time, to make sure the window looked intact. It wouldn't last past dawn, but at least I'd be able to sleep, especially if I added an alarm spell to it.

I thought about the demon that had appeared. I'd been pushing that to the back of my mind, but with the apartment clean and the carpet re-rolled out, it had returned to my thoughts. Who had it been? It sure as heck wasn't Vine. I'd seen him summoned numerous times. He'd been the go-to demon for *Haul Du*.

A vision hit me of that smoke demon appearing the next time *Haul Du* summoned Vine. Could they hold him? Being used to Vine, the experienced mages didn't always take the precautions I'd just done. If that thing showed up instead of Vine, a whole lot of mages could die. I wasn't very happy with the members of *Haul Du*, but I didn't exactly want them slaughtered by a minion of Satan.

I picked up my phone and scrolled through my contacts,

hesitating a few moments before dialing Raven. It went to voice mail four times before she finally answered.

"I'm not supposed to be talking to you." She was whispering, like others were nearby, listening in.

"This is urgent. Have you guys summoned Vine lately?"

She hesitated. "That's not… I can't talk to non-members about such things."

Damn it. "You've got to tell the others, Raven. I summoned Vine tonight and another demon came. He was not friendly, and I barely managed to send him back. Cross Vine off your list and use another Goetic demon."

"Maybe you made a mistake with the sigil?"

A valid assumption for someone who'd only been an initiate for eight months. Raven was forgetting something, though. "I'm a Templar. I've been drawing sigils in a null room for over a decade."

"Maybe the incantation—"

"Something is wrong with Vine. Either he's dead, or he's been subsumed by this other demon. Trust me, Raven, you don't want to deal with this guy."

"They won't believe me, Aria. And I'll be in big trouble just for talking to you."

These idiots were going to get themselves killed. There were a few of them that I wouldn't mind seeing in the obituaries, but I liked Raven. There had been a time when I'd considered her my best friend.

"Tell them that I left you a message. As a Templar, I'm tasked with protecting Pilgrims on the Path. This is my public service announcement to you *Haul Du* pilgrims, warning you of danger ahead. Okay?"

She laughed, and for a second I felt a lump lodge in my chest. We'd been friends.

"Okay. Take care, Aria."

She hung up before I could reply. Damn, that lump in my

chest hurt. I had two quick spells to do before bed and I was an emotional wreck. Time for drastic measures. Time for the Emergency Beer.

Everyone should have an Emergency Beer. Not the light stuff that you drink after mowing the lawn, or something happy and fruity. No, Emergency Beer should be dark and rich, with enough alcohol to be noticed, but not enough to put you in a stupor. I carefully choose my Emergency Beer, replacing it with something else when it had been consumed. This one was a barley wine that had been in my fridge for five months.

I got out a brandy snifter, wanting to honor the Emergency Beer with an appropriate container. Then I reached in to grab it, the bottle of barley wine in my almost-empty fridge sat next to a bottle of mustard and a white box.

Huh? I pulled the white box out with the care of a bomb-squad technician. The way my evening was going, I wouldn't have been surprised to find a bomb in my refrigerator. I stared at it as I poured my beer, but there were no red or blue wires to snip, just a piece of twine looped into a bow on top.

I pulled the thread, eased open the lid, and looked inside. There, nestled in wax paper, sat six cannoli.

I wasn't sure whether this was an apology or not, but any guy who brought me pastries, even if he broke into my apartment to do so, was pretty close to winning my heart. Too bad he was a vampire.

CHAPTER 5

My landlord was pissed. Not only was he up early on a Friday morning supervising my window replacement, but he'd needed to pay the contractors the emergency rate. Correction, *I'd* needed to pay, because as I'd been informed many times in the last thirty minutes, these sorts of repairs were not his responsibility.

I'd thought about lying and saying some drunk threw a rock at my window last night, but I just couldn't. It *was* my fault. So instead I lied and told him I was practicing tai-chi and had a mishap with my bo staff. I think the only reason I wasn't out on the street with all of my belongings was my payment of last and this month's rent in cash. That meant I was caught up. And it also meant that after paying for the window, I'd have about fifty bucks left in my tampon box.

Which was just enough to get me to and from Middleburg, Virginia.

The summoning hadn't worked, and given the results I was reluctant to try again with another Goetic demon. My call with Raven last night made it quite clear that I shouldn't expect help from *Haul Du* or any of the other ceremonial magic groups in the northeast corridor. That left my family.

It says a lot that I was weighing the risks of attempting another summoning against the unpleasantness a family visit would bring. I knew I'd eventually have to go home and make nice with everyone. My parents had been leaving the occasional message on my voicemail. There were regular deposits in my old checking account—money I refused to touch. They were extending the olive branch, and I knew I looked like a jerk for not accepting it. Of course, that olive branch was full of thorns, and any return of the prodigal daughter would be celebrated with constant questions about when I was going to be a responsible adult and take my Oath.

Ugh. Luckily I had to work later this afternoon and could delay this trip until tonight. Weekends were usually family time, and there was a good chance my brother and sister and their families would also be in residence. I'd soldier through Sunday, and head back that night using work as an excuse. Hopefully I'd not need to repeat this trip for another six months.

By the time the contractors finished with the window it was nearly noon and I'd eaten three cannoli for breakfast. Hyped up on sugar, I locked my door and headed for the police station.

The records division was in the Baltimore City Archives, which luckily had a parking lot that didn't charge an arm and a leg. Once in, I made my way to the information desk and asked where to file a request to see a cold case file.

"Online."

Crap. "Can I fill out the form here?"

The woman shoved two papers at me. "Fill out the registration form, and the research appointment request."

I thanked her profusely and went off to fill out the forms. When I returned the woman was gone, and a man was at the desk. He was a balding guy with a skin tone that desperately needed some sunlight and a paunch that desperately needed some time on the treadmill. Although if I had this job, I'd probably be deathly pale and fat, too. There's only so much sitting a person can do in one day, and the boxes of donuts on a table toward the back probably didn't help with the weight issue. I eyed them, but was still buzzing from my cannoli fest this morning.

The man looked over the forms and nodded. "Seems complete. We'll order the files and call you when they arrive to schedule a time for you to see them."

Government. Moving at the pace of an advancing glacier since the dawn of time. We Templars weren't much better, but sheesh, I needed to see the records now, not in eight months.

"Is there anything I can do to speed this up?" I tried on my best smile. My looks weren't movie-star beautiful, but I'd been called pretty.

Not pretty enough, evidently. "They might not even be here. A good number of the records are kept at the Maryland State Archives in Annapolis and we have to order them. If you want to pay a fee, we can make copies for you and mail them."

I figured that would take even longer. "No thanks. Is it possible they're on microfiche or scanned electronically? I don't need to see the originals, just read the files."

He smiled sympathetically and gestured around the room at their antiquated equipment. "It's not like in the television shows. Unless something is going to trial and we need to get copies to the fifty lawyers on the case, it doesn't get scanned. Reports are electronic, but they're archived after a certain length of time, and lots of notes are still done by hand."

Drat. "Thanks anyway. I appreciate it." I did. He'd taken the time to explain, hadn't dismissed me or bitten my head off. Working in a coffee shop for six months had taught me how hard it was to remain friendly and cheerful with grumpy, demanding people on the other side of the counter.

"Want a donut?"

This dude needed a promotion. He was giving government workers a good name.

"I thought you'd never ask."

He waved me around the desk over to the table where the square boxes were lined up. They were half empty, and of course all the chocolate ones were gone. I had my pick of glazed, jelly filled, and some mystery cake-type donut.

"I'm Rob." He pointed at the mystery donut. "They're apple spice. Don't tell anyone, but they're the best ones here."

Guess my smile worked better than I thought it did. "Aria. And your donut secret is safe with me." I pulled back my sleeve so it didn't drag in the powdered sugar and reached for an apple spice.

When I looked up, Rob was staring at my wrist. "You're a Templar."

How did he know? Most humans went about their normal lives thinking we died out with the Crusades. "Yes, I'm a Templar." I didn't feel the need to explain my non-Knight status. "Thanks for the donut, Rob."

"In fourteen twenty-eight a group of travelers was captured just outside of Vaucouleurs, France. Half of the party died, but the rest were rescued by a Knight of the Temple." His wide eyes met mine. "I'm descended from one of those survivors."

Hundred Years War. Joan of Arc. It was way past the heyday of the Templars but some of the families in France had survived the purge and continued their duties in stealth. It warmed my heart to hear his story. It had been so long since we did that sort of thing. It was nice to know this tale had been handed down through generations, that this man remembered and appreciated our protection.

Rob looked around, as if worried he'd be overheard. We were the only ones in here beyond an ancient woman nodding off at her desk in the far corner and a young man bouncing his head vigorously to whatever was streaming through his headphones. "Look, those files really do take forever to get here, but I'm due for my break. I'll pull a couple boxes of microfiche and let you look through them in one of the rooms."

"I don't want to get you in trouble," I protested. I didn't, but I did really want to look at those files. I had a couple of hours to kill until my shift started. Might as well root through a few boxes of microfiche.

"No one will know. It's Friday. Most everyone is off today anyway." He grinned. "Besides, I can trust a Templar. If it weren't for your Order, I wouldn't even have been born."

I don't know how trustworthy I was, but I certainly wasn't going to run off with a bunch of microfiche or some giant heavy piece of viewing equipment.

Rob ushered me into a small room with two desks, two chairs, and two viewers. I sat. And waited. The donut was long gone and I was wishing I'd brought a bottle of water by the time my-man Rob came back in, two boxes stacked high in his arms. He slammed them down on the table, his face red with exertion.

"I had to hurry, they were back farther than I expected." He waved a hand at the dusty boxes. "This is all I have onsite from forty years ago. I can't guarantee you'll find what you need."

"Fingers crossed," I told him, lifting the lid off one box and staring at the little rolls of cartridges inside. "Thanks for this."

Rob went back to work, leaving me with the sterile room

and a daunting amount of tape to search through. I felt like that miller's daughter in Rumpelstiltskin, facing a room full of straw and expecting to spin it all to gold. I had two hours. Better start spinning.

Half an hour later I was regretting my decision. There had been a lot of crime in Baltimore forty years ago. There was probably just as much now, but catching the news every now and then meant I missed a lot, and I'm sure many robberies and petty crimes didn't make the papers. This was all laid out in front of me—day after day of car break-ins, assaults, thefts, drug arrests. It was hard, reading all of this. And it was hard not to get sucked into the details of cases that had nothing to do with the Robertsons. One carjacking of a priest had me especially intrigued.

Finally I found something, but it wasn't exactly what I'd been looking for. Shay Robertson had been reported missing by her parents four months before their murders. Interesting. She'd been listed as pre-deceasing her family in the obituary, so I'd just assumed she'd died much earlier. Turns out she must have passed away not long before her parents and three of her siblings.

Lincoln and Tanya had reported that their eldest daughter, aged fourteen, hadn't come home after school one day. They suspected she had a boyfriend, but had never met him. The officer taking the report noted it as a possible runaway, although the parents had insisted they had a good relationship with Shay and there hadn't been any arguments or friction at home.

Three days after her parents visited the police station, Shay Robertson was officially listed as a missing person. The officer assigned the case had spoken with her friends, and they stated she'd been sneaking out of her house to meet a boyfriend late at night—someone older, someone her parents definitely wouldn't approve of.

The case remained open. Shay was never found. I frowned at the casual detective work in the case, the lack of urgency. Nowadays there would have been amber alerts and the girl's picture on milk cartons all over the country. Fourteen, and probably run off with some creepy pedophile. Had things been that different forty years ago? Had the race or economic status of the girl played into the less-than-adequate police attention?

And just as important, how had her relatives known she was dead? They'd listed her as pre-deceasing her family, but the case was still showing open.

I made a note and kept going. With just fifteen minutes to go before I needed to leave I found the microfiche, buried deep in the second box of tapes. It was a grisly murder, attributed to gang revenge, although the detective assigned to the case could find no evidence that any of the Robertsons were involved in gang activity. A few neighbors wondered if they'd maybe angered someone involved in organized crime. A few connected the case to Shay's disappearance, conjecturing that she'd become involved with a gang member who was upset with the parents' attempts to find her. Ultimately the case went cold with lack of leads and evidence.

Not much more than the paper had reported, except the microfiche had scanned copies of crime scene photos and the coroner's report. I wrote frantically, my hand cramping as I tried to get it down as fast as possible. The pictures I snapped with my cell phone were less than ideal, but they'd have to do until I could see the originals. I hastily boxed everything back up, and went out to thank Rob.

All the murdered Robertsons had died the same way. Their throats had been cut from side to side, in a slash so deep it nearly decapitated the younger ones. They'd died from blood loss, and there had been quite a mess of red on the carpet. But I didn't need to be a CSI junkie to know something was wrong with that crime scene—very, very wrong.

It was the blood. The coroner's report said the family had bled out—completely bled out. But their room hadn't shown anywhere near the amount of blood it should have. Lincoln would have had about 8 pints of blood, the rest of his family a bit less. All totaled, there should have been approximately twenty-two liters of blood on that living room floor. The place should have been saturated, painted in blood. The carpet would have been soaked. From what I could see, over half the blood was missing.

And there were no signs of struggle, no evidence of drugs or other wounds that would have rendered the family unconscious. Just a whole lot of throat cutting. I wasn't an expert on gangs, but far as I knew they didn't waltz into your house and convince you to politely stand still while they slit your throats and carted away half your blood.

I was an expert on plenty of creatures that *did* do so. I wasn't ruling out humans, either. There were plenty of texts in the Temple documenting death magic rituals where a spell held the victim in a state of compliance and blood was collected in a bowl.

"Thanks, Rob." I gave the man a slip of paper with my phone number on it and grimaced at his excitement. "Can you give me a call once the files come in? I'm particularly interested in the crime scene photos. The microfiche ones weren't the greatest resolution."

His face fell. "Sure. I also looked through the log, and last year a reporter with the Sun had requested the same file. Evidently she was doing an article on crime in the area back then versus now. She might still have her copies."

Whoa, that would be a huge stroke of luck. Rob handed me a sticky note with the reporter's name and phone number, and with his own name and phone number written below. "Just in case you need me to help you with anything else," he added sheepishly.

I really needed to watch that smile. I was breaking hearts all over the place. "Thanks. I work at Holy Grounds on Pratt. Stop by some time and I'll comp you a chai latte."

His face brightened. "Will do."

I pocketed my notes and the reporter's information, and ran to my car. The rest of my research was going to have to wait until later, because I was about to be late to work.

CHAPTER 6

I was late, but managed to sneak through the back and clock in without anyone noticing. Sean and Petie were working this afternoon, and I slid right in beside them, calling orders and frothing milk as needed. By five, things had tapered off, the work crowd heading to happy hour to start their weekend. By seven, we were the only ones in the shop and I was helping Petie stock shelves in the back while Sean twiddled his thumbs up front, just in case someone stumbled through our door.

I loved working when it was busy. There was no room for anything in my head besides coffee orders and the customers lined up in front of me. I could let my mind wander, imagining who these people were with their iced espresso, sugar-free caramel mochas, their double-shot dirty chais. What lives did they lead outside the doors of my store? What kept them awake at night? What brought them joy? They fascinated me, and for a portion of my day I got to forget all about my abandoned Templar duty, the responsibilities that had been assigned me by accident of birth.

What if I didn't want that life? What if I wanted something else? I hefted a box of cinnamon dolce syrup and looked down at my Templar tattoo. Branded, before I knew what this really meant. My life given over before I was even eating solid food. Yes, the research and the guarding of the Temple were important. Yes, it was essential for Templars to continue doing what they had been tasked with since the day they received their message from God. Yes, I felt like a complete loser for walking out on that. We all had burdens in this life. Every one of those people I handed a coffee cup to had their own cross to bear. Who was I to refuse mine?

Not that taking an Oath and spending the rest of my life guarding a bunch of magical artifacts and researching dusty manuscripts was a cross to bear, especially not with the lifetime stipend all Knights received. It wasn't the duty that bothered me, it was the lack of meaningfulness in that life. A Knight today wasn't what the job was a thousand years ago.

"Hey Aria, can you get down that box of Kenyan beans?"

I hopped up and climbed the ladder. Petie had pulled his shoulder a few months back and struggled to handle boxes above his head. That, and I think he liked looking up my shirt as I reached my arms up to grab stuff. These button-down blouses they had us wear came right to the waist, which meant I showed a ton of skin every time I lifted a box. No biggie. I liked Petie. If it gave him a thrill to see less than I showed in a bikini, more power to him.

"What the heck did you do to yourself, girl?"

"Where?" I climbed down and sat the box to the side. Had I cut myself cleaning up the glass last night? I'd been careful, but between the wine bottle, the goblet, and the window I might have sliced myself and not noticed.

"There." He pointed to my left side. "Looks like a burn."

I'd had burns before and they weren't anything a reasonable person could ignore. They throbbed and ached, driving every other thought from your mind. It can't have been all that bad if I didn't even know I'd done it.

I lifted my shirt and squashed my boob, trying to see the spot on my waist Petie had indicated. He was of no further help, transfixed, no doubt, by the cleavage effect of me squishing my ta-tas.

It did look like a burn—an old one. It was circular, like someone had singed me with the lit end of a big, fat cigar. I touched it and felt nothing. The skin was numb, the white scar raised and bumpy. When had I gotten that? It was summer, and I'd sported plenty of sports bras, bikinis, and halter-tops over the last month. Someone would have mentioned it before now. I should have seen this in the mirror. Although it was in an odd place, hidden from my view by my breasts, and I wasn't exactly the sort of girl who was always examining herself in the mirror.

"Curling iron accident?" Petie teased. Brandi was always claiming her hickeys were the result of a hair styling mishap. Nobody was that clumsy with a curling iron, and Brandi's boyfriend clearly had a neck fetish. But this wasn't on my neck. Admittedly it had been a long time since I'd seen any action—so long that my memory was probably a bit fuzzy on the details—but I didn't recall getting a hickey on my waist so violent that it would leave a scar. And this was a weird shape, as if something with tentacles, or an eel had attacked me.

And no, I'm not into being burned as a part of sex. Thanks for asking.

"No idea," I told Petie. "Must have been really drunk to have slept through that one, huh?"

"Damn, girl." He gave me a thumbs up. "Can't say I've ever partied quite that hard. Shame it's scarred like that. You've got real pretty skin."

Yeah, the parts that didn't have sword-fighting scars, road

rash scars, magical weapon burns. Oh and the skateboarding scar. That was one sport I didn't try more than once.

I winked at Petie. "Just gives you one more thing to look at when I'm pulling boxes of beans off the shelf."

He smiled, like a little boy caught with his hand in the cookie jar. "Maybe we need one more box of Java."

I swatted him lightly on the arm and picked up the box of Kenyan. "Think you've seen enough today, big boy."

By the time I'd driven home the sky was orange and violet with the setting sun. Warmth rose from the asphalt into the cooling evening air. Locusts sang from the scant trees that had managed to find a withered life in this urban jungle. Somebody's battered Honda was in my space so I found a spot on the street and walked a couple blocks back to the apartment building. I'd be leaving in a few hours, and calling the tow truck in this neighborhood had repercussions. People had long memories, and I rather liked my little car. If it happened again, I'd make a charm for my spot. Something long term. Maybe an illusion of lots of vomit. Nobody wanted to park in that.

Upstairs, I finished off the last cannoli—yes, that was six in one day plus the donut—and listened to my messages. Brandi left one saying the LARP people wanted to meet Monday evening to strategize our plan of attack for Saturday. I was starting to get pretty excited about this whole thing. Armor, sword, some kind of warfare simulation and a potluck afterward. It sounded a whole lot more fun than the practices I'd done with other Templars. We never had a potluck.

The second message wasn't as pleasant. It was my mother, reminding me that this was family weekend, and that she expected me to put aside my sulking for a few days and come home to do my duty. Mom was all about duty. She also took it as a personal affront that I hadn't taken my Oath.

Mom was the Guardian of the family, the warrior, the protector of the Temple. She'd had big plans for me, envisioning her daughter a high level Knight influencing Templar policy and perhaps even becoming an Elder. I can't say my running off had ruined her plans, just delayed them, as well as irritated her that I wasn't already on my way to Templar greatness.

Well, she'd soon get a chance to tell me all of this again in person. Erasing the message, I went into my room and started to pack. I didn't need to take much. I'd left a lot of my clothes at home. A barista in Baltimore doesn't need formal dress, tennis outfits, or jodhpurs. I had a go-bag pre-packed. Just needed to add some casual clothes, some makeup and I'd be ready to leave.

There was a knock at my door. Then the squawk of hinges as it opened. I'm sure there were many beings, paranormal and otherwise, who could open a locked door, but only one seemed to be regularly stopping by my house. I slung my duffle bag over one shoulder and walked into the living room. Dario was still standing in the doorway. I knew he could walk right on in after the first invitation, but appreciated his manners in waiting. Plus I couldn't be too pissed at a guy who'd brought me cannoli.

"Come on in." I tossed my bag on the table. "I'm sorry for losing my temper and storming out last night. I hadn't slept. Not that it's any excuse. Anyway, I appreciate the dinner. And the cannoli."

He eyed the white box crumpled in the trash. "You ate them all?"

I shrugged. "What can I say? I love my pastries."

His lip twitched, and I smiled in response. It was good to see something on his face beyond that bland, mildly alert expression.

"I'm sorry, too. I didn't speak to you with proper

respect, and I apologize. I've never been around Templars and I find it hard remembering that you're not just another human."

I wasn't sure how to take that. I *was* just another human, circumstances of my birth aside. Did he treat his victims that way? Some women might get off on that domineering approach, but I didn't. I'd like to think if a woman was going to risk losing her life, she'd at least get the white glove treatment beforehand.

"All is forgiven," I told him. And I actually meant it. The residual anger I'd felt at being left up in the northern part of the city had faded away. Friends forgave each other stuff like that. Eventually.

Was Dario my friend? Oh good Lord, how insane that I was counting a vampire as one of my besties. I needed to get out more.

"Where are you off to?" He patted the top of my duffle bag.

"Home." I grimaced. "I need to look at a few of the books Dad has in his vault. And it's family weekend. If I go now, then I can probably cry off for the next few months. Sorry to dash, but I was actually just leaving."

Dario nodded. "Okay. Let's go."

What? Did he mix up some pronouns there? I know he was supposed to be my minder, but coming home with me to meet my parents was out of the question. "No, *I'm* leaving. I'll give you a call Monday when I'm back in town to let you know what I found out."

"I'm coming with you." He picked up the duffle bag. Great. Now I'd need to wrestle him to get it back. The prospect of rolling around on top of Dario was pretty enticing, but I had no time for that.

"Why? It's a family thing, like with *family* and all that. Heck I don't want to go and they're *my* family. You won't be allowed in the vault. There's no reason for you to waste your weekend tagging along."

His eyes met mine. "I'm coming with you."

Was that look supposed to be some sort of vampire mind control whammy? If so, it failed miserably. Now if he'd said "come to bed with me" or "take off your shirt" with that sort of look, I might have done it. Although my compliance wouldn't have anything to do with a mesmerizing trick. Lust, pure and simple. Sheesh, it really had been too long. I needed to get a boyfriend. Or some kind of battery operated device.

My dirty-thoughts tangent aside, I was sure what was driving Dario's insistence on accompanying me into family hell. He was my minder. I shouldn't read too much into a box of pastry in my fridge. He was establishing a connection with me, making sure he could follow me around and ensure I got the job done—and that I reported every detail back to Leonora.

Friends. I sure can pick them, huh?

"All right hot-stuff. Don't say I didn't warn you." I locked up, leaving the living room light on to give any potential burglars the illusion that I was home. Not that there was anything in my apartment to steal. I was taking my sword and my laptop with me, the tampon box was now empty of anything except tampons. It was still best to take precautions. The landlord had been upset enough about the broken window, a broken door might have me homeless on the street.

I insisted we take my car. There was no way I was going to be trapped in Middleburg, Virginia with my parents and not have a getaway car at my disposal. Dario eased the passenger seat back to accommodate his long legs and folded his arms across his chest. He looked bored. Too bad.

Interstate 95 was busy day and night. Friday night was no exception. Cars whipped across four lanes of traffic, veering onto exits at full speed. Trucks clogged up the right lanes. Signs announced lane closures for road work, even though no one was within the sectioned off areas. We'd left Baltimore behind, and Washington D.C. was lighting up the horizon before I spoke. I wasn't about to drive two hours in silence. Might as well break the ice.

"I didn't tell my family I was coming."

He continued staring straight ahead. "So this will be a happy surprise?"

"Oh the fatted lamb will definitely be killed. There's a good chance I'll be the fatted lamb on the skewer, though. Just warning you."

"Warning taken. I'll try to stay out of the way if dishes start flying, or whatever you Templars do when you have a family argument." The vampire didn't look too thrilled to be thrown into such family dynamics, but he was the one who'd insisted on coming.

"Plus, my parents are going to have a problem with 'us'," I added, moving my index finger back and forth between us.

"Because I'm black?"

I couldn't help a quick smile, having gotten used to Dario's deadpan delivery of humor. "That may raise a few eyebrows, but the fact that you're a vampire is going to really upset the familial apple cart."

Given the truce between us, Templars were in theory okay with vampires. That didn't mean anyone wanted their children to date one. We'd spent centuries killing them left and right. Vampires weren't considered moral beings. They were technically dead and had sold their souls for the curse of immortality. And then there was that whole "purity of the gene pool" thing. The sanctity of the Templar blood must not be sullied. My great-grandfather may have gotten away with bringing home a Hungarian gypsy witch as a bride, but that was a rarity. He'd been a twenty-ninth level Knight. When you're that good, you can get away with just about anything. I wasn't that good, and Great-grandma Essie might be a blotch on our lineage, but at least she wasn't a vampire.

"Do they have appropriate accommodations?" Dario asked, finally becoming serious. Not that I could tell the difference from his facial expressions. I thought about telling him "no" just to mess with him, but that seemed kind of mean. Vampires could make do, but no one liked sleeping in a dark corner down in the basement.

"Sort of." The thought of my proper mother with her pearls and sweater set, throwing together a light-safe vampire resting area with no notice made me rather gleeful. We had bedrooms that could easily be made vampire-friendly, but it's not like we were prepared for one as a guest. In fact, I don't ever remember a vampire visiting a Templar household. Huh. There's a first time for everything.

"I'll assume I'm going to be fasting while I'm there?"

There would be plenty of food, but that wasn't what Dario meant. Vampires could go several days between meals, so I wasn't particularly worried. Dario hardly looked like some freshly turned newbie who might snap at any moment.

"Sorry, yes. We don't exactly have blood slaves on standby."

I just couldn't help but dig at this guy every chance I could get. I expected him to snarl at me again about watching my tone, but instead he just raised an eyebrow.

"If I get too hungry, I'll just have to feed on you."

Yeah, I probably deserved that after my quip about blood slaves, but still the reminder that I sat in very close proximity to a predator that could kill me in a blink was unnerving. It's not like I could get to my keychain in time, swinging from the ignition like it was. Time to move creating a vampire protection amulet to the top of my list.

In spite of my quick shiver, I knew I was safe—for now.

There was that whole Templars-are-off-limits thing. And he needed me to get this information for Leonora. It's not like he could waltz into my family home covered in my blood and ask my father to help him out. Plus there was some instinctive part of me that felt I had nothing to fear from Dario. He was controlled and elegant, in spite of the weird leather getup the other night. I got the feeling he wouldn't kill me, even if the impossible happened and he fed on me.

"You might not want to bite me," I teased. "How do you know I don't have hepatitis or some kind of Templar blood-borne disease? Don't you guys screen your food first? Is there some kind of vampire USDA?"

"I can smell you." His voice got sexy, but all I could think of was whether my deodorant was working or not. "And some diseases lend a lovely flavor to blood. You should try it."

Ick. We loved our veal, and that was seriously anemic calves, so I guess I couldn't judge. "No way. I'll stick to steak and potatoes, thank you very much."

His lips twitched. "Your loss."

The last half of our drive went quickly. Dario was a pretty interesting guy, weird dining habits aside. He liked modern music, had a thing for craft beers, and confessed that he'd always wanted a cat. I didn't ask whether he meant to eat or as a pet.

What he didn't have were a lot of hobbies outside of hunting for a meal. Vampires liked to lay low, and it was difficult to completely satisfy their hunger without killing their human prey. Every now and then they could get away with murder, but with the number of vampires in a *Balaj*, it had to be a rare occurrence. A rapidly vanishing population would be noticed, as would a stockpile of dead, bloodless bodies.

Which reminded me of the autopsy report on the Robertsons. I'd thought about the possibility of vampires as the killers, but there were too many other suspects to start pointing fingers. Still, it seemed a good moment as any to dig for information.

"Let's say you kill your victim, either accidently or on purpose. Would you try to cover it up somehow? I can't imagine it would do you all any good to have a vampire scare in Baltimore."

"Are you trying to pin some murders on me?" he teased, cutting a bit close to the truth. "It would be stupid to kill on purpose in your own territory and potentially bring notice to yourself, as well as put your Mistress and *Balaj* in danger. If there's an accident, it's best that the body never be discovered. That rarely happens, though. Leonora doesn't punish those who have such accidents with a slap on the wrist."

I winced, my vivid imagination supplying me with plenty of ideas of Leonora's punishments. "But what about on purpose? Let's say you have a score to settle with someone, or you need to set an example."

He eyed me steadily. "Leonora would need to sanction that sort of thing. And there would be no need to 'cover it up' since we would want the message to get across loud and clear."

Made sense. Without coming right out and asking, I couldn't see a scenario where the Master, or Mistress, of a *Balaj* would want to kill an entire family and make it look like their throats were slit. I was leaning toward death magic.

"Not thinking of becoming a Paladin, are you?" There was a note of ruthlessness under the wry tone. I had no doubt what he'd do to me if he thought I was going to turn into some kind of Batman in plate armor.

"Do I seem like the Paladin type to you?"

He snorted. It was the closest thing to a laugh that I'd ever heard him make. "So how is this thing going to go at your parents' house? Do I have any hope of being back in Baltimore by sunrise?"

It was my turn to snort. "Sunrise Monday, maybe." I turned off the main road and started down the long drive that lead to our house. "It's late in human-time, so we'll have a lovely, tension-filled meet-and-greet, then be packed off to bed. While you sleep through the day, I'll be subjected to the torture of family activities while my mother snipes at my life choices. Then after dinner, which will be insanely late because Mom will demand we have it when you're up and about, I'll finally get into the vault. It will hopefully only take me one night to find what I need. Normally I'd bug out Sunday after brunch claiming to have the plague or cramps or something, but since you're not able to travel in daylight without a movable crypt, I'll need to stay one more agonizing day before heading back."

We sat in silence, the tall oaks on either side of the drive like an endless row of giant fence posts in the dark.

"Sorry."

Whoa. Two apologies in one evening. That had to be some sort of vampire record as far as humility and manners went.

"No biggie. I survived twenty-six years with them. One weekend won't kill me."

We rounded a corner and the house appeared ahead. There was pretty much no need for headlights at this point. Every light in the place was on. Spotlights out front highlighted the three story Georgian façade. Little globes lit the circular drive and the way to the garages. As in garage, only plural. Even the stables were bright as day. I can't imagine what kind of electric bills my parents had been paying over the years.

"Seems like someone is afraid of the dark," Dario drawled.

"We're Templars. The dark is afraid of us."

That shut him up. Well either that or the over-the-top ostentatious splendor that was my family home. It was *Gone With The Wind* meets Versailles. I loved it the way I loved the Temple, the way I loved the Smithsonian Museums, but in spite of the sheer beauty, I longed to be back in my apartment with the ratty carpet, stained padding, and newly replaced window.

I parked smack in front of the main steps, figuring I'd move the car in the morning. The place had alarm wards as far out as the highway. My parents might not have known I was coming until I turned down the driveway, but they'd known there was a vampire in the area from the Berryville exit on Route Nine.

Dario was gentlemanly enough to grab my duffle bag. He followed me up the marble steps half a pace behind. Close enough to indicate his equality in status to me without seeming rudely dominant. The guy was pretty savvy about human non-verbal cues for a vampire.

My parents might not have rushed out the door to welcome me on the steps, but they were excited enough about my attendance to be waiting in the hallway. A chorus of greetings hit me before I had the door half open, and I realized that it wasn't just my parents in the foyer, but my brother and sister, their families, and a couple of cousins, as well as the black sheep of the family before I took her place—Great-grandma Essie.

"Aunt Ari!" My nephew Bors plowed into my legs, his face buried in my stomach. I hugged him back and greeted the rest of the clan, overwhelmed by hugs and cheek-kisses. It was an excessive display of affection from a family that was normally reserved about such things. It made me feel guilty for being away so long, for not returning half of the phone calls I'd received, for thinking all of those bad thoughts on the way up.

"So, you're back to take your Oath?"

Mom. And now I wasn't feeling so guilty about those bad thoughts. I was barely five feet in the door and she was nagging me about my Knighthood again. And ignoring Dario. Not one of them had asked who he was. Not one had greeted him or introduced themselves. I wrestled free from Bors's embrace and reached out to put a hand on Dario's arm, ignoring his slight flinch.

"Everyone, this is Dario."

There was a moment of silence while my family waited for me to elaborate further. I didn't. Let them think whatever they wanted.

"Dario, this is my Mom and Dad, my brother Roman, his wife and two kids, my sister Athena with her husband. Over there are my cousins Bran and Cesare. And this is Great-grandma Essie.

"He's a fucking vampire," Essie announced. She seemed rather cheerful about the whole thing, as if I'd brought a much needed bottle of Jack Daniels to Sunday church service.

"Yes he is," I responded.

Essie walked around him, inspecting him as though he were a horse at auction. Dario looked appropriately terrified.

"Can I kiss him?" she asked. Actually, she shouted. Essie was somewhere over one hundred years old, and although she walked around like she was a spry eighty, she was losing her hearing. Thus, she assumed everyone else was losing their hearing, too.

"Later, Gran."

"Welcome, Dario." Finally someone besides my crazy great-grandmother spoke up. Mom had obviously felt the silence had gone on long enough to get her point across and it was time to once again be the gracious hostess.

"Well, it's pretty late," Dad chimed in. "Time we were all in bed. Early start tomorrow, you know."

It was just past one in the morning. Dad routinely stayed up until three and had always seemed to thrive on a mere four to five hours of sleep per night. Either there was something especially exciting planned for tomorrow, or Dad felt everyone needed to go to bed and process the fact that I'd brought a vampire to our home for family weekend. Yeah, probably the latter.

Everyone chimed in their good-nights as if we were the Waltons, and made their way up a staircase so wide four could walk abreast. I waited, knowing what was to come.

"Aria. A word with you in the kitchen, please?"

Mom. Dario raised a questioning eyebrow at me and I waved for him to follow. The kitchen was in the rear of the house, through a maze of rooms and hallways. If I hadn't grown up here, I would have been tempted to leave a trail of breadcrumbs to find my way back.

The house layout may have been for the convenience of a lifestyle long ago, but the kitchen had been remodeled for modern needs. I'm sure it was huge two hundred years ago, but it was even bigger now that two of the old servants' rooms had been demolished in the expansion. One pantry had been converted into a walk-in fridge, two others retained their original use. A fireplace big enough to roast a horse took up one entire wall. It was totally impractical, but Dad adored it and refused to see it walled in. I adored it, too. The brick had chips, patchwork, and tiny carvings where Ainsworths of old had etched charms and, no doubt, curses. A heavy black metal arm on a hinged pole was still in place inside the fireplace, its hook holding an antique cast iron pot. I used to sit at the kitchen table eating my cereal and imagine that I was a witch with potions boiling away over the fire. In reality, that pot hadn't seen use in close to fifty years. And the housekeepers we'd had over the ages always complained about having to clean the thing of cobwebs and dust.

I waved Dario to the huge butcher block we used as a kitchen table and grabbed a couple of beers out of the fridge. Dad may be a wine kinda guy, but he always had a good supply of beer for us kids.

"When are you taking your Oath, Solaria?"

I totally expected this. Mom never pulled her punches. "I'm not ready. Should I show Dario to the dragon bedroom? I'm assuming that's where you'd like him to stay?"

With twelve bedrooms, we'd taken to naming them by décor. The dragon bedroom had tapestries on the walls showing Saint George's legendary battle. It also was north-facing with electronic privacy shutters. Perfect for a vampire, or for guests who had been partying very late and wanted to sleep the day away undisturbed by sunlight.

"Of course. Your Oath, Solaria—"

"I'm not discussing my Oath. Can we please change the subject, Mom?"

We weren't always this way, my mother and I. There was a time when I'd cuddled in her lap while she sang me songs of Charlemagne and Genghis Khan. She'd taught me sword-play at three with a red plastic Excalibur. She'd bandaged my cuts and scrapes, kissed my boo-boos. She'd held me as I cried in her arms over some boy. Something changed between us and I wasn't sure exactly when it had happened. All I felt from her now was pressure. And disappointment.

Her blue eyes, so like my own, were steely as they met mine. "For the sake of your guest, who I'm sure is uncom-fortable with this discussion, I will change the topic. But be aware, Solaria, we will speak of this again."

Dario didn't look uncomfortable. Actually he looked intrigued at the tension between us. I drained half my beer and nodded. I was starving, cannoli didn't make for a very filling dinner, but I wasn't willing to hang around my mother long enough to raid the refrigerator.

Mom chatted about family news, careful not to discuss anything too personal around Dario. I was saddened to hear we'd lost one of the mares to colic last week, and excited to hear Sasha had a litter of puppies two months back. Knowing my family, there would be time carved out of this weekend for riding. I was looking forward to getting out to the stables to see the horses and cuddling with a bunch of rowdy pups.

"I know you are both eager to head to bed. You must join us for brunch tomorrow, Dario." My mother smiled, her teeth perfect and white, her eyes guileless. "Solomon makes the most wonderful French toast."

Here we go again. I rolled my eyes. Not that Dad's French toast wasn't something to write home about, but Mom was baiting Dario, and thus me, in her usual passive-aggressive manner. "Is brunch now at five in the morning, Mom? How kind of you to offer to accommodate my vampire boyfriend with a time change but I would hate to inconvenience everyone else."

Dario started at my titling him "my boyfriend". He was normally so controlled that the expression on his face nearly cracked me up.

Mom's eyes met mine. "Touché," they said. "We'll be sure to schedule a late dinner and leave plenty in the fridge. I'm assuming Dario has the means to take care of his other needs?"

Ah yes. Dario, addressed in the third person as if he were not standing right in front of her. The chilly tone of her last sentence was just as much about the "ick" factor of the vampire's other needs as the disapproval she felt that my "boyfriend" must surely be slaking his needs by means of my veins.

"Not to worry, Mrs. Ainsworth. I fed before I left town and should be fine for a few days. If such activities are not allowed in your home, I'll be more than happy to pop down to the neighboring village each evening." I choked back a laugh at Dario's cheerful tone. It was as if he were discussing a tobacco habit. "Just to ensure I'm not seen, I'll make sure I fly there and back as a bat."

Shit. I tried to hide my laughter as a coughing fit, but Mom knew better. "That won't be necessary, Dario. As long as you are discreet, we will tolerate your taking care of these things within the home."

We barely made it upstairs before I collapsed on the bed laughing. I knew Mom would put me in my old bedroom, the one that hadn't been redecorated since I was twelve. I'd rebelled against all the jousting and hand-to-hand combat lessons by painting my room bubble gum pink. Fuzzy kitten pictures lined the walls, side by side with sparkly unicorns. My bed sported a million lace pillows and a lace draped canopy. The joke had been on me, though. Mom had refused to let me change it back, and I'd been in girly-girl hell ever since my teen years.

"Did you see her face? Sucking lemons couldn't be more appropriate a term." I started laughing again. This guy was hysterical. Maybe hanging with a vampire wasn't so bad after all.

Dario tossed a few lacy pillows to the floor and sat down on my bed. "I'm beginning to prefer the rest of your family's icy silence."

I snorted and sat up. "Except for Essie. Better lock your door. She's pretty spry for her age and I think she fancies you."

"I'm worried *she'd* bite *me*. Can you loan me a sword or a javelin or something? I wouldn't be surprised to wake up tonight with her on top of me."

I fell back onto the pillows laughing at the image of my great-grandmother, naked and sexually assaulting a vampire. The beer on an empty stomach was getting to me, and I found myself in a happy buzz-land place, where it was perfectly okay for me to be sprawled across my bed next to a vampire. There was one of those odd moments where his eyes met mine and the silence held all sorts of meaning.

Dario cleared his throat. "So where is this dragon room? I'm assuming there aren't actually dragons there. Surviving your great-grandmother is going to be difficult enough without having to fend off fire-breathing reptiles, too."

"It's early. What are you going to do all night?"

I knew I was treading on dangerous ground, that I really didn't want to go there, but I couldn't help myself. Blame the beer, or sexy vampire come-hither magic, or the tension of being around my family, but I didn't want to be all alone in this pink bedroom.

The vampire gave me an odd look. "Read a book or something. Maybe prowl around your gardens if you'll assure me that there aren't any spells to set me on fire, or launch a stake through my heart."

I rolled around on the bed, knocking pillows to the floor. "Nah, you'll be safe. Although I'd rather you stay here." I looked upside down at the wall beside my bed and began to laugh uncontrollably.

Dario had that look on his face. The same one he'd had when Essie had been eyeing him up. "What's so funny?"

"The pictures," I gasped. "Can you imagine having sex and looking up to see some unicorn smiling benignly down on you? Would you be able to keep it up with all these fluffy kittens staring at you with their big eyes?"

I looked up at Dario, my grin fading. There was no doubt he'd be able to keep it up, and he was indeed imagining the very thing I was. I held my breath. Waiting.

"How are you drunk on one beer?"

Guess that was a "no". Not that I was really sure I wanted a "yes". Sex with Dario sounded really good right now, but I had a feeling that activity and drinking blood went hand-in-hand with this vampire. I wasn't about to head down that slippery slope.

"All I've eaten today is six cannolis and an apple spice donut."

Dario swore and stood up. "Stay there. I'll be right back."

I was half asleep when my door opened again. Dario set two plates and a bag of chips on top of my bed, and a huge glass of water on my bedside table.

"Here." He stuffed a sandwich into my hand. Crumbs rained down on my lacy pink comforter. "Eat. Drink. Then show me where this dragon room is before you go into a food-induced sleep coma. This house is huge and I'm worried if you don't show me which room is mine that I'll fry come morning. Or worse yet, climb into bed with your great-grandmother."

I giggled with my mouth full. I was coming down off my one-beer buzz but still feeling silly. Dario joined me, eating the other sandwich and sharing the bag of chips. It was fun. More fun than I'd ever thought I'd have in this god-awful pink bedroom.

We tiptoed down the hallway and up one more set of stairs to the upper floor which had once housed servants and provided storage for generations of crap. The dragon room was at the end of the hall, next to the wooden door that led to the attic. I flicked on the light as we entered and admired what had been one of my favorite rooms as a child.

Each wall boasted a huge tapestry, hanging ceiling to floor from sturdy brass curtain rods with gold embossed pineapple-style ends. They made the room cozily warm on damp, chilly winter nights, and provided a perfect spot to hide. Many times I'd snuck between a tapestry and the wall, avoiding Latin lessons or the dreaded herbal identification quizzes our tutor insisted on torturing us with. The old fabric smelled of dust and incense, and I'd always pressed my nose against them, trying to hold my breath until our tutor gave up his search.

"Nice," Dario commented. "Not many humans enjoy sleeping with scenes of beheading and fatal gut wounds surrounding them."

"Would you rather have the kitties and unicorns?"

"No." He shot me a quick smile. Guess Dario wasn't as expressionless as I'd thought. Maybe he was warming up to me. Maybe I shouldn't think about that at all.

"Here's how you work the blinds." I showed him, then flicked off the lights to illustrate the completely light-proof nature of the room.

"I'll admit I thought I'd be down in the wine cellar," he confessed. "Judging by your family's greeting, I didn't assumed they ever had vampire guests."

"Uncle Beo," I told him. "He gets out-of-his-mind drunk and goes on a rampage if there's a hint of sunlight in his room before late afternoon."

"Part vampire?"

I didn't know someone could *be* part vampire. I'd always read it was an all or nothing kind of thing. I made a note to research further. And remember to take my birth control. Just in case.

"Nope. Just an old Knight who hits the scotch rather hard, especially during the equinox. He's been a bit off ever since that sand *wyrmm* incident in Egypt a few decades back."

Dario nodded. "Well, I think I'm good. Thanks."

I winced at the dismissal, lingering just a second longer than I should. "Goodnight."

Idiot. I cursed myself the whole way back to my Pepto-

Bismol colored room. Yeah, Dario was mighty sexy, but he was a vampire. I'd had no problem keeping myself from doing anything but ogling and mild flirtation back in Baltimore, but here among my family I was grabbing at him like a drowning woman clinging to a buoy. Luckily he hadn't been the type to take advantage or I'd probably be showing up to breakfast claiming a curling iron mishap. Then moving in with him once we were back in Baltimore, never to be seen alive again.

And I was clearly insane that the thought of a vampire related death seemed more sexy than terrifying. I needed to snap out of this, get the information I needed, high tail it back to Baltimore then stop indulging in this death-fetish fantasy I had going on.

And find a boyfriend. Or at least some guy willing to participate in regular booty calls. Because curling up in bed thinking about what sort of other facial expressions I could coax from Dario wasn't healthy.

CHAPTER 7

$\mathcal{D}$ad was serving up a dose of fatherly advice along with his famous French toast. Luckily I was the only one awake to hear it. I hated getting lectured in front of an audience, even if that audience was my family.

"I get it, Solaria, really I do." He flipped the bread expertly and it sizzled in the pan. "We all need to sow oats, some of us more than others."

He winked, and I knew what he meant. Great-grandma Essie's blood flowed through our veins. We might not talk about it, we might pretend that she was just an eccentric branch off of our stately family tree, but in spite of our ability to deny what was right in front of our faces, we all knew. Essie was a witch, a gifted woman of the wild, a dark-haired gypsy from Eastern Europe. And thus she was the scapegoat for every undesirable trait her descendants possessed. I felt a stir of anger about that. I was more than a mish-mash of my family's genetic pool, I was me. And only *I* was responsible for my life choices.

"I'm not sowing oats, Dad. Nor am I planning on harvesting grains of any kind. I'm just living my life, which happens to be different than the one you and Mom had planned for me."

He smiled and shook his head. Mom got angry. My sister, my brother, and I got angry. Great-grandma Essie *really* got angry. Dad never got angry. I mean never. He'd get that stern look in his eyes sometimes, but that was as close to a display of temper as I'd ever seen. He was the most controlled man I'd ever met in my life. Dario came close, but his dry humor put him a lap or two behind my father.

"Come on. Your mother and I both know that vampire you brought home isn't your boyfriend. Aren't you a little old to be acting out like this? I get it that you feel this need to express your individuality, to rage against the family way, but this sort of thing is juvenile."

He slid the French toast onto a plate and handed it to me, just a hint of disappointment in his bright blue eyes. It worked. I felt like shit. Why was it that when it came to my family I always reverted into an immature, rebellious teenager?

"He's not my boyfriend. I'm researching something for the vampire *Balaj* up in Baltimore, and he's allegedly facilitating."

"Ah. Making sure you get the job done, huh?" Dad. There was no fooling him. "What are these vampires paying you?"

"Nothing," I lied.

He smiled again, and this time it reached his eyes. Just barely. "Good. That's my girl."

Templars weren't supposed to take payment for our work. It was all for the betterment of humanity, for the glory of God and the Righteous Path of Truth. Of course, even guardians of the Path can't exist without food and shelter. There were donations, tithes. Substantial ones, and I suspect many of them were not voluntary. Basically we were all trust-fund babies, each earning according to the level of their knighthood. Inheritance rights also had some play in the matter. I'd never been privy to the details, but we had an estate in horse country, went to private schools, and enjoyed regular vacations in Europe.

I didn't get a stipend. I wasn't a Knight and thus was not eligible. Those regular deposits into my other, untouched checking account were courtesy of my parents. Yes, it stung to be the black sheep of the family, on a sort of allowance at the age of twenty-six, but I'd been raised to be a Templar. There weren't exactly living-wage opportunities for those skills outside of knighthood, and slinging coffee on the corner didn't even pay for my lousy apartment. Still, it would take a lot for me to swallow my pride and accept what I'd come to view as charity. Demanding payment for my work for the vampires somehow seemed better than dipping into my "allowance".

"So, let's see it."

"Huh?"

A tiny frown creased Dad's brow in response to my speaking with my mouth full of breakfast. Swallowing, I tried that again. "See what?"

"Whatever it is that brought you home this weekend." He reached out a hand. "Normally wild horses wouldn't drag you here for family time, so I'm assuming your visit has something to do with your research for the vampires."

Did I mention that nothing got past Dad? Well, nothing except my lie about not taking payment. I took another bite of French toast and dug in my pocket, unfolding the crumpled copy of the symbol.

Dad ran a finger over the creases, smoothing them and tracing the lines of my photocopied version. "Got some Mars influence here, it seems."

I felt a swell of pride. Yeah, I'd seen that.

"Did you check Cicero?" he asked.

"Yes." Sheesh. I might not be a Knight, but I knew the basics.

"Swift and Beachum?"

I nodded. "Yes. It doesn't match anything there either."

Swift and Beachum's Cabalistic Rites was a huge, heavy tome only printed in eighteen-by-twenty size. Thus I'd left my copy here. After I'd left Dario's room, I'd been unable to sleep, so I'd stayed up nearly all night scouring the enormous book.

I leaned over, my shoulder touching his. "I thought this circle here could be the one for health, but maybe it's life?"

His finger traced the symbol again. "I wish you had the original. Pressure points in the ink often reveal the individual symbols and which one is predominant in the spell."

A warmth washed over me. This felt so good, so right, to be here with my father discussing the finer points of symbolism in magic. God, how I'd missed this. Had I made a mistake to leave all this behind? Then I remembered the joy I felt in the summoning circle—and the fear when the demon broke free. Never had I been so close to death, and to life.

"I also saw the symbol on some graves this week—graves where magic raised five specters."

He nodded. "Necromantic?"

"That's what I was thinking. The symbol on the graves was very faint. I'm thinking whoever the mage is, he or she figured it would have washed off before anyone noticed it. I don't know how that relates to the vampires, or what their interest is in the symbol."

Dad turned the paper upside down. Sometimes viewing from a different angle brought a revelation. "Well, technically they're dead, too. Could be this is something that could be used against them?"

That was one possibility. "Or it could be they have an

interest in the necromancer for other reasons, and are trying to find a way to track him or her through the symbol."

Magic was personal. Even following a ritual from someone else's grimoire didn't keep a mage from leaving what amounted to a graffiti tag of magic on the sigil, the site, even the spell's residual energy. Every practitioner knew to be careful with hair, fingernails, and especially blood. There wasn't much they could do about magic tags, though. No matter how skilled, everyone left a calling card.

"We'll need to check the vault tonight."

I felt a tingle of excitement at Dad's words. The vault could only be opened at certain times, and was sealed with a blood lock. The books there were some of the most definitive works on magic and the divine ever written. We were honored to be caretakers for a few original versions, but most were copies, laboriously scribed hundreds of years ago.

"Bible of the Curses?"

Dad nodded. "It's a good place to start. Or possibly Peterson's Monsters of the New World."

I frowned. "You don't think it's European?"

My father folded the paper and handed it back. "I think it's custom crafted, an amalgamation of European and North American magicks."

I tucked the paper back into my pocket and thought as I finished my breakfast. Initially I had assumed that whatever this symbol did, it was detrimental to the vampires, rather than a method for them to trace the practitioner. To track down the necromancer, they'd need a magic user of their own. A Templar Knight was supposed to freely give information, but concocting a trace spell was beyond our duties and responsibilities. I doubted Leonora had a mage on retainer, or she wouldn't have come to me for this information, so I was banking on the first theory. The symbol was involved in raising dead spirits, and something about that made the vampires very uneasy.

A custom symbol was one that only worked under the hands of a powerful magician. A question to add to my growing stack was one about the caster's intent. Was he purposely targeting the vampires, or was the effect toward them only a byproduct? Hopefully we'd find out tonight once Dad opened the vault.

"You know, if you'd stayed, you would have had access to the vault yourself."

I cringed, covering my reaction up by taking my plate to the sink to rinse and stack in the dishwasher. My brother and sister were good Knights, really good, but I had been the golden child. The youngest of three, I'd shown the most promise. The power of the third, Mother had always said. And thus the pressure, and the ultimatum.

"But that's history." Dad waved his spatula. "Go get your tennis clothes on while I finish cooking these up for your lazy siblings. We've got a busy day ahead of us."

Shit. Tennis. I closed the dishwasher and glanced over toward my father. The bones in his hands were sharp; brown spots that I didn't remember now dotted the skin. Time was a foe none of us could conquer. We'd had our differences. I still dreaded family time. But deep down, there were memories of my childhood that I'd always cherish, long after my parents left their mortal shells behind.

"Love you, Dad." I kissed him, and saw him flush with embarrassment at the physical affection. "And this time I'm going to kick your ass on the court."

He transferred the spatula and swatted at me. I easily evaded his hand. When had I become quicker than my Dad?

"Watch your language in this house, young lady," he scolded. "And you most certainly won't 'kick my ass'. Not this time. Not ever."

CHAPTER 8

I came in dead last at tennis. Again. Which is the reason why the entire family always argued over who was going to be my partner. Great-grandma Essie finally yelled that she'd participate. I wasn't hoping for much, especially since I doubted she'd ever played tennis in her life. She hadn't. It didn't matter because she broke all the rules and used magic to return the ball, cackling gleefully when she managed to slam it into an opponent's legs or torso.

Gran was finally banned from the court. Well, bribed by mimosas, actually, because no one banned Great-grandma Essie from anything. Which left me with Roman's youngest son, Ajax...who was five.

Croquet was minimally better. By the time lunch was over, I'd had my fill of genteel sports and smoked turkey sandwiches and was glad that we had "free time" until tea.

Yes, tea. Because in my family it was a crime to go more than three hours without eating something. The fine china and tea growing cold in the pot were our nod to the customs of our ancestors across the pond. Tea in the Ainsworth family meant it was time to bring out the whisky and more sandwiches—ham this time. Evidently I wasn't the only one who needed hard liquor after ten hours of family time. I was eagerly anticipating tea, err, whisky.

But first, the stables. I snagged a few carrot slices off the luncheon tray and made my way across the thick green grass to the picturesque brown and white building surrounded by looping rows of painted wood fencing. First things first, I searched the freshly cleaned stalls in my quest to find the puppies.

Oh, they were adorable. At eight weeks they were rowdy, plump little balls of white and brown fur. Their terrier of a mom had come to us pregnant, and I'd been told by a very sad Ajax that the rescue already had homes for all six of them. I wished I could take one back with me, but my land-lord would have a fit. I'm sure a puppy would be happy to add to the collection of stains on the carpet padding, but I really didn't have time for a pet or the money. Sheesh, I could hardly take care of myself.

I left the pups and went to visit another animal I wished I had the time and money for—the horses. We had quite a few here, and the staff to handle all the poop, feeding, and turnout schedules they required. There were four draft crosses, six hunters, and three feisty ponies. I checked the status board in the stable to see if any were lame or injured, then grabbed a grooming box and loaded up my arms with tack.

Peace was my choice today. My siblings usually went for the bigger horses, but I liked the ponies. Being able to hop off in the field without worrying how the heck I was going to climb back on was a plus, as was not getting constantly whacked in the head by tree branches. Peace and I had a lovely ride, and I fed the little gray mare my leftover luncheon carrots after we returned.

"Tea" required a quick shower and a change of clothes. Even taking my time, I'd beat most of my family downstairs. Roman was the only one in the sunroom when I came in. He already had a tumbler of whisky in hand, and quickly turned to pour one for me.

"So, how long did it take Mom to jump all over you about taking your Oath?" he asked, handing me the glass.

"Pfft. I don't think you all were even in bed yet. Heck, my car was still warm from the drive up."

He laughed, leaning back against the mahogany buffet cabinet. "Just do it, Ari. You know she won't give in until you do."

I gulped whisky, enjoying the burn and the warmth as it went down my throat. "It's my life, Roman. I spent every moment except the last six months living it as others wanted me to. No more."

He saluted me with his glass. "It's not that I don't admire your little rebellion, baby sis, but you haven't toed the line since birth. In fact, you've done nothing *but* dig your heels in. The pink, frilly bedroom? Hiding from your tutor nearly every day? Sticking a giant dildo on the end of your lance at the tournament? Shall I go on?"

There was no rule against jousting with a penis. None. I'd checked. "I won that tournament. The youngest by five years at the least, and I won."

"Because everyone tends to be thrown off their game seeing an enormous phallus coming at their heads. You won because you danced your way around the rules, Aria. Just like you dance your way around all the rules."

There was a tinge of bitterness in Roman's voice. It was the familiar bitterness of the eldest who'd always done as he was asked only to be upstaged by his wild, reckless youngest sister. I understood. And I also knew he was right. Still, even though I hadn't always lived my life the way others wanted, those "little rebellions" hadn't done much besides allow me to lodge a protest. I still learned Latin. I still jousted in the tourney. And I had to sleep in that pink bedroom. This was different. This was me deciding to be me.

Roman lifted his hands in surrender. "I get it. You don't want to be a Knight. What *do* you want to be, Ari?"

That was the question I still hadn't found the answer to. I liked living in Baltimore, liked my coffee shop job, but these last few days of researching for the vampires had taught me that I needed more than that. What that *more* was, I hadn't figured out yet.

What I *had* figured out was that it was time for me to change the topic before my eldest sibling started channeling my mother. "Hey, do you have any idea what LARP is? I'm supposed to wear armor to one and I'm wondering whether to grab the plate or the chain mail."

Success. Roman shook his head, clearly intrigued. "I've never heard of a LARP. Maybe you should bring both sets, just in case."

Ugh. That was a lot of weight to be lugging around. "Maybe chain mail and just knees and elbows?"

Roman pursed his lips. "I'm a fan of full plate, especially since you don't know what you'll be encountering."

That was going to be pretty hot in August, but my brother was right. He was a Guardian like Mom and Athena. When you were in charge of defending the Temple, it paid to be cautious. Not that anything had attacked in over a century, but it was best to be prepared for anything. Kind of like the Boy Scouts.

Before I could respond, we were interrupted by the arrival of the rest of my clan. The whisky flowed, sandwiches were consumed, and before the untouched pot of tea had a chance to get cold, we were all drifting off with excuses of checking e-mail, escorting the kids out to see the puppies, or taking a nap before dinner. I snuck into the library, grabbing the decanter of whisky on my way. This is how family time always went. Frantic togetherness activities in the morning the first day quickly devolved into meals together and everyone off on their own toward evening.

I wasn't alone in the library.

"'Bout time someone got here with more booze," Great-grandma Essie shouted. "Solomon waters this one down, naughty boy. And it's almost gone."

I passed her the decanter, not surprised to see her swig it from the bottle. Whisky dribbled down her chin and onto her bright yellow shirt. "Where's that hot piece of ass you brought home?"

Dad really needed to limit her internet usage. Hearing that sort of language from a coworker at the coffee shop was fine, hearing it from an elderly woman chugging whisky was disturbing.

"He's a vampire, Gran. No one in this household is going to be enjoying that 'hot piece of ass'."

She eyed me in disappointment. "Just as well you're not letting him climb on top of you. He'd bite you, and we all know how that would end. He could bite me all he wants. I'm almost dead anyway. It would be a lot more pleasant way to die than a heart attack in my sleep. That's how Tarquin died, although he wasn't sleeping. We were rocking the bed and all that excitement was too much for his old heart."

Great-grandpa Tarquin *had* died of a heart attack, but it had been while having breakfast at IHOP, not sex with Essie. Although I'm sure he did plenty of the latter activity right up until he died.

"I'm not going to let Dario or any other vampire bite me, Gran." Best to steer this conversation back to vampires before Essie started revealing the details of hers and Tarquin's sex life.

"Good." She took another swig of whisky. At this rate, liver failure was looking a more likely death for Essie than a heart attack. "Maybe when you're old like me you can let him stuff your muffin, but not now. You've got things to do with your life. People depend on you. You've got to protect the Pilgrims on the Path as Tarquin always said." She peered at me, her dark brown eyes intent. "You look like him, you know. Those cheekbones, that sexy mouth, that same determination in your eyes. You're a great Knight."

"I'm not a Knight. I haven't taken my Oath."

Essie made a dismissive noise, waving her hand for emphasis—the hand not holding the decanter of whisky.

"Oath-smoath. You're a Knight. It's here, my girl. Here." She was grabbing her left boob, but I think she meant to be indicating her heart.

I smiled, trying to keep my expression as non-committal as possible. The feelings I'd had during my tea-time chat with Roman came back. I wasn't a Knight, didn't want to be a Knight *or* spend the rest of my life as a barista in a coffee shop—at least not full time. What was a woman with a degree in European History to do? Museum jobs were insanely competitive, and my knowledge was unusual in its specificity. Add in my prowess in swordsmanship, jousting, and illusion magic…

And I came up with a job at the Renaissance Fair. Which paid about as much as the coffee shop job and was only four months out of the year. Maybe these LARPing people had a paid position open?

"Pilgrims on the Path," Essie repeated. Her voice softer, her head lolling to the side. "Someone has to keep them safe. Pilgrims on the Path."

A light snore came from her, and I dove in to rescue the

whisky before her tight grip loosened and it hit the floor. Booze safely on the table, I found a pillow and made my great-grandmother more comfortable. She smiled in her sleep, and I left, hoping she was dreaming of younger times with her dashing husband by her side.

CHAPTER 9

There was a knock on my bedroom door. Before I could respond, it opened and Dario stepped in. I froze, not sure what my reaction to him would be, or his reaction to me. I had sort of thrown myself at him in a moment of low-blood-sugar drunkenness. He'd declined. And that was part of the embarrassment. It's a woman thing. *Oh my God, I hit on a vampire,* and *I'm not attractive enough for him to even consider the offer* both were equally mortifying.

It was as if last night had never happened. That bland expression was back on his face.

"Whose monkey suit did you borrow," I pointed at his tux.

"I believe this is your brother, Roman's." Dario straightened the sleeves. "He's about my size. I found it hanging in the closet."

I doubted anyone went into his room while he was in slumber. Mom must have delivered it last night, while we were in my bedroom. I bit back a smile, knowing she'd been imagining all sorts of naughty goings-on between me and Dario.

"Ready? I fear your mother's icy glare if we are late to dinner."

He wasn't the only one. "Ready."

It was a sacrilege to miss dinnertime growing up, and we all were expected to be clean and appropriately attired. Family Time warranted the ridiculously formal outfits, Mom's attempt to compensate for the fact that her children were all grown and she only saw them every other month. I secretly loved it. The huge silver candelabras were all ablaze. Gold rimmed plates, crystal goblets, and solid silver were artfully set on the long table. My long dress brushed against my legs, every step a seductive caress. I was well aware with my hair done up that the long column of my neck, my shoulder, and the top half of my breasts were exposed. I felt the weight of the jewelry against my skin, the burn of Dario's gaze as his eyes roamed. I felt sexy, powerful, privileged.

"Ma'am." One of the staff extended a silver platter offering me a martini with an olive rolling about the bottom of the glass. I took it as if I were accepting the Holy Grail. This was ceremony, familiar and scripted. They knew what I drank and had it ready for me to take with a gloved hand. This could all be mine. It was my legacy. It was part of who I was.

But as much as I reveled in it, I missed my ratty apartment and the hiss of the espresso machines at the café.

The waiter took Dario's drink order, and scurried away while I sipped my martini, my other hand resting on the crook of the vampire's elbow. The bite of juniper melded with the bitterness of olive and tonic on my tongue.

"This is insanely over-the-top," Dario muttered.

It was, but something in me bloomed with the pomp and circumstance, as if it were my right to have this. I remembered the little I knew about Dario's history. Life in Haiti as a human, then what amounted to the exile of his *Balaj,* roaming north across America until settling in Baltimore. Did they have to oust another *Balaj*? How hard had those decades, possibly centuries, been? I looked at our priceless dinnerware, handed down through generations and felt a stab of shame.

"Enjoy it. Patrick makes a good martini."

Mom and Dad arrived last, entering with great ceremony. I felt a swell of pride. Mom was turning sixty this year. She was beautiful with a slim, muscular body, her natural blond hair streaked with silver and just brushing her shoulders. The laugh lines at the corner of her eyes and the parenthesis that bracketed her upturned mouth were the only concessions to her age. She used to smile a lot when I was young. And laugh. I missed that.

Dad was a decade older, his black hair long gone. He was still in good figure, although I'd witnessed the broadening of his waist across the years and seen the shadows darken and sag beneath his eyes. I remembered his hands as he flipped the French toast, fine-boned and spotted.

When had my parents grown old? Was it just six months away that had brought this home to me? It was like a stab in the chest, this realization they wouldn't live forever. Great-grandma Essie seemed to be on the road to rival Methuselah, but her children and grandchildren hadn't been graced with such longevity. There was Dad, his two sisters and a cousin left out of Essie's dozen grandchildren. My heart ached.

Dario grabbed my hand and gave it a quick squeeze, then left my side to approach my parents. I watched in horror, as if a friend had jumped into the lion's den at the National Zoo. He spoke to the pair of them. They nodded stiffly, then Mom took his arm and walked alongside the vampire to her place at the table. I noted the little smile curling up one corner of her lips as well as the slight flush on her cheeks.

Seemed that Essie and I weren't the only ones who admired the attractive vampire.

I walked to Dad and he extended his arm, his grey eyes twinkling as they met mine. I looped my hand around his and leaned my cheek against his shoulder, breathing in the familiar scent that had always meant love, approval, and security.

"I think your Mother has been seduced to the dark side," he murmured.

I laughed. "One wrong move and his head will be rolling across the oriental rug."

And it would. Dad was the only man who had ever swayed Mom into losing her warrior caution.

Dinner was a ceremony unto itself. Seven courses with non-confrontational conversation. As we rose, Roman's wife, Hilda, took the children upstairs. Athena and Mom went for a moonlight walk in the gardens. My sister's husband, Pietrus, took a quick look at Dad and I, then excused himself to smoke a cigar on the terrace. Dad poured us each a glass of port. I glanced at the mantel clock and knew it was time.

I touched Dario's arm. "There are some books I need to peruse. With any luck, I can find what I need and we can be out of here and back in Baltimore before sunup. If not, I'll work through the night, sleep tomorrow for a bit, then we can leave at sundown."

His dark eyes bore into mine. It was unnerving, having someone stare directly at me for so long. "I'll come with you."

It took me a moment before I realized that he meant the vault. "These documents are for Templar eyes only. I'll let you know as soon as I find something."

"Unacceptable. I've received word that we must return tonight, and that I'm to assist you in any way necessary to ensure you have information for the Mistress when we return."

Why was he suddenly so stiff, so antagonistic? I felt like the last few days we'd moved past that. Honestly, we'd always seemed to have something more than this cold, impersonal, business-like thing between us. From day one when I'd been sending him Bloody Marys and he'd sent back martinis filled with little plastic swords, we'd had a connection. What had happened over dinner to change that?

"Dario, there's no need for this. Dad and I will go through the documents, and I promise I'll let you know anything I find."

Dad's eyes went back and forth between the pair of us. "I'll meet you at the vault, Solaria." He bit back a smile as he left the room. I watched him leave, waited until the door closed, then turned to Dario.

The vampire set the untouched glass of port on the table. "Aria, there is more riding on this than you know. I need to review these documents with you."

"What's riding on this, Dario? You haven't told me shit. I can't violate the sanctity of Templar property without good reason, and you haven't given me that good reason."

He turned his head. "I cannot give you the reason. You need to trust me."

For Pete's sake. "And I cannot let you in the vault. You need to trust *me*."

There was that standoff between the pair of us, tension you couldn't cut with a two-handed sword.

"Let me help you, Solaria."

His voice was like velvet and chocolate, like warm spiced wine on a cold snowy night. I fell into the dark promise in his eyes, felt the urge to reach out and run my fingers over the curve of his lips. But of all the magicks I'd played with in my life, illusion was my strength. And enchantment was but a sister to illusion.

Fine. If he was going to pull the seduction thing, then I

would, too.

"I would love to, Dario," I purred, pressing my hand against his chest and leaning in to brush my lips along his jaw. "If only you would allow me to help you first."

I heard the snick of his fangs descending, felt the touch of his tongue on my neck. His hands encircled my waist, holding me ever so lightly. "Do not play with me, Aria."

I stepped back, knowing that I was treading on dangerous ground. Knighthood or not, it was time to bring on my inner Templar. "Then don't play with me. I agreed to research this symbol, to give information to the head of the *Balaj*. I've prioritized this request, giving it my every attention. And in return I get saddled with a vampire minder. And now my minder insists on entering a sacred space, viewing documents that are forbidden to his eyes." I straightened, gritting my teeth. "I believe that both my patience and my hospitality have reached an end."

Was I imagining it, or did I see him wince, his dark eyes flashing a sadness I'd not seen before?

"Fine. I'll wait in the library. Please send word as soon as you've discovered something."

I gave a sharp nod and turned.

"Aria?"

I hesitated at the doorway.

"I don't normally have such poor control over my baser impulses, but you...you are so very tempting."

My breath quickened at his husky voice. The thought of his teeth against my neck, the hunger in his dark eyes, the scent of cinnamon and myrrh. I closed my eyes and forced away the visual of his body above mine.

"Forgiven. Just don't let it happen again."

I walked out of the room without looking back, well aware that part of me longed for it to happen again, for *it* to go all the way to completion. And well aware he knew it.

CHAPTER 10

I felt like my eyes were about to bleed. Or fall out. Either one. We'd been at it all night. I wondered if Dario was still hanging out in the library or if he'd gotten bored and went off to…I don't know, play X-box or something.

"Here." Dad pushed a book toward me. It smelled of mothballs, which didn't say much for whatever preservationist had worked on it.

"Voodoo? In Baltimore? I'm thinking more like this." I shoved a different book his way. One that smelled a whole lot better.

"Wendigo. Peterson did know his stuff."

"This symbol here that we thought might allude to Mars? I think the rounded end here is actually part of this other section with the circle, which would turn this into—"

"Saturn. Good job, Solaria." Dad's smile was unusually warm. "Saturn fits in with the whole dead theme we've got going on here."

"Voodoo doesn't normally employ sigils, so if the practitioner is incorporating that branch of magic into his spell, he'd also have a focus item. A lock of hair or something similar."

"Wendigo would mean cannibalistic undead. Did your vampires have any evidence of eaten corpses?"

"They didn't elaborate. All I got from them was the symbol. The specters raised at the cemetery had malevolent intent, but they were non-corporeal. They might kill, but I doubt they'd consume."

Dad sighed. "I'm wondering if the practitioner isn't using a voodoo symbol in combination with European necromantic practices. I wish we knew more about how the Baltimore *Balaj* got ahold of this. Vampires. Not the best at communication, are they?"

Understatement of the year.

"You've worked with vampires before?" He knew about them, obviously. He'd probably encountered them off and on during his studies. But, the way he'd said that last sentence, the easy tone, led me to believe he'd had a far more intimate encounter with this particular branch of the undead then I'd ever suspected.

"Yes." His smile was a hint nostalgic. "And they are difficult to resist. Almost as seductive as magic's left-hand path. Don't let that sexy boy out there turn you into his blood slave, Aria. He'll be your friend, lure you in with mystery and the promise of knowledge. Then the monster will appear when you are too far gone to resist."

"Did you…?"

"No. I've never been so tempted that I've allowed one to bite me. But I've seen it happen. And I, myself, have felt that temptation. Once you give in, you are forever lost. Like an addict, all you'll think of is him. You'll only exist for those moments with him, for the times when he feeds from you. You're strong, but don't become overconfident. Vampires love those who have a toe in the water of sin, and pride is their favorite."

His words were painful. I knew I couldn't go there, but part of me toyed with the idea of sex with Dario. Part of me wanted to experience the feel of sharing blood with a vampire. Part of me just wanted to lose myself, my identity, in a sea of lust. Forever and ever, amen.

Then my thoughts shifted from Dario to a non-corporeal being of black vapor and red coal. That had not been sexy. That had been terrifying. Still, the thought of magic, that gray area where black wasn't really black, appealed to me. It drew me in even more than Dario's dark eyes.

"What about demons?"

Dad closed the Peterson book and pulled a grimoire toward him. "I didn't see any sigils that I recognized in the symbol, but we can check."

I put a hand on the leather cover. "Not the symbol. I mean, have you ever worked with demons."

His hand rested on top of mine. Again I saw the mottled skin, the bones beneath, and wondered how much longer I'd have these conversations with him. Great-grandma Essie had gotten me used to the idea of longevity, but she had outlived her husband, her children, and most of her grandchildren. Who's to say she wouldn't outlive *this* grandson?

"I worried when you started associating with those magicians up in D.C. I let it go because knowledge is critical to all Templars, and it's always beneficial to have contacts in the magical community. If I'd had any idea they were summoning, I would have put a lid on that right away."

It was one of our mandates, to escort Pilgrims on the Path. My dad felt that it didn't matter which path as long as it led toward the light. Associating with demons was not a rung on the stairway to heaven. Still, there was plenty of gray area, and we Templars argued about it endlessly. *"Haul Du* only summoned information demons."

I heard his sharp inhalation. "That's cheating. Summoning a demon for what you could obtain through research is lazy. And any contact with demons comes with a price. Information demons may not be the most dangerous of hell's minions, but it's a slippery slope, Solaria. Don't risk your soul for a shortcut."

I winced. "There are many magicians throughout time who have summoned demons. The grimoires are full of rituals and sigils for doing so. King Solomon commanded demons."

His head pivoted, and I felt the weight of his stare. "You are no King Solomon. And those magic-users from history eventually came to a grisly end. Demons always demand their pound of flesh. Just bringing them into this world can establish a permanent connection. And once they have their claws in a soul, they never let go."

I felt sick. Really, really sick. Maybe some demons were like that but the Goetic demons were helpful. Angels rarely answered a summons, why not turn to those who actually would? We don't judge. Not after our shameful acts during the crusades. Judging good and evil was for God, not us mortals, so shouldn't we take information where we found it?

"Knowledge is Truth," I recited.

"Knowledge is Truth," my father repeated. It was one of our mantras, one of the Templar code phrases. And it was my justification for delving deeper into ceremonial magic than Templars usually did. Knowledge was one thing, practice was another. I'd crossed the line as far as my father was concerned, but I wasn't a Knight, and I wasn't bound by the same convoluted set of rules as he was.

And it was time to get back to the topic at hand, because I

really wanted to wrap all this up, get some sleep, survive tomorrow's "family" activities, then get back to Baltimore and make some lattes.

"We know the ritual has an appeal to the dead," I said. "I saw the specters raised from the graves, and that's illustrated by this sigil representing Saturn. Then there's the invocation to life—the double circle. These dual lines lead me to believe the summoning involves a physical body, and that's backed up by the portion we're attributing to voodoo or Native American rituals."

My father adjusted his glasses and peered closer at the paper. "But the spirits raised in the cemetery were spirits, not zombies or ghouls. Did the physical portion of the symbol not work correctly?"

I shrugged. "No idea."

I had what the vampires wanted. This was a personal symbol for use in a necromantic ritual to raise the dead—raise a physical form of the dead regardless of the state of decomposition. I wasn't paid for my concerns about its effectiveness given what I'd seen at the Robertson's graves. Case closed. Convey the information to Leonora as soon as I was back in Baltimore, collect my money. Hide it in the tampon box, and go back to my life.

But I couldn't quiet the questions hammering their way through my mind. Why were the vampires interested in a mage who raised specters, or even the dead in physical form? And voodoo or wendigo? Which path was the spell oriented toward? Because that meant a whole world of difference when it came to the intent behind the spell. Plus there was the question I'd had for days—what did the Robertsons have to do with any of this?

Dad shrugged. "I think you've gone as far as you can without more information from the vampires. It's a custom crafted spell to bring the dead to life. What kind of dead, and what sort of purpose they are resurrected for has yet to be seen."

"We know the practitioner is a necromancer. They summon the dead for servitude, to commune with lost loved ones, or to determine past events."

"Necromancers in the past have summoned armies of the dead to fight for them. Modern ones are not always so violent. As you mentioned, this necromancer's intentions may be benign, but don't discount a darker motive."

Parents. They were always warning their children to be careful.

"Got it." I scraped my chair away from the metal table. "Love you, Dad."

He squirmed when I kissed his cheek. I didn't care. This was who I was, and I wasn't about to leave this house without my father knowing how much I cared about him.

"Should I give your excuses to your mother?"

"No. I'll be here for breakfast. And basket weaving or whatever she's got planned for tomorrow."

It was four-thirty in the morning. Even if I drove like a bat out of hell I couldn't get Dario back to Baltimore before he turned into a pile of ash.

"Your friend is still waiting for you. Want me to put together an early breakfast?"

I shook my head. "Go to bed, Dad. It's late and I know you'll be up with the sun frying French toast. Dario and I will raid the fridge for leftovers. Then we'll go upstairs and swap bodily fluids."

Dad hugged me tight and kissed the top of my head. It was an unusual display of emotion. "I'm so glad you're here, Solaria. And you, my little Knight, are incorrigible."

I was. I didn't have any intention of changing. And I wasn't a Knight.

CHAPTER 11

*D*ario was waiting for me in the library. He appeared composed as usual, but I felt an odd tension radiating from his body.

"If we leave now, we'll be close to D.C. come sunrise. There's a sanctuary you can drop me at for the day."

I plopped down on the sofa next to him, exhausted. "I know I said I didn't want to go through another day of 'family time', but I don't trust myself driving right now. It won't be a big deal. You can spend one more day in the dragon room. I'll probably sleep until noon anyway, unless Mom gets some wild hair and decides we all need to go to early church service. We'll leave right at sunset."

"I think we should leave now. I can drive if you're too tired."

Why the hurry? And why hadn't he asked me about what I'd discovered while in the vault? I would have thought he'd be eager to pump me for info. Although maybe that's why he was so eager to get back. Had something come up that made him want to rush back to Baltimore?

"Uh, no. The last time you drove I got abandoned in a

scary section of town without so much as a goodbye kiss. One more night won't kill us."

"It might," he muttered as he stood. I bit back a smile, wondering if Essie had cornered him in the library while I'd been nose-deep in dusty manuscripts. The mental image of my great-grandmother chasing a vampire around the room was pretty amusing.

"Let's grab some leftovers out of the fridge. It's been forever since dinner and I'm starving."

I walked past him and he followed me into the kitchen where we stood and ate chunks of cold roast beef without plate or utensils. I was practically asleep on my feet, but I followed him up to his room and dropped down on the bed, covering a yawn with my hand.

Dario stood in the doorway. "I thought you were tired."

"I am." I patted the bed beside me. "I figured you'd want to hear what I discovered before you went down for your daytime slumber."

He hesitated, then walked over to lean against one of the bed posts. "It can wait until tomorrow night."

"Why not now? I found out that the symbol is part of a necromantic spell to return the dead to life. The symbol was personally crafted, a blend of different magicks, so whoever put it together is an experienced mage—someone who knows their stuff. Probably someone older. That level of magic usually requires many decades of dedicated study."

He sat down, reluctance vanishing. "What kind of life does it grant to the dead? Ghosts? Zombies? Are they just animated or sentient? How long do they live once risen, and what determines which dead it brings to life? Is it an area of effect or targeted? If targeted, what kind of focus or personal item is needed?"

Whoa. Like seriously, whoa. Dario was far more knowledgeable about necromantic magic than I'd suspected. And the questions he was asking were a whole lot more than I'd bargained for when I'd asked Leonora for five grand. I doubted I could answer half of them without some kind of Vulcan mind-meld with the caster.

"The symbol indicates a physical body will be risen, but the one time I've seen it used it only brought forth specters."

The vampire leaned closer to me. "You've seen it used? When? Who cast the spell?"

I got the uncomfortable feeling that I'd said too much and frantically wondered how I was going to backpedal on this one. "I didn't see the caster, only the specters. The mark was on the graves. I'm assuming it might have been a test run—one that failed since no physical body rose from the grave."

He nodded, apparently satisfied with my explanation. "How long did the specters remain?"

"They weren't friendly, so I didn't hang around. They were gone the next morning."

"How can you discover more? I'm assuming since it's a personal symbol, you've exhausted all your Templar resources?"

I felt sort of nauseous as I nodded. "Will that be enough for Leonora? Without knowing who the caster is, I don't think I can find the answers to your other questions."

My words were greeted with silence. The roast beef in my stomach threatened to come back up. If I hadn't demanded payment, I could have held firm on only giving her the knowledge we had as Templars, but I'd demanded payment.

"Leonora will not be satisfied," he admitted.

Yep. Gonna puke. "So I won't get the rest of my money?" If I needed to return what she'd already paid me, I'd have to dip into the other checking account—the one I hadn't wanted to touch. Maybe she'd take it in payments?

"She'll consider it a breach of contract."

I understood what Dario meant. If she was really pissed,

I'd be dead. If she was feeling charitable, I'd be passed around as a blood slave for a few days before being dumped in an alley to crawl my way to the hospital. I might have some immunity from retribution as a Templar, but to an angry vampire, payback trumped immunity.

It wasn't fair. I knew the vampires were withholding information from me. How the heck was I supposed to find the caster when I didn't know what was going on? They couldn't just shove some piece of paper at me with a symbol on it and expect me to wave a wand and know all.

Wand. It made me think of the demon who'd come when I summoned Vine. It had to have been a fluke. Maybe I could summon a different Goetic demon and get the information that way. One who had some skills in divination, perhaps? But before I went down that road again, I had one more angle to check out. The Robertsons hadn't been a test case. They were significant somehow. If I could get to see that reporter, swap some information with her, then maybe I could figure out who the caster was without having to summon a demon.

Although if it came to a choice between facing Leonora or risking a summoning, I'd take the demon. Ironic how I was more afraid of a vampire Mistress than a being from hell.

"I've got a few more avenues to explore. Just let Leonora know what I've found out so far, and that I'll have the other answers to her by the deadline." I would, even if I had to replace another window in my apartment.

"Good." Dario leaned closer and inhaled. "I'd hate for Leonora to kill you. Although I might be able to convince her to give you to me instead."

I froze like a rabbit in the briars. "I'll get her the information by the deadline. Then I'll collect the rest of my money and be on my way."

He edged nearer. I couldn't move, could barely breathe. "I'd make it enjoyable for you. Weeks, months if I can keep control. I like you, Aria. Maybe enough to turn you so you'd always be mine."

What the hell was going on? I caught my breath and leaned back. *No sudden moves.* "That won't be necessary. I'll get the information and we'll never see each other again."

We wouldn't either. I'd completely avoid those pubs he liked to frequent, stay as far away as possible from the side of town he'd clearly claimed as his hunting ground. Heck, I may never go out at night again.

"But we will see each other again," he murmured. "I'm your boyfriend, remember? We're supposed to be having sex right now. Isn't that what you led your parents to believe?"

Shit. I tried to break out of the deer-in-headlights reaction I was having. "I was joking, messing with my parents."

I reached out to push him aside and turned to swing my legs off the bed, well aware that I needed to get out of here and fast.

Touching him was a bad idea. Dario shot forward with inhuman speed. I recoiled, twisting to roll-off the bed. I've got good reflexes from a lifetime of training, but there was no way I could evade a vampire this close to me. In a blink, I was on my back with his arms on either side of my shoulders, his legs pinning mine to the bed.

"Boyfriends get certain benefits." He shifted, his thighs straddling mine, his upper body completely supported by his arms.

"Get off me," I choked out. "Dario, snap out of it and let me go."

I felt ready to burst into flame. The nearness of him, the smell of myrrh and cinnamon on his cool skin, the intense way his gaze traveled over my face and neck, lingering on the pulse in my throat. If he'd been human, if I'd had any confidence in his ability to keep this just sexual, then I would have lost myself in the feeling of his body against mine. Instead all I could think of was his fangs sinking into my neck, and how that was beginning to sound like a good idea.

"Words have power," he whispered. "You've called me your boyfriend repeatedly. It is too late for you to take that back now."

The part of me that was screaming a warning faded away, hidden beneath a fuzzy-headed lust and need. My breath caught as he bent his head, moving his mouth lightly across my jaw and down the side of my neck. His hips brushed against mine and I arched my back upward to touch him, something between a whimper and a moan escaping from my throat.

"Do you want me, Ari?" My hands clawed at him in an affirmative response. I couldn't think straight beyond my desperate need to feel his naked skin against mine, to have him fill me.

His kisses grew more insistent, teeth nipping along my skin. "Can I share your blood, Ari? You've never experienced ecstasy until you've had the double hit of coming while I taste the sweet nectar of your gift."

I was gone. Drunk. High on the equivalent of a vampire roofie. He could take anything he wanted—blood, my body, anything. Just let this liquid pleasure washing over me continue, let me come in his arms with his teeth buried in my neck.

Dario shifted backward, crossing his arms as he stripped off his T-shirt. I couldn't move. I could do nothing but watch him. Then I reached for him, welcoming the weight of his body on mine, welcoming the press of him between my thighs.

Sharp fangs glinted between his lips. His eyes were dark, expressionless. He moved against me and although my body was completely with the program, my mind suddenly wavered, then rebelled. This wasn't the Dario who ate Linguini Alfredo with crab meat, who dryly annoyed my mother, who teased me about my love of pastries. This wasn't Dario, this was a predator. And I was held tight in his grasp.

"No. Don't. Dario, please don't do this."

I'd cast no spell but still he froze, the muscles in his jaw tensing as he stared down at me. Slowly, careful not to brush against me, he rolled away and sat up.

I didn't say another word, just bolted out, down the stairs and into my room. There I leaned against the closed door, stared at the pink walls decorated with kittens and unicorns, and tried to catch my breath.

Close call didn't even begin to describe this. I'd been ready to give in. Part of me still wanted to go back up there and let him do whatever he wanted with me. Instead I went into the bathroom across the hall and took the coldest shower I could. Then I lay wide awake in bed until the first rays of dawn crawled across my floor.

CHAPTER 12

Normally "family time" dragged, but Sunday afternoon went by in a blink. As expected, I slept in until noon, had lunch, then played bridge and swam in the pool as the sun raced toward the western horizon. I dreaded seeing Dario, dreaded being in a car with him for several awkward hours as we made our way back to Baltimore. I prayed there wouldn't be the usual traffic and that I could speed like a maniac and end what was best case scenario going to be a horrible drive, worst case scenario a deadly one.

I ate dinner, said my goodbyes, packed my bag, and met the vampire as I was throwing the duffle, along with a giant sack full of armor, into the back of my car.

"Ready?" I wasn't sure what else to say to him. I didn't even want to look at him directly.

"Mmm."

That was it. The lack of communication on his part was actually a relief. He could have been a mannequin for all the interaction we had as I drove home. My mind made up for the silence by thinking of last night, of how I would have been completely willing to have sex with this guy if it hadn't involved the aftermath from the donation of blood. Why couldn't vampires be like they were in the movies, all sex and little sips from your neck now and then? I could totally get into that if it was just some kind of kink like rubber nun's suits or ball gags. Booty call, little biting action, then see-ya-later, gator.

I had a feeling it wouldn't be just a sip if things went that direction with Dario and me. And I worried it would be the beginning of a serious addiction on my part. Whatever was in vampire saliva that made the experience so pleasurable for victims also left the blood donor craving a repeat experience. The need eventually subsided—unless the vampire came back for more, setting up a cycle that resulted in the stereotypical blood slave/master relationship.

I'd seen those one-time victims the day after, dazed and still floating, then seen them later in the week with shaking hands and hungry eyes.

I had no desire to go through that kind of withdrawal, and from what Dario had said in the heat of the moment last night, I doubted his control. If he caved and came back to me, if I somehow managed to find him and talk him into a round two, three, and four, I'd wind up a blood slave. And blood slaves died. His promise of a few months would probably be optimistic.

Dead. I needed to keep reminding myself of that. Dead.

"Remember the hunger I told you about?" Dario's soft voice jolted me out of my thoughts. "It's no excuse for what happened last night. I'm surprised you trust me enough to let me come with you back to Baltimore."

"Well, I was hardly going to leave you there with my family," I snapped back. I wasn't really angry at him. Yes, he'd lost control and crossed a line, but I should have seen the signs. Wait, no. That was the equivalent of saying I was almost raped because I'd drank too much and wore a short skirt. Actually, I *was* angry at him. "What happened to your being able to go a few days without feeding? I thought you had more control than that."

He flinched at each statement, as if I struck him. "We are careful not to kill our victims, not to overindulge when we take blood, not to draw notice to ourselves by feasting too often. Every one of us constantly hovers on the edge of starvation. It's no excuse. I *should* be able to go two days without losing control over my hunger."

"Why?"

Out of the corner of my eye I saw him turn to face me. "Why what?"

I wanted to ask him why he'd lost control this time, but I wasn't sure I wanted to know the answer, so I asked my other question.

"Why are you on the edge of starvation? There are six hundred thousand people in Baltimore. Are there really that many vampires that you can't get enough blood without killing?"

Dario sat back and stared out at the traffic for a moment. "We can't over graze. If we're careful about tourists, and we take a small amount from only one or two victims per night, then we'll have enough without needing to go beyond the city limits. We'll also have reserves if we need to feed heavily to defend our territory."

It was such a famine mindset. I just couldn't wrap my head around the logic. "But you don't have to stay within the city. Baltimore County is huge, and the nearest other *Balaj* I know of is in Philadelphia. Heck, you all could even pop over to D.C. if you wanted.

He turned to me. "I'm trusting that you will keep this between us."

I nodded, wondering what he was about to say and if I

could keep his confidence or not. Templars were not to judge, but something in me tensed as I waited to hear his secret.

"There are solitary vampires, ones without a *Balaj*. There are also *Balajes* that do not have territories. They roam and exist in the fringe areas around claimed cities. Since they have no land to call their own, they don't care about killing. They're reckless. If we hunt in the borderlands, we could be killed by these rogues. The only safe way to hunt there is in a pack of our own, which would leave less of us to defend the city if need be."

I had no idea all this was going on right under my nose. "Do you all police the borderlands for these rogues?"

"Only if they stay and their activities threaten to bring notice to us. Otherwise, we let them be and they quickly move on."

I had a sudden urge to start checking crime stats and tracking murders in these borderlands, but something else Dario had said struck me.

"When your *Balaj* came from Haiti, when you all were kicked out of your territory in Florida, you were one of these rogue bands."

"Yes." He practically spat out the word. "I'm not proud of what I did to survive, or what my brothers and sisters did either. It was a precarious existence until we managed to take Baltimore. Living like that changes a vampire. Some of us manage to regain control once we have the safety of a territory, but some never do."

"What happens to those who don't? Regain control, I mean."

"We do our best to help them. No one wants to lose a brother or sister. No Sire wants to put down a child of their making. If they are a threat to the *Balaj*, then that's what eventually must be done."

"I'm sorry." I couldn't imagine how difficult that must have been for him. I'd never been in the position where I had to make a difficult decision like that about a loved one, and I hoped I never was.

"About last night…if it had been simple blood lust I wouldn't have tried to take you like that. I don't spend a lot of time with humans who aren't my targeted prey for the evening, and I usually only spend a few hours with them at the most. Being with you over these last few days, actually having conversations with you…I'll admit it's caused me to have some rather lurid fantasies."

His tone had turned light, teasing. I knew he meant what he said, but I also knew he wouldn't attack me. It lifted a burden of anxious fear I'd been carrying since I'd climbed into the car with him.

"You're not the only one with lurid fantasies. I seem to remember I threw myself at you that first night. Yeah, I didn't try to bite you, but I guess that makes us kind of even."

And just like that the tension was gone and we were back to our weird, easy friendship.

Dario tapped me on the arm with his fist. "I want to hear these fantasies. Do they involve me sharing your blood? Biting you in all sorts of sensitive spots?"

I laughed. "More like me having sex with you while wearing one of those whiplash collars so you can gnaw away at my neck without actually biting me. I could even duct tape a pint of bagged blood from the hospital to it so you can pretend you're drinking from me."

"Ugh." He wrinkled up his face. "I tried that stuff once. It's horrible. Even if you warm it up, it's flavorless and doesn't do anything to fill you. Maybe you can have me bite on a piece of wood like they used to do when they amputated some-one's limb. Chain me up to the bed with gold-plated hand-cuffs so I can't take it out."

I recoiled in mock horror. "Dario! What sort of porn have you been watching? Nice Templars like me don't do things like that. Besides, I like a man to have his hands free, otherwise why bother?"

He smiled at me. Even in the dim light I could see his eyes crinkled up, the white of his teeth, the faint dimple on his left cheek. "If you ever grow tired of this life, Aria, if you ever desire immortality such as mine, or if you want to lose yourself in the life of a blood slave, let me know. I'll not say no."

He wouldn't say "no". Which is the reason I could never say "yes".

anice Oswald was a tall woman with a runner's build and a thoroughbred's face. I'm very fond of horses, so I took to her immediately, especially after she offered to pay for lunch. Gas to and from Middleburg had taken the last of my cash, and I didn't get paid until Friday.

She was just as eager to see me as I was to see her. Folder after folder came out of her briefcase until there was barely room on the table for our soups and salads.

"I was originally researching changes in crime statistics in the different parts of Baltimore, but this case caught my attention. A family of five murdered in their home, and no one was ever charged." She shook her head and made a *tsk* noise.

"And one daughter who died only a few months before that," I added. "Were you able to find out what happened to Shay Robertson? I read the missing persons reports, and the records show the case remained open, but the family obituary said she predeceased her parents."

Janice tapped one of the folders. "That's one of the other odd things about this family. Shay was never seen again, and there was never a body found. In spite of that, the family was absolutely convinced of her death."

"A few months and they're assuming she's dead? I thought most families held on hope for years."

"Every family member I interviewed was convinced she was dead. I got the impression that they'd received some sort of proof."

I winced, thinking of a finger in a box, or an ear. Although neither of those would necessarily mean Shay's death. "Did they know who killed her?"

"Yes, and none of them would say. A cousin finally admitted the family believed it was her boyfriend."

"The older guy? The one she was supposed to have run away with?"

Janice nodded. "Bit of a mysterious character. She'd sneak out at night to see him. None of her friends ever met the man, but they said she was infatuated with him. He was all she could think about, all she could talk about. Teenage love is so obsessive."

My breath caught, wondering if there was more behind the obsession than just teenage hormones. "Were there any descriptions of this boyfriend?"

"No. The detective on the case thought he might have been into organized crime and when Shay's parents started figuring out what happened to their daughter they were killed."

Was I seeing vampires where there were none? From what Dario had said it seemed unlikely that the *Balaj* would have killed a local family and covered it up. Women certainly turned into fools over human men often enough. But still, I remembered the look in Dario's eyes as he pressed himself against me...

A vampire bites a young girl, a fourteen-year-old girl, and can't stay away. Eventually he takes her, and inevitably kills her. If the family discovered who—and what—he was… The *Balaj* couldn't risk exposure. They'd need to ensure the family never revealed their secrets. An entire family killed, either with the consent of the Mistress, or without her knowledge, by a creepy, pedophile vampire Lothario.

"Here are the victim photos you wanted to see." Janice pushed a stack of eight by ten glossies toward me.

I stared at them closely. If vampires had done this, they'd been handy enough with a knife to destroy any evidence of bites.

"There wasn't enough blood and there was no sign of struggle." Janice's laugh was short and bitter. "It's almost like they were horribly anemic and too weak to do more than sit there as they were killed."

I wondered about the connection between the symbol and all this. A family long dead, possibly killed by vampires. Was Leonora afraid of what their ghosts might say? Was that why she wanted to know about the symbol? How far would she go to silence the necromancer who dared attempt to air their dirty laundry?

"If only the dead could talk," I mused. "I wonder who they would accuse."

"Probably the same person that did this." Janice tossed a newspaper on top of the folders.

The circled front page article detailed what police were calling a possible gang related murder.

"I've got a source with the Baltimore City P.D.," Janice continued. "He says the four gang members had their throats slit nearly ear to ear, but the blood at the scene is far less than it should have been. And there was no sign of struggle. Four armed men—suspicious armed gang members—brutally murdered without lifting a finger."

I felt like time stopped around me. Dario had led me to believe that vampires wouldn't kill like this, that they'd either dispose of the bodies or send their fang-punctured corpses to others as a warning. With this newspaper article in front of me, I found myself having a hard time believing Dario. The details were eerily similar to the Robertson case, except the family forty years ago hadn't been involved in any kind of illegal activity. "Why now, after forty years, would the same person strike again?"

"I'm not saying it's the same person." Janice nudged the paper. "Could be a gang M.O. Could be they always take out their enemies this way and nobody ever connected the dots before. I've got more research to do, but I seriously think we have a connection here."

Gang. As in gang of vampires. I couldn't completely rule out death magic but that seemed like an increasingly remote possibility. No practitioner of the dark arts would subdue and drain four gang members when there were far easier victims to choose from. Vampires. Growing up I'd read about their brutalities in history, our justification for what had been genocide. With the truce, I'd come to believe they'd changed, that they had become a kinder, gentler predator. Clearly I'd been a fool.

Even more a fool for trusting Dario.

"I'd love to know what the connection was." Janice gathered her folders up. "The crime status study on the Robertsons was pretty dry, but if I can link it to other murders in the last forty years… well, breaking open a case like this would make my day. Heck, it would make my year."

I'll bet it would. I had every intention of looking on this in more detail myself, as well as holding the vampires accountable for mass murder. Feeding on humans was one thing, intentional killing was another. First things first, though. I needed to discover as much as I could about this symbol and fulfill my contract with the vampires. Then I'd deal with their more recent activities.

I gestured toward the folders. "A whole family murdered. Well, except for Russell Robertson."

"Russell Findal now. His aunt and uncle took him in after the murders and adopted him."

That was odd. The boy had been eight. I would have thought he would have wanted to keep his family name, to honor the parents who'd died so violently. Unless he was afraid the killers might track him down. He was only eight. Perhaps his aunt had the same fear. Perhaps I was being a weird paranoid woman after my close call with Dario.

"Did you interview Russell Findal? Can you share his contact information with me?"

"Sure." Janice jotted down a name and phone number on a slip of paper and passed it to me. "He's a bit odd, I'll warn you. Not that I blame him, losing his family so young."

"Odd how?" I didn't have a gun, but maybe I should bring my sword. If only it weren't so huge, and… obvious.

"He's one of those intense sort of guys. You know, the ones where you wonder if they don't wear a tin foil hat when no one's looking. He moved back to Baltimore a few months ago. Unmarried. Works warehousing jobs—forklift operation and that sort of thing. When I spoke to him last he was between jobs."

"Are any of his family still in Baltimore?" It seemed kind of odd to move back here otherwise.

"No. The aunt and uncle that took him in are down in Florida. Everyone else is spread out across the U.S. He was the only family member I was able to interview in person."

"Thanks. I really appreciate your meeting me and sharing your research like this." I was. She'd been really forthcoming, and even bought me lunch.

Janice grinned. "I have an ulterior motive. It isn't every

day that a part-time coffee-shop employee takes an interest in a forty-year-old murder of people she didn't know, so I did a little bit of digging of my own."

No biggie. We weren't a secret society or anything. The whole idea of Templars was that you should be able to find one when you needed one. Of course few, including us, knew what our purpose was in this modern day beyond safeguarding the contents of the Temple and acting as an archaic Wikipedia of the supernatural.

"Templars, huh?" She stuffed the folders into her briefcase and finished her iced tea in a quick gulp. "Sword and armor and horses and all that?"

"Yeah. Although I can't exactly go trotting my steed around the city wearing full plate and sporting a claymore. The police frown on that sort of thing, and I'd probably get shot by a paranoid drug dealer."

She laughed. "Still, if there's something that comes up, say with that coffee-shop job of yours that might be worth investigating, or if you find out the connection between the Robertson murders and the gang ones, you'll let me know?"

It took me a second to realize that she thought we were some kind of vigilante group and my coffee-shop job was a cover for my superhero activities. Templar Batman. That would be funny. "Sure. Just to get you caught up to speed, there's someone raising the dead on the Northside, and the vampires are probably involved."

She stood, her grin so wide I swear I could see every one of her teeth. "Thanks for the tip. And given the amount of illegal Viagra sales in the Northside, I'm not surprised the dead are getting it up."

I watched her leave, her long legs taking her to the curb in four strides. Janice was a good contact to have. A savvy reporter would make an awesome resource if I ever needed to do this sort of thing again. And all I had to do was keep her in the loop, even if she didn't believe me about the necromancer or the vampires. Yet.

CHAPTER 14

I'd snuck into the back room during my shift and tried to see if I could reach Russell Robertson/Findal. Time was running out and I didn't have much more to tell Leonora than I had yesterday. If I couldn't glean anything from this guy, I'd need to either try summoning an information demon again or lie. Lying to the vampires didn't seem like a wise thing to do, but I might not have a choice.

Russell's phone was no longer in service. I searched both his names and couldn't come up with a Baltimore address for either. Reverse tracing the phone revealed nothing. It was a dead end—for the investigation, and probably for me.

I had one more day before my deadline ran out, but there was no doubt in my mind that Dario would be banging down my door tonight, pressuring me to wrap this up. I got the feeling he didn't want to see me dead either, at least not unless it was his sort of dead. I didn't need any more pressure and there wasn't anything he could do to help me. Plus I wasn't sure I wanted his help. If this crazy idea bouncing around in my head turned out to be the truth, then the vampires had a lot to answer for, and I wasn't sure

I wanted to give them information that might lead them to Russell.

There was one last place I wanted to try. One hunch to follow up on, but it would have to be later tonight, because I had to meet with my new friends about the upcoming LARP right after my shift finished.

I probably could have walked to Brandi's apartment from work, but I needed to go home first and stuff my armor and a sword into my car. Thankfully, none of the people walking by or the other building tenants batted an eye over a woman juggling a Santa-sized bag, a sword, and a peanut butter sandwich in her hands.

Turns out Brandi lived in a nicer neighborhood than I did. Passersby and other tenants here *did* stare as I hauled my stash through the front door and into the elevator.

"Nice evening, huh?" I commented to the elderly man next to me whose eyes kept straying from the lighted numbers above the door to my sword. He made a noncommittal noise, and practically ran once the elevator opened to his floor. Maybe I should have left all of this at home until the actual LARP event.

Brandi's apartment wasn't much bigger than mine, although it seemed smaller with all the furniture and knick-knacks scattered around. The six other people plopped on sofas, chairs, and the floor left little room for my bag of armor, so I stashed it against the closet next to the front door.

"What the heck is in that?" Brandi pointed to the bag, then proceeded to make ooo noises over my sword. That got everyone moving and suddenly I was surrounded by seven people eyeing my weapon. At least they were respectful enough not to touch it.

"A real bastard sword," one large man announced. "Looks like it's been used, too."

Well, yeah. Why would I have something like this and not use it? "Others in my Order use rapiers or two-handed swords, but our family favors a hand-and-a-half. I've had Trusty since I was nine."

"More like Rusty," a guy with glasses commented, lessening the rudeness of his words with a friendly grin. "The edges don't seem very sharp either, is this a practice sword?"

"I only sharpen the last ten inches or so of the blade, so I can half-sword—grip it midway down and thrust it like a lance. That's how you kill someone through the gaps in their armor or holes in their helmet. The wedge design of the tip is for forcing its way through chain mail. The blade actually spreads and breaks the links at their joint."

There was a poignant silence after my monologue, then a soft "whoa" from a woman with green dreadlocks.

"I don't know about you guys, but she's got my vote." Glasses guy had a glint of appreciation, as well as something more lustful, in his eyes.

"What's in the bag?" The large guy asked.

"My plate mail and my chain mail. I wasn't sure which you guys use during your LARP." I held my breath, worried that maybe I'd screwed up. This was turning into a giant show-and-tell, and I couldn't see that anyone else had brought either armor or weapons. Hopefully I hadn't ruined my chances with these people.

My fears were unfounded. If the sword hadn't captured their interest, my armor did. Next thing I knew, everyone was trying on knees and elbows, admiring the articulation in my gauntlets, and the tight weave of my mail. I thought glasses guy was going to hump me on the spot, but he restrained himself and instead offered me one of his beers. Which I gratefully took. I'd been so busy loading up all my gear that I'd forgotten to bring drinks.

"You do know that we don't use this real stuff in the

LARP?" Glasses guy took a swig of his beer, standing as close to me as possible without touching.

No. I didn't know. "Ummm, I thought you guys might like to see…"

"We use foam padded wood or PVC core weapons, and armor is usually a few pieces of aluminum chain or molded plastic armor."

Shit. Good thing we were meeting tonight. I would have shown up Saturday and killed all my new friends. It would have been a Massacre in the Park instead of a LARP in the Park.

Glasses guy must have read my expression because he smiled reassuringly. "I've got a spare sword you can borrow. It won't be as nicely balanced as yours, but at least it won't kill anyone. You can use your knees and elbows, and maybe your gauntlets and helm. We have a team tabard that goes over top so you don't accidently whack any of your teammates."

I understood. This would be a war exercise, only with minimal armor. The intent would be mostly tactical and skills testing, as opposed to actual combat training. "How hard do I need to hit for it to count as a strike?"

He eyed the muscles in my arms, then his gaze shifted to the neckline of my tanktop. "Be gentle."

I got the feeling we weren't talking about the LARP any longer.

The rest of the meeting went quickly with everyone discussing logistics and determining who was bringing what for the potluck. I discovered that Glasses Guy was named Zac, and that he was determined to ply me with beers as fast as I could drink them. I steadily resisted, keeping to water after the first one. I'd been excited about Saturday's event before I even knew what we were going to be doing, but as the group discussed tactics and strategy, I felt my adrenaline surge. This was going to be a freaking blast.

After the meeting Zac insisted on walking me to my car while I eyed the sun low on the horizon. As much as I wanted to take him up on his offer to go get a cup of coffee, I really needed to get going.

"What RPGs do you like?" he asked, opening my door for me after helping me shove the bag of armor in the trunk. I sat my sword carefully on the passenger seat and pondered his words. LARPing was soft-weapon war games. I assumed he meant a rocket launcher that propelled beanbags as opposed to grenades.

"I've got an airsoft one at home just for fun, but I've shot both the Redeye and the Stinger a few times. I prefer the Stinger due to missile range and maneuverability when tracking the target, but I'm not really proficient in either one. Templars are more sword-and-shield fighters."

Zac's mouth dropped open in astonishment. "Just throwing this out there, but the thought of you firing an anti-aircraft gun turns me on beyond belief. Unfortunately I meant role playing games. You know, like D&D or Warhammer?"

I shook my head and shrugged, past being embarrassed by my ignorance of these things. Nobody seemed to mind that I was a total noob, and I doubted Zac was going to suddenly stop admiring my chest because I'd confused the acronyms. "I've never played any of those."

He chuckled. "A virgin! A beautiful virgin who could kick my ass and leave me bleeding by the side of the road. Can I see you tomorrow night? Dinner and an introduction to some of my favorite games?"

He was cute, and the attention flattering although bordering on the edge of creepy-stalkerish. The only male interest I'd had the past few months beyond Petie looking up my shirt was Saturday night's near miss with Dario. I should take Zac up on his offer, but I had to deal with the vampire issue first.

"I'm kinda busy this week, but I'll see you Saturday at the park," I told him, sliding into my car before he got any ideas and tried to plant one on me. Friends. I finally had some people to hang out with and an admirer of sorts. Maybe now my evenings would consist of more than hanging out in cheap pubs waiting for a sexy vampire to show up.

$\mathcal{I}$ typed an address into my GPS, and started driving, feeling increasingly nervous as the busy streets grew empty and the occupied houses were separated by rows of boarded-up ones. I parked a few blocks down next to an area that looked as if people still lived there. Then, feeling rather foolish, I slid my sword off the passenger seat.

Old Trusty wasn't as fancy as my great-grandfather's sword. It was just a plain old bastard sword, perfect for thrusting through your opponent, breaking a few ribs with a flat blow, or smashing in skulls with the pommel. And I felt like a total idiot walking down a Baltimore city street in khaki pants, a cheery light-blue button-down shirt, a designer cross-shoulder bag, and a large sword.

Some guy sitting on his porch steps eyed me curiously as I walked past. "That dragon be a couple blocks down on the left."

"Thanks." I saluted him with the sword, then flipped it around my wrist in a flourish that had nothing to do with fighting. Whatever. It impressed the guy on the porch enough to get a whistle of admiration out of him.

Once I neared my destination my stance changed, and I held the sword across the front of my body, point down. I'd gotten out of practice in the last six months, and the sucker felt heavier than it should have. Three pounds doesn't seem like much but when you're supporting the weight by only a few muscles in your arm and wrist, after a few minutes it starts to feel like you're lugging an anchor around.

The house was boarded up, the plywood old and covered with black mildew and worn graffiti. The brick crumbled around the porch where straggly, determined weeds reached upward. I pushed aside a rotted, grass-choked gate and waded through the unmown jungle to the back yard. At one time this had been a nice row house, but now it was a hazard. I wasn't even sure if the joists would be sturdy enough inside to hold my weight.

They'd held someone's weight. One of the boards over the back door had a half-circular scrape in the grain. Shifting my grip on the sword, I grabbed the board next to it and slid it sideways, creating a narrow opening.

I let Trusty enter the house first, one hand halfway up the dull-edged portion of the blade, and the other braced on the knob of the pommel. This thing worked best as a sort of multi-purpose spear, and if anyone jumped at me, they were getting shishkabobbed.

My footsteps were the only ones on the alarmingly spongy floorboards. The disturbed dust indicated that others had been there before me, and I was very aware they might still be there, hiding in case I was the police, or possibly sleeping off their last fix. Either way, this place had served as a flop house for quite a while. Doors had been torn off the kitchen cabinets. The carpet was sliced to ribbons. The entire place stank of urine, unwashed bodies, burned trash. Something scurried in a corner and I froze to watch a rat dash from one open counter to another.

There was nothing that indicated someone had been here who hadn't been high as a kite and less than picky about their living quarters. I hesitated at the stairs, eyeing them skeptically. If the main floor was dicey, the top floor was liable to give under my weight. Holding my breath I went a few steps up and stopped, my palms sweating. There was no sense in breaking a leg, or worse, on this fool's errand. I backed down the stairs deciding to check the cellar then write this whole thing off.

The cellar stairs were even more rickety than the ones leading to the second floor. I used my cell phone for light and brushed the thick cobwebs aside for a quick look-see. Dirt floor. A chipped cement slab in the corner. Broken glass and splintered wood. And a whole lot of spiders.

Scurrying back up the stairs, I spent a few moments brushing off the cobwebs and spiders that I was sure had covered every inch of exposed skin. Nothing. Just another abandoned house in Baltimore. Taking one more look at the stairs to the second floor, I gritted my teeth. I really, really didn't want to go up there, but I'd driven down here, walked a few blocks with a big sword in hand. I might as well be thorough about this.

Two steps up, and my palms started sweating again. The wood creaked beneath my feet, the railing rocked with the slightest touch of my hand. By the time I was halfway to the landing, I was nearly hyperventilating. I was going to fall. I was going to crash through the stairs, then through the shitty first floor onto the dirt basement covered in cobwebs and spiders, and probably impaled by my own sword.

Why was I so terrified of climbing a set of stairs?

Shit. How many times had I used this very spell? It was a close cousin to the one I'd used on my tampon box, as well as the one I'd cast to keep any intruders from taking Trusty or my armor. How embarrassing to be almost done in by such a simple hex.

I had the means to break through it, but didn't. Breaking a hex, even one this simple, took a good bit of magical energy —energy that I wasn't willing to expend with a potential vampire meeting awaiting me this evening. Plus there was a decent chance that this was a layered spell, and that something with more whomp would come at me if I disabled this one.

And busting up someone else's spell was damned rude. I didn't own this building. I was trespassing. Yes, whoever put this hex in place was most likely trespassing, too, but courtesy between magic users meant one didn't go around disabling others' workings without good reason. Me feeling like I was going to die if I took one more step wasn't reason enough. So I pressed on, clenching my jaw and breathing as slowly as I could. When I reached the landing, relief washed over me. I'd passed the area of effect for the spell. Hopefully there wouldn't be others—especially lethal others—ahead.

Left or right? Neither choice looked particularly appealing, so I headed right. The bathroom was at the end of the hall. All the fixtures had been ripped out and the walls smashed in, no doubt to scavenge any copper pipes. The sink and toilet lay in white porcelain chunks, the tub filthy and cracked. Some artist had written slanderous comments about a woman named Bethany in what I hoped was brown marker. I backed away slowly and checked out the bedrooms on this section of the hall.

The one next to the bathroom used to be pink, then white, then yellow judging by the layers of peeling paint. There was a stained mattress on the floor next to a garbage bag. I peeked inside the bag and wished that I hadn't. Old aluminum cans, dirty clothes, and newspapers. Ugh. I hastily closed the bag up, pinching my nose to try and get rid of the memory of that smell.

The only other interesting thing in the bedroom was a doorway to a balcony. I didn't venture out onto the sagging structure, but I envisioned little girls looking out over the back yard and alley behind, perhaps sneaking down the support post to the soft ground below and running off to meet a boy—or a vampire.

The two bedrooms that flanked the stairs both had one window and their own dirty mattresses, these with a variety of drug paraphernalia next to them. So far I'd seen nothing worthy of a keep-away spell. I doubted a junkie would have the control needed to put it in place, but there weren't any indications that someone beyond the homeless and drug addicts used this house.

At first glance the master bedroom was equally disappointing. If I hadn't noticed that someone had pried the boards covering the windows aside to allow thin beams of light into the room, I might have given up. It wasn't just the late day's sunlight that piqued my curiosity. This room felt lighter. In spite of the soiled mattress and general filth, it smelled like…cinnamon. And sandalwood. Like Dario only without the odd cool smell of vampire. Cinnamon and sandalwood, both used throughout time to anoint the dead and prepare them for their eternal rest. It wasn't the acrid smell of unwashed addicts.

I moved the mattress, and there it was: A large, flat, clear plastic container. Not in plain sight, but not well hidden either. Either the owner had great confidence in his keep-away spell, or he had something else in place to protect his belongings.

It might be a terrible breach of etiquette, but I wasn't about to risk blowing my arms off opening this case. Pulling a piece of chalk from my pocket, I wrote a few runes on

Trusty's blade, then sent my energy into them. They glowed blue, then faded, leaving my sword appearing to be the same old battered weapon as before. Extending it full length so I was as far away as possible, I hooked the tip of the blade under the lid of the plastic box and flipped it open.

Unfortunately I also flipped the box over. The contents slid across the floor, but nothing exploded. I frowned at the box. There was no spell. Who kept belongings important enough for a hallway keep-away spell in a box without any additional protection? It was as if the owner wanted them to be found, although not without some minor effort.

I'd made the effort, so I righted the box and examined each item as I put it back. A pocket knife, the red plastic handle missing on one side. A faded loop potholder, the kind children made on a square loom as a craft. A teddy bear with one eye missing. A silver comb. A cat's-eye marble. A pipe, still with the faint aroma of tobacco. Six items for six dead. I picked up a picture in a cheap wooden frame, smoothing my hand over the unbroken glass. It was yellowed, a picture taken long ago with a film camera. A man and a woman were smiling out at me. A teenage boy trying to look tough. A little girl, her braids tipped with colorful beads. Two twin boys with mischievous grins. And another girl—one on the edge of womanhood whose eyes held a secret.

Russell would have been one of the twins. My heart ached to see the picture, to know that the items I'd just placed back into the plastic bin had once been touched with love. They were focus items, holding not just the energy of their dead owner, but serving as a means for a magician to connect and summon their spirits back to this world.

If I'd had any doubt before stepping into this building, I didn't now. Russell Robertson, or Findal, was my necromancer. He looked about eight in the picture. If he'd been his brother Hector's twin, then that would have been right. Forty years was plenty of time for a driven boy to hone his magical ability. I put the picture back in the box and picked up a notebook, leafing through it. A grimoire. I shut it hastily and placed it with the other items. Searching what amounted to a magical diary without the owner's permission was equally as rude as breaking their spells.

I didn't have the same reservations about the actual diary that the second notebook held. In it were page after page of Russell's memories of his lost family, all the things he wanted to ask them, all the events of his life he wished they could share. My throat was tight as I turned to the last page, dated two months ago.

No one would ever believe me if I told them what really killed my family. Aunt Lisa knows, but is afraid to say it—either afraid people will think her crazy, or afraid that if she mentions the word they'll come to her door one night and kill her, too.

I saw Shay sneak out to meet him, saw the bites she tried to hide. They started like needle marks on her arm and leg, then on her neck, carefully hidden by her hair. She couldn't stay away, and when she didn't come home that night, Linc went to bring her back.

He returned with a message, looking like a dog had attacked him. We were to give up, to forget about Shay.

When you love someone, you don't forget about them. Dad and Mom searched for her for months, then one night Dad came home crying. I overheard him tell Mom that Shay was dead, that they'd killed her right in front of his eyes, holding him back and laughing the whole time. They wouldn't even let him have her body.

We never spoke of Shay again, but I would see Dad leave late at night, coming back before dawn smelling of smoke and gunpowder. Then the night came when I stayed with Aunt Patty. Hector was supposed to go, too, but he'd gotten a stomach bug and stayed home. I'll always remember that evening, coloring, eating cupcakes with sprinkles on the icing after dinner, staying up too late playing with my cousins. Then the morning came and when I ran through the door of my home ahead of Aunt Patty, I saw them all. They were dead, tossed aside like garbage on the living room floor.

The vampires killed them. I thought my life changed forever that morning, but it had actually changed months before, on the day Shay first caught the notice of a monster.

When you love someone, you don't forget about them.

I went to put the notebook back, then hesitated. Carefully I tore out a sheet of paper, took a pen from my cute little designer purse, and began to write.

CHAPTER 16

The sun was below the rooftops, tinting the clouds scarlet and tangerine in a dusky-gray sky as I made my way back to my car.

"Did ya get your dragon, hon?" The man on his porch called out.

"He wasn't home. I left him a message."

I heard him chuckle as I walked past. "Girl, you can come slay dragons in this neighborhood anytime."

I looked around at the boarded up buildings, the shadows rapidly engulfing streets and alleyways. Night was falling and the dragons—human *and* vampire—would soon be out. Maybe I would be back. This neighborhood looked like it could use a woman with a good sword arm.

But that would be later. Right now I had a vampire mistress to see and I wasn't sure exactly what I was going to tell her.

Vampires occasionally killed their prey. It happened pretty much every time they fed a thousand years ago but when we'd come to the table and agreed on what amounted to a cease fire between us, they'd vowed restraint. Understandably, blood slaves who willingly entered into what amounted to a deal with the devil would eventually die. Beyond that, there might be the occasional mishap and the vampires were supposed to take care of those offenders who killed.

Since last week, I'd begun to have a whole new view on vampire society that was completely different from what the Templar texts taught. *Balajs* were independent. There was no central authority that I could see—no one to enforce the terms of our truce. Solitary vampires wandered the edges of territories, killing at will.

Those gang members were killed. That had been a mafia-style hit for God knows what reason.

What happened to the Robertsons had been murder. They killed Shay right in front of her father, held him, made him watch, and mocked him. Then when he didn't give up, when he proved to be a pest, they killed him and his family. They probably forced him to watch as they killed his wife and other children, too.

Last night they killed four people. Yes, those people weren't exactly pillars of society, but it was still murder. Vampires killed the Robertsons, killed the gang members, and no doubt killed many more people who stood in their way.

It made me sick. These vampires slaughtered without conscience. If they'd killed the Robertsons with so little care, then they'd kill Russell to cover any trace of their doings.

How many others had they murdered? They were the same brutal thugs we'd taken down for centuries. There was no truce. It was a lie, a worthless agreement that allowed us Templars to turn a blind eye to injustice. I could go to the Elders, show them what was happening, and demand they take action.

They'd do nothing. No, they'd actually investigate and

discuss, which would allow them to do nothing while claiming to be taking the whole thing seriously. Only God can judge, they'd say, citing the shameful atrocities we'd committed during the Crusades as evidence of what happened when we tried to usurp God's role. Hypocrites and cowards, too comfortable with their scotch and twelve-ounce filets to get their hands dirty protecting the pilgrims on the path. As long as the vampires covered it up, kept their activities cloaked under the guise of human crime, the most we Templars would do is post a few Facebook memes.

I was going to do more. I wasn't going to stand for this bullying, these vicious murders in *my* town. They'd brutally killed Shay in front of her father, murdered Russell's entire family. I had no idea what the necromancer had in mind, but I had his back. It was time to expose the vampires for what they were and bring them to justice.

I'd already told Dario too much. If he connected the specters I'd told him about to the cemetery near where he'd dropped me off that night, it would be no time at all before he linked this all to the Robertsons. How long before he found out about Russell? How long before they tidied up all the loose ends by killing the one remaining member of the family?

I lugged Trusty and my bag of armor up the stairs to my apartment. My front door was unlocked and Dario sat on my sofa, watching two politicians verbally duke it out about firearm licensing and the second amendment. I hesitated when I saw him, images of the Robertsons flashing through my mind.

"Hey. I hope you don't mind my letting myself in. I was worried if I hung around in the hall too long, someone might come after me with a crucifix or something."

I fingered my keychain and put my sword and my backpack on the table. "No problem. Want a beer?"

Seemed a better thing to say than accusing him of slaughtering two adults and three children four decades ago.

"Sure. What's your stance on assault rifles? I mean, seems someone can do just as much damage with a pistol and they're easier to hide. It's not like someone could walk around with an AK in their hip pocket. Although what do I know?"

Yes, what did he know? Vampires had other methods of killing. Still, his easy conversation made me ache. I'd be losing this. I'd be losing one of the first friendships I'd managed to make in Baltimore. It was hard to reconcile that the vampire I thought was my friend was part of a *Balaj* that killed the Robertsons in cold blood. They murdered a fourteen-year-old girl right in front of her father.

Maybe he hadn't known. Maybe he was innocent, clueless about the ugly side of his *Balaj*. Then I remembered the look in his eyes that night in his bedroom, the brutal tone he'd taken at Sesarios, his tale of when his *Balaj* had been without territory. I remembered all that and realized that I had been a fool wishing a vampire, a ruthless predator, into someone I might fall in love with.

Time to stop being a fool.

"You can't really do a sniper hit with a handgun, it's more of a personal kill. Although not as personal as me walking around Baltimore with a forty inch long sword. Can't put that in your hip pocket either." I kept my tone casual and handed him a beer. He looked at the cap and yanked it off with his fingers. It wasn't a twist off.

"Yeah. Why are you carrying that thing around? I understand a woman's need to defend herself, but aren't you better off with a can of mace? You're going to get arrested."

I did have a can of mace as well as a gold crucifix, a spelled servingware knife, and an amulet I'd whipped up last night. "Where I went tonight, no one was going to call the police." At his raised eyebrow I added, "I heard about a place that had a really good corned beef on rye, but it was in a bad neighborhood."

He shrugged and turned back to the television. "Guess I can't point fingers. I've gone out of my way often enough for a decent O Negative."

Yesterday I would have laughed at the comment, but today it made me shiver. I needed to get this all over with, get this vampire out of my living room and have nothing more to do with him. I had always been taught not to judge. That was so easy when I was living at a giant estate in Middleburg, playing tennis, or studying artifacts at the Temple. How could I *not* judge when I'd just read the pain a whole family had gone through at the hands of another.

This was ridiculous. I couldn't sit here and make small talk with him knowing what I knew. I sat my beer on the table, pulled the newspaper out of my backpack and shoved it at the vampire.

"Last night four men were murdered, their throats cut." I threw it out there and just let the words sink in, waiting to see how the vampire would respond. He read the article, the look of cool indifference returning to his face. I'd almost forgotten how unapproachable he could seem now that we were kind-of friends.

But were we really friends? That wariness behind the bland expression made me wonder. "I see that. Is there something about this incident you wished to discuss with me?"

He was dancing around the topic, waiting to see how much I knew, or didn't know, before he spoke. A wise move —one that made my spark of distrust flourish.

"The amount of blood on the scene isn't sufficient. Either these four healthy men were severely anemic, or vampires enthralled them, fed on them, and then sliced their throats to mask the bite wounds."

Something unreadable flickered in the back of his eyes. "The *Balaj* was attacked Saturday night. We needed to retaliate, to exterminate those who would do us harm as well as send a message to others who might wish to do the same."

I remembered our conversation in the car on the way to Middleburg. "But how is this sending a message? You cut their throats to hide the bites. The police think this is a gang killing."

He nodded. "But those in this gang who work with the *Balaj* will know differently. We made sure of that."

Great. That distrust was now a full-blown paranoia. There was this tiny part of me that didn't want to believe the worst, that wanted to rationalize the killings last night.

"So a local gang stormed a vampire enclave knowing you were all vampires? Were they armed with holy water? Had a priest in tow?" Because it didn't make any sense at all that humans with a reasonable IQ would attack vampires with guns—at least with non-magically enhanced guns.

Dario turned off the television and took two steps back around the sofa to face me. "We were attacked by ghostly beings who were insubstantial enough to resist damage by us, but corporeal enough to do harm. Three vampires died and the others in the house at the time were severely injured. We've had to abandon use of that location as a precaution."

The paranoia receded a notch. It had been a serious attack. Perhaps the retaliation was justified. But ghosts? That sounded too much like the specters in the graveyard to be a coincidence. Was Russell working with a local gang? Somehow I couldn't see the possibility of a connection there. Necromancers weren't common among magic users, but they weren't a rarity either. The gang attack could have been a coincidence, but I had my doubts.

"How do you know the gang instigated Saturday night's attack?"

Dario waved a hand. "This is an internal matter. It's not something you need to know about."

I snarled, my hand tightening into a fist. "It *is* something I need to know about. I'm not joking around here, Dario. You need to be straight with me about what's going on."

His eyes met mine, and for a second I'd thought he'd retreat further behind that cold mask, or turn on the seductive compelling stuff. A muscle twitched in his jaw.

His voice was soft when he finally spoke. "They've employed magic users in the past against us, plus negotiations over a contract dispute took a bad turn last week." Dario reached out a hand as if to touch me, then quickly dropped it back to his side. "This isn't any of your business, Aria. It's an internal matter. Let it be."

So it was unrelated. Two necromancers, one trying to find answers about the murder of his family, and another working as muscle for a gang. A turf war wasn't anything the Order would stick their nose into. Feuds often had bloody resolutions, and this is what happened when humans chose to make deals with the devil—or in this case, vampires. I remembered the memorabilia in Russell's plastic bin, the picture of a happy Robertson family. The Order wouldn't bother with that either, but I would.

"And you're *sure* it was the gang who attacked you? Not someone else? Absolutely, without a doubt, sure?"

Dario's eyes narrowed. "What do you know?"

There was a sharp edge in the question making it a command. I shrugged. "I have reason to believe that your *Balaj* has employed these execution methods before. How do I know you've got the right people? Or that their attacks on you aren't justified?"

His expression grew even more remote. "This isn't your business, Aria. They were members of a *gang*. Drugs, human trafficking, protection rackets. Plus they invaded one of our homes and killed. Why are you so concerned over their deaths?"

Not exactly pilgrims on the path, but did that still excuse their murder?

I couldn't tell him my dogged questions were was because of the similar murder forty years ago of a family who had just been avenging the cruel death of their daughter. I needed to wrap up this business with the vampires, and have no further dealings with them that didn't involve them being on the opposite side of my sword. These vampires were bad news, and Dario wasn't who I'd thought, or maybe hoped, he was.

"So how do I present my findings to Leonora? I've gathered all the information she requested. Does she want it in writing? Or should I show up and personally discuss it with her?"

Dario blinked at the abrupt change of topic. "You have all the information? Because last night you didn't and I know you had to work today. What did you find out?"

I stalled. "I'd rather relay it once, if you don't mind. Would Leonora have time to see me right now?"

The vampire leaned in uncomfortably close to me and I struggled to maintain eye contact. "What's wrong?"

"Nothing." The word came out as a squeak and I silently cursed my inability to remain calm when he was this near.

"No, there is something." His voice was silky smooth and he took a step closer, putting him inches from me. "Suddenly you're worried about the death of society's worst and out of the blue you've acquired knowledge on this symbol that wasn't available in your father's extensive library. What's going on?"

Did vampires have some kind of lie radar? I hoped not. "Nothing. I was up late last night researching, and at it again first thing this morning. I'd like to go ahead and wrap this up so I can get the first decent night's sleep I've had in a week."

He reached out and put his hands on my shoulders. I forced myself to relax. "You just seem…upset. And afraid. Are we okay from the other night? I've fed. I won't lose control like that again."

I was afraid *and* upset. I'd come to terms with the predatory nature of all sorts of beings—including humans. It was possible that the murders last night had been justified, but what had happened to the Robertsons was beyond killing in self-defense. It was cruel. It was a bunch of bullies with sharp teeth who thought they were beyond the law, slaying an innocent family. And Dario, the vampire I'd taken to my family home, the vampire I'd flirted with, the vampire I'd fantasized about—he was a member of this *Balaj*. He had to have known what happened, even if he didn't participate in it. I could never look at him the same way. I just had to get through tonight, then make it clear I was done with them.

"Well, finishing this up with less than twenty-four hours to spare and a death threat over my head tends to make me upset. Let's go and get this over with so I can go to bed."

He stared at me for a moment then lowered his hands and stepped back. "Okay. Leonora will want you to discuss this in person. I'll drive."

"No, I'll drive. Last time you drove I wound up walking halfway across the city." Just in case, I grabbed my sword, slinging the scabbard over my shoulder and waiting for Dario to walk out so I could lock up.

Once in the parking lot I realized I had a problem. If I drove, then I'd be expected to bring Dario back for his car. If he drove, I'd be reliant on him to get me back home. I thought about having to make a quick escape from Leonora's. Would it be better to have my car there, or would I evade them easier through the city on foot. I'd need to return for my car, and I wasn't sure that would be a good idea if things went south, even during the day.

Was the place where I'd met Leonora before their home base? Did they rest the daylight hours somewhere else I didn't know about? And they knew where *I* lived. If things went bad tonight, they could come get me at any time. My wards, my spells would only hold them back so long. One slip, and they'd have me. My mind whirled, paranoia reaching a fever pitch. If I was going to go head to head with these creatures, to hold them accountable for their actions, then I needed to be strong enough to face them. I needed to be secure in my apartment, protected from any retaliatory attack. That meant I'd need to put some long hours in on home security, get back to regular sparring practices, and seriously hit my magical studies. No more slacking off in pubs.

Not that I'd be hanging in pubs after tonight anyway. The nights of flirty Bloody Marys were over. Forever.

"I changed my mind. Why don't you drive? I'm so tired that I'm worried I'll wreck."

He gave me another odd look. "Why don't you just wait until tomorrow? You've got one more day until your deadline. That way you can sleep tonight and meet with Leonora with a clear, refreshed mind."

Snap out of it. "No, I'm good." I forced myself to relax and smiled at the vampire.

He peered at me over the top of the car. "Are you sure? You're tired and hungry. I can hear your stomach growling from here. I'll buy you dinner. We can take some cannoli back to your house for a sugar-filled breakfast tomorrow, and we'll crash."

Netflix and chill? I don't think so, although the idea did make everything below my waistband rather warm. The thought of dinner was appealing, too. My lunch with Janice seemed like it was a decade ago, and my stomach was making ominous grumbling sounds.

"No, I'm good," I repeated woodenly, trying to ignore the protests from my empty digestive system.

We drove through the city, and I rehearsed what I would say to the vampire Mistress, what I'd do if things went bad. I also turned off my phone, worried that Russell might get the note I'd left for him and contact me at the absolute worst time. Dario called Leonora as soon as we got in the car to let her know we were on our way. It made me think—did she ever leave the safety of their house, or whatever dwellings they used? I couldn't imagine her out in pubs picking up prey like Dario did. Was her dinner delivered to her?

And how had Dario "fed" tonight when he'd been at my house right after sunset? There hadn't been time for him to go pick up some tipsy woman. Did he just grab someone off the street, or did they have communal blood slaves at their house? How long did those slaves live before the constant anemia did them in?

"Who did you feed from tonight?" I should have shut up, should have just kept silent, delivered my report, and left it at that, but I had to know. Something inside me ached at the thought that this vampire I'd come to regard as a friend wasn't what I'd thought he was.

His hands tightened on the steering wheel, his eyes remaining fixed on the road ahead. "Why?"

"Because you didn't have a lot of time between waking and showing up at my house to woo prey. Do you have a regular donor? I thought you said that your *Balaj* tries not to target the same person more than once?"

A muscle twitched in his jaw. "When I have time I prefer to be more selective and choose someone new, but we do have groups of individuals that we can rely upon if we need to feed quickly."

"Blood prostitutes? Like drug addicts? You take their blood, they get a hit and money? Was that the nature of the business that you had with that gang?"

I could practically hear his teeth grind. "Yes, it was. Some people are willing for the right price. And unlike you, many find what we offer to be pleasant."

I found the idea more than pleasant, except for the addiction and eventual death part.

"What do you do with the bodies?"

Shit. Was I suicidal? I just couldn't stop my damned mouth.

"What the hell is wrong with you tonight, Aria?" Dario swerved over to the curb and slammed the car into park. "Are you jealous? Because I've told you I'm more than willing to take you to bed, share your blood, and more."

And part of me really wanted to. I got the feeling that Dario wouldn't drain me and kill me, that he'd restrain himself as much as he could, and turn me if things went too far. But this wasn't about me. This was about Shay, about the Robertson family, about all the other men and women who had been murdered, treated like throwaway toys, about a supernatural group of thugs who thought it was fine to treat humans like disposable objects.

"How many *have* you killed, Dario? Since you became a vampire, how many have died either a victim of your blood lust or for other reasons?"

His eyes darkened. "More than I want to admit. I've lived nearly three hundred and fifty years compared to your twenty-three. Let's see how many terrible things you've done in the next three hundred years then we'll talk."

I winced. It was easy to condemn him when I'd never feared for my life, been at the edge of starvation, wandered homeless with my family. But just as I began to feel sorry for him, the remembrance of that picture in the abandoned house came to mind. Shay...so young, those deaths...so brutal.

So I sat, silent, and refused to look at him again.

"There are many times I've gone hungry, struggled to control my needs and won so that I could live with myself the next day. I try...but why bother telling this to you, a Templar whose ancestors slaughtered vampires without a care. How many died a victim of your people's misguided ethics? Or died because of their greed for money and magical items?"

He made a low noise, something between a growl and a snarl, then put the car in gear and squealed the tires. I flattened against the seatback with the g-force, feeling sick. I wanted him to be a friend. Had my desperate need for companionship, for a friend who actually *got* me, made me blind to who he really was?

CHAPTER 17

We pulled up outside the same house as before, only this time I felt tension in all the eyes that watched us as we climbed out of the SUV. The vampire that walked down to meet us visibly recoiled as I pulled my sword from the car and strapped it to my back.

"Leave that here," Dario commanded.

I don't think so. "I'm a Templar. I need to have my sword by my side."

"Since when?" Dario walked around the SUV to stand beside me. "You can't carry a weapon into an audience with the Mistress. You've got to leave it in the car."

There was no way I was going to leave my sword in his car, not after what I'd discovered today. "I'm not going to remove it from the scabbard or anything. Think of it as part of my attire, sort of a Templar uniform. It's not like you all have anything to fear from a sword."

His eyebrows shot up. "Thousands of dead vampires would beg to differ. It's a blessed sword, a holy weapon. It needs to stay in the car."

I wavered. I had an amulet, a butter knife, and a can of

mace. Still, the thought of leaving my sword behind nearly sent me into a panic attack. "I will disarm while in audience with your Mistress, but I'm not leaving my sword in the car."

There was silence while the vampires eyed the weapon in question.

"I'm not holding it for her," the guy who came to meet us protested.

"How about you leave it on the table in the foyer?" Dario proposed. "Trust me, none of us want to touch it. It will be safe there, and you won't be delivering an aggressive slap in the face to the Mistress of our *Balaj*."

I wasn't thrilled, but I knew I couldn't very well present my findings to Leonora with Trusty on my back. "Fine. I'll leave it on the table."

Dario didn't take my arm, instead motioning for me to precede him into the house. A different set of leather-clad vampires served as our escorts this time, every one of them baring fangs and sending hostile glances at the sword on my back. Once inside, I slid the weapon from my back and carefully laid it on the side table in the foyer. The last six inches hung over the edge of the table, the hilt crowding a decorative lamp. The vampires glared at it, giving the sword a respectful distance as we continued down the hall to the throne room. Once inside there was the same wait as well as the same silence as before. The vampires on either side of me were far from relaxed, and I got the feeling their agitation wasn't only due to my sword in the hallway.

"Solaria Angelique Ainsworth, I hear you have news for me." Leonora spoke before she'd even taken her seat. There was something off about the way she crossed the room, the way her eyes sought out Dario's. Had she been injured in the fight last night? Had her authority somehow been weakened from the attack?

I straightened my spine, very aware that I was

surrounded by vampires with my sword out of reach. "Yes. I have the information you requested which will satisfy the contract between us."

The vampire mistress sat and motioned for me to get on with it. This whole meeting lacked the pomp and circumstance of the last. The vampires were in a hurry, although I wasn't sure if it was for my information, or for me to get the heck out of here so they could take care of some other pressing matter.

They'd killed the people they thought responsible for the attack, but there could still be unfinished business that they needed to handle tonight. I bit my lip, trying to process my mixed feelings over the gang murders. According to Dario, the gang had attacked them unprovoked, killing three and wounding many more. They were defending themselves. As a Templar I should be okay with that.

But maybe… I again wondered if Russell was involved in last night's attack, working with the gang. If so there might be a repeat performance either tonight or in the near future. How often could he raise spirits from the grave, how much energy could he amass in a twenty-four hour period?

If Russell was involved, how long before the vampires traced it to him? And if not, the vampires still might want to silence him, to keep him from airing the dirty laundry of those murders forty years ago.

I shook the thoughts out of my mind and took a steadying breath to focus. "The symbol is necromantic in nature and combines foundational as well as European, voodoo and possibly Native American elements. It takes considerable energy to activate and would require either a high level mage, or the extra power of a full moon or weather event to successfully work the spell. The intent is to call back the soul into either a raised physical form or as a specter with control over the physical plane. A focus is required specific to the soul being summoned."

Leonora nodded, her hands restless on the arms of the chair. "Does the spellcaster control the specter? You mentioned voodoo—is the raised spirit in thrall to the one who brings them back?"

Hell if I knew. Based on what I'd seen in the cemetery, I had a good hunch, though. "No. Friendly spirits can be questioned or become helpful to the summoner if they so choose. Control of the undead would require something beyond this symbol."

"Such as?"

That was way beyond what I'd been paid to research, but I wasn't about to point that fact out. "There are some artifacts that allow the holder to control the undead. I can assume that there might be a very high level necromantic spell that does so too, although I have no knowledge of one."

"What are these artifacts and where are they? Are there any mages alive today with the skill to perform such a level of spell?"

Leonora was leaning so far forward in her chair that I expected her boobs to pop free of the corset at any moment. Her dark eyes were wild with anger…anger and fear.

Fear. Russell had already summoned his dead family, presumably to question them about their murders. It was possibly that he was instrumental in the specter attack Saturday night. Were they afraid he'd spread the news of their misdeeds, afraid of the specters returning for another attack, or something else entirely?

"I must ask, is there someone in particular that you worry might be summoned? An old enemy perhaps?"

Her eyes flickered with anger. The atmosphere in the room grew decidedly chilly.

"That is none of your business. Answer my question."

There was more to their worry than random attacking specters. Who didn't they want the necromancer to summon —and most especially control? Could it be Shay, the long dead blood slave? I couldn't see how the spirit of a dead girl could be any kind of threat to a powerful *Balaj*. Why were they so worried about the ability of a necromancer to bring a spirit from the dead and possibly control it?

Russell already had the information he needed from the spirits of his family. What would he do next that had Leonora so very afraid?

"There are two artifacts within the Temple that deal with undead. I am unaware of any mage with the power to perform that level of spell without their assistance."

There. Done. Contract with the vampires satisfied. I could leave and have no further business dealings with them. At this point I didn't even want the rest of my money. I just wanted to get the heck out of there and back to my apartment where I would continue to research the vampires' activity without their deadline looming over me. What *was* Russell planning to do? And who was Leonora so worried that he'd raise from the dead?

The vampire mistress relaxed. I felt the need to tell her there were tons of unknown artifacts still outside the Temple, that magic users were a secretive bunch. There could have been an adept level Necromancer right in my apartment building, and I wouldn't know unless he started casting spells in the parking lot or in his living room.

"Do you know who crafted this symbol?"

Here's where I hoped vampires didn't have any special lie-detection skills. "No, I don't."

She exchanged another silent glance with Dario. This wordless communication between the pair of them was making me uneasy. I held my breath, but before Leonora could give my continued existence the royal thumbs up or down there was a deafening crash and a scream from the hallway.

I jumped, my heart nearly exiting my chest. The two vampires beside Leonora dove in front of her, shielding her. Spinning around I saw the other vampires, including Dario, had already raced out into the front hallway. My Templar training kicked in and I ran after them.

I should have hid behind a chair instead. There was another crash, this time followed by a series of shouts as well as screams. I hesitated at the doorway, yanking my butter knife out of one pocket and my gold crucifix from the other. Then I quickly looked into the hallway.

There was blood, a whole lot of dark red blood with chunks of flesh splattered on the walls and floors. Semi-corporeal specters fought, tearing limbs and pieces from the vampires. I stared, unable to process what was before me. I'd trained my whole life as a soldier, but never seen anything like this.

We were under attack, and me without my sword. I couldn't even see it since there was a battle in the hallway, between me and my weapon. I swear that was the last time I got talked into leaving it behind. Although I wasn't sure what good my sword could do even if I managed to reach it. Each time the vampires got a grip on a specter, the beings turned to smoke, resuming a physical form once they'd shaken off their opponent. Vampires could take a lot of physical damage, but they were being torn apart bit by bit while the spirits remained unharmed.

What the heck? Was this Russell's retaliation? The gang continuing their war with a different necromancer? This wasn't my fight. The vampires weren't blameless victims. It wasn't my duty to defend them, or even get involved. Not one Templar would blame me for ducking out the back door and leaving the vampires to reap whatever shitstorm they had sown. In fact, this was the perfect distraction for me to get away without any unpleasantness regarding the completion of my contract with Leonora.

Except that would mean I would be leaving my sword behind. Yep, that was it. I was going to get my sword then get out of here. I wasn't going to engage in battle or defend a bunch of murderous vampires. Not at all.

I had a butter knife, a keychain, and a can of mace. None of them were effective against spirits. I'd come here prepared to defend myself against vampires, not specters. There was only one thing in my bag of tricks that might work, and I wasn't sure what effect it would have on the vampires. I couldn't just stand here and do nothing, though. If I did, I was going to witness a massacre, and there were no guarantee that these spirits wouldn't turn their fury on me when they were done.

I stepped into the hallway, hugging the wall as I made my way forward. I needed a specter that wasn't touching a vampire, but they were all in the middle of combat. Some of the vampires were teaming up on the spirits, but the damage they were inflicting was far outweighed by what they were receiving. I needed them to step back so I could have a clear shot at one of the spirits.

"Hey," I shouted, dodging a vampire's back-swing. "Fight me instead. Me. Templar. Come get me."

No one paid any attention, so I picked up a spindly, decorative hallway table and swung, bashing a vampire in the face when it passed right through the spirit.

Oops. The vampire's head snapped backward from the impact, and he slid on the bloody carpet. That hadn't worked out as I'd planned, and I wasn't sure the six inches of space between them would be enough to protect the vampire, but it was all I had.

I raised my crucifix. *"Jesu, luys im chanaparhy."*

The tunnel shot out in front of me. The vampire had good reflexes, throwing himself backward away from the light. The spirit didn't have such skill. The three foot wide beam hit him square on, blasting him into a shower of sparks. The tunnel of light vanished the moment it exploded the specter, but the vampires hit by the sparks shrieked, their skin burning.

Not the best of solutions, even if it was all I had. I didn't have an opportunity to think of something else, because now I had the attention of the other spirits. Five of them abandoned their attacks on the vampires to come straight at me.

"Jesu, luys im—" My blessing ended with a scream as they tore into me. I swung blindly with my knife, but it passed right through them.

I'd spelled this knife thinking I'd need to defend myself against vampires, not bodiless spirit beings. I needed my sword. I could see it on the floor next to a broken lamp and a smashed table, far out of reach. Swinging the knife like a wild woman, I tried to push past the spirits and the wall of vampires toward my sword. How could something be solid enough to feel like they were ripping my flesh while they were still non-corporeal?

It was then I realized the spirits weren't actually tearing my body. They were passing their hands through flesh and bone and pulling at my very soul. I kept stabbing with the knife, in panic mode and unable to concentrate enough to repeat the blessing. Fine droplets of blood flew in an arc following my arm, and I realized they were from me. I was bleeding out my pores, and when they managed to get a good grip on my soul, I'd be dead.

My knife was a flash of metal. I held the cross aloft and tried again to say the blessing, but nothing came out of my mouth. The pain was horrible, my arm continuing to swing on a form of auto-pilot, no doubt from my Templar training.

Something large hit me, knocking the breath from my lungs and crashing me to the floor. I was face down, finally sheltered from the specters, well aware that my savior was taking the brunt of their attack.

"Get her out of here."

It was Dario's voice. A wave of relief crashed through me as I realized it wasn't him on top of me being torn apart by the specters but some other vampire.

"No, my sword. I just need my sword."

Hands grabbed me, yanking me out from under the vampire and hauling me out of the foyer toward the back of the house.

"Get off me." I struggled in vain against the vampire's greater strength. I hated I was being hustled to safety like some helpless damsel. I was a Templar. I'd been trained my whole life to fight. I just needed to get my sword.

"Dario says get you out of here, so that's where you're going. Come on." The vampire half-dragged me through a back room, swinging a large metal door open. A burst of cold damp air hit me and I shivered, pulling back. The vampire paused, and then tightened his grip. As he turned to face me I saw his eyes black and feral, as well as the sharp points of his fangs.

Shit. I knew Dario had intended to get me safely out of the house, but from the look in this vampire's eyes he'd changed his mind.

Injured vampires needed blood. This guy was injured, and beyond caring how much he took. I reached for my crucifix keychain, dismayed to find that both the keychain and the knife had fallen from my hands as I'd hit the floor. I looked down and saw my hands, as well as the front of my clothing, splattered with blood—my blood. I was a walking buffet standing right in front of a vampire lost in blood lust.

"Dario said to get me out of here, to let me leave out the

back door." I halted and tensed. If he was going to continue, he was going to either have to drag me or give me a good reason for proceeding forward.

"No. We're not." The vampire's grip tightened, and he pulled.

I leaned backward, remembering how my tussle in the SUV with Dario had turned out. I had more room to maneuver this time, and my goal was escape, although that goal seemed unlikely given this guy probably didn't care whether he broke my arm or not.

"You're going down those stairs if I have to throw you down them," the vampire snarled.

My whole body went cold.

I'd read enough true crime novels to know that chances of escape, let alone survival, diminished significantly once captors got their victim where they wanted her, but Dario had said the vampires would think twice before harming me, that there would be repercussions for killing a Templar.

There were repercussions for killing an entire family in their home, but that hadn't seemed to stop them. And this was one vampire, injured and hungry. He wouldn't care one bit about repercussions right now. Hunger.

I had a choice, fight this guy and probably die. No one would hear the struggle or hear us scream, and I had nothing but my bare hands as a weapon. Or I could let him chain me up somewhere. I could try to escape once he left me alone, possibly be somewhere with a weapon I could use to protect myself.

Screams and sounds of smashing furniture intensified from the hallway. The vampire yanked, nearly pulling my arm from its socket.

"Come on. Get moving now."

He needed to get back to the battle, and if I didn't go willingly, I was going to find myself trying to escape with a dislocated arm and probably two broken legs.

So I went, easing my weight forward as the vampire lead me down the stairs, wincing when he tightened his grip just a hair shy of bone-crushing. We went toward the back of the basement and down a second set of sturdy stairs into an empty, dim room with a steel door on the opposite wall. The vampire jerked me forward, slid the bolts, and opened the door. I had a split second to look around, hoping there was something I might be able to use as a weapon, assuming I got out of this locked cement-and-steel room the vampire was about to put me in.

Rope. Chains. What looked like a leg-hold trap. Some well-used wooden benches stacked against the wall. And another set of stairs leading further downward. I squinted at them, trying to see how far they went. Was there a sub-basement? A sub, sub-basement?

"Dario isn't going to like this," I told him in a last ditch effort to get through the hunger to whatever humanity was left in him. "He'll kill you once he finds out."

I hoped so, although maybe not. This guy was family. The two of them might have known each other for a hundred years. I was just an intriguing meal. I'm sure Dario would be pissed, but I wasn't sure he'd be angry enough to avenge me. Would he even survive the battle upstairs? Would anyone come for me at all, besides this vampire who wanted to drain the blood from my veins? Whatever happened, I had no one to rely on but myself.

"Shut up." The vampire slammed me against the wall. I turned my head just before I hit, taking the impact to the front of my body and the side of my face. Once again I felt blood, this time trickling down my cheek.

I was yanked back from the wall as quickly as I'd been slammed into it, then thrust forward through the doorway. It was dark, so dark I truly couldn't see my hand in front of my face. Vampires must have superior night vision, as I felt myself guided forward and nudged backward into a chair. I tensed, ready to fight if I heard the slightest rattle of chains.

Instead I smelled the familiar scent of cinnamon and myrrh, shuddered as a tongue traveled its way up my cheek. "I should drink from you right now," the vampire murmured, "but my absence will be noted and others will come. I don't want to share."

The only thing saving my life right now was this guy's greed. If I was going to die at the teeth of a vampire, I'd rather my executioner be Dario, not this guy. Still, every second I lived gave me another second to try to survive, to escape. And as soon as this guy left, I was going to do everything in my power to get out of here.

I felt him step away and took a breath of relief. There was a moment of light as the door opened, then darkness as it slammed shut again.

I couldn't hear the battle from down here, had no idea how much time I had, but the sand was quickly running out of my hourglass.

$\mathcal{I}$ sat stock-still, holding my breath as I listened for any noise that might indicate I wasn't alone in the room. Nothing. I couldn't even hear sounds from the other part of the basement. I stood, holding onto the chair to orient myself in the darkness.

Haxa Luz

And then there was light. Well, not as much light as I'd hoped for, but at least I could explore my surroundings without doing a face-plant onto the concrete floor. Cement block walls made up the tiny six-by-six room. There was the chair that my hand rested on with a pile of chain and locking cuffs next to it, what looked to be a blanket balled up in a corner, and something that I strongly suspected was a dogfood dish.

I blinked back tears. There was no sense in giving up hope now. A dish, iron chains, a blanket, and a metal chair weren't much, but MacGyver wouldn't let that stop him from using all this stuff to break free and rain down a world of hurt on these vampires. I was a Templar. That had to give me a whole lot more ingenuity and strength than a fictional television character.

Using my floating ball of light, I flipped the chair over and examined it. If I snapped off the legs, I'd have some stakes, and more importantly supplies to create a makeshift crucifix. The vampires upstairs had been burned by the blessing. If blood-starved vamp came back, I'd light him up and run for it. Or try to light him up. My sword and keychain were consecrated. I'd never done a blessing without a sanctified crucifix, but I was hoping two crossed chair legs would do in a pinch. Hey, it worked in the vampire movies.

Clearly I lacked faith, because I wasn't willing to put my one chance of escape on a makeshift religious symbol. If the blessing didn't happen, I'd pivot that asshole around and jab him through the heart…hopefully. Tapping on the chair legs I noted they were hollow. With the cement walls and floor, or the metal of the door, I might be able to squeeze the end together to form a sharp point. It wouldn't be the traditional wooden stake, but it would give me a weapon.

Crucifix to the face, a few chair legs to the heart, and my attacker would be down. Then I'd get out and hide until dawn. If any of them came after me, I'd call my family and bring the holy wrath of the Ainsworths down on them.

I got to work, wincing at the noise as I banged the chair against the wall. The thing was better made than I had thought, and I'd worked up quite a sweat by the time I managed to snap the legs off and splinter the rest into jagged chunks.

It gave me time to think. Did Dario believe I was safe in my apartment? How long would it be before he knew differently? I hoped he'd go to check on me before sunrise and realize something was wrong. I wanted to be optimistic about my chances of getting out of here, but just in case things went horribly wrong, I'd hoped Dario would avenge my death. Or at the very least let my family know what had happened to me.

Or not. I still didn't trust my judgement when it came to that vampire. Was I letting my hormones sway me? The murder of the Robinson family weighed heavily on my heart, but part of me *wanted* to trust Dario. He'd said he'd done things in his three hundred and fifty years that he regretted, who's to say he hadn't been forced to turn the other way when Shay and her family were killed? If keeping silent was the price for him staying alive or for not being cast out of his *Balaj*, then perhaps he was less to blame than the others.

I'd never been in a position where someone was going to die whether or not I stood up for them. And I'm sure his standing up for Shay would have meant Dario's death. What if he had no choice in the matter?

What was I doing? I was sitting in a tiny basement cell, bashing a chair against a wall and making excuses for a vampire that I desperately wanted to *not* be guilty of ruthless murder. I was such a fool. How could I be so blind as to think that Dario wouldn't put his family as well as his own safety before the life of a fourteen-year-old girl? I might desperately want to think him innocent, to forgive him in this crime, but deep down inside I'd always see the face from the picture, the girl-almost-a-woman with the secret in her brown eyes, every time I was with Dario.

He might have had good reasons, but that didn't mean I couldn't judge him for doing nothing as Shay Robertson died, as the vampires fed from and kill her parents and siblings.

My head came up, my fingers stilled as I felt the familiar tingle across my skin of a vampire approaching.

Fue.

With the word, my light was extinguished, hopefully giving me a few more seconds to surprise my kidnapper. I readied my makeshift crucifix and another unsharpened, chair leg. There was the click of a key in a lock. The door opened and I saw a figured shadowed against the outside light before I lunged forward.

"*Ansurb.*"

The original Templar incantation of protection had been *Jesu, pashtpanel indz bolor ansurb eakneri,* which had been so long that it had resulted in a lot of dead Templars. Thankfully the shorter version worked as did my chair-leg religious symbol because I'd barely gotten the word out of my mouth before I was punched in the face.

I heard a scream that sounded more like a roar, smelled the sizzle of burned flesh, then I was slammed against the block wall, my head making an alarming crack on impact. No pain registered, but my legs wobbled, and my left arm felt partially numb. I'm sure the room would have been swimming before me if the door hadn't slammed shut leaving me blind in the darkness.

I couldn't hear shit from the ringing in my ears, either, so I let my instincts guide me, stabbing with the chair leg at the scent of cinnamon and myrrh. I hit something with give, felt sticky liquid on my hand, and swung my other hand forward to strike again with my crucifix. Again the aroma of burning flesh.

Hands tried to grip me but I struggled, twisting and attacking with both of my makeshift weapons. Wet ran down my head and into my mouth as I tasted the tang of my own blood. Oh God no. I was bleeding. If the vampire hadn't been ramped up before, he would be now that he'd scented my wound. I felt a surge of adrenaline at the thought and battled like a cat about to be bathed. I kicked, hit, head-butted, and kneed, determined to subdue the vampire and escape.

As if from down a long tunnel, I heard the sounds of flesh hitting flesh, of our feet, of the vampire's muffled curses. My blood ran into my ear and eyes, my head began to ache and the floor seemed to sway under my feet. If I didn't take this guy down soon, I was going to pass out.

I was desperate, so I did the unexpected. I dropped to the floor, taking my assailant down with me, then rolled, slamming the end of the crucifix toward where his eye should be. Hands gripped my wrists before the cross hit its mark, and my arms were slowly forced backward and twisted until my weapons dropped. I went to head-butt the vampire, but my head only lolled to the side. So tired.

"Aria." I heard Dario's voice as if he were inside a mattress filled with cotton. "It's me. Stop fighting."

Shit. I hadn't seen him in the darkness, nor recognized his voice since my hearing had gone out once my head had hit the wall. It was kind of funny that I'd just beaten the crap out of the only vampire here that might be on my side. I wanted to laugh, but a sob came out instead.

The sob turned into a torrent of tears that drove my headache into migraine proportions. I felt like I was either going to pass out or throw up. It embarrassed me, a Templar not-quite-a-Knight crying from fear and relief in a dark cell. Dario seemed to realize my shame and instead of comforting me, just waited out my flood of emotion with a steadying hand on my arm.

Finally I gulped, regaining control.

"You okay? He didn't hurt you, did he?" Dario's hand caressed the side of my face. I winced as his fingers traced cuts and bruises. I didn't have the heart to tell him that the vampire who'd locked me down here hadn't hurt me nearly as much as he had.

"He was going to come back and drain me. That's why I attacked you. I thought you..."

Dario pulled me close and I breathed in his cinnamon and myrrh scent, so comforting now that I knew it belonged to him and not some other vampire. "Yeah. Well, that's *not* going to happen."

There was a fierce possessiveness to his voice that warmed my heart as well as other, more hormonal parts of my body. Slowly my panic receded and I felt more like a Templar and less like a woman afraid for her life.

"How many of your *Balaj* are injured? Will they be able to heal before dawn?" I didn't dare ask how many had died. I didn't want to know. And I didn't want to think about who the vampires would retaliate against for this night. I wanted to tell them about Russell, to keep innocent people from suffering for tonight's events, but I saw the necromancer as an innocent, too.

But was he? Yes, his family had been slaughtered, but did that give him the right to kill vampires who hadn't even have been turned at the time his parents and siblings had died? There had to be a better way to deliver justice—on both sides of this issue.

Sitting there wounded, in the dark, in the arms of a vampire, I came to a sort of epiphany. Well, an epiphany for a Templar, anyway. There was no good guy or bad guy in this thing. Both sides had made horrible decisions, and both were somewhat justified in their stance. This gray area was why our Order had backed away from society so long ago and become the obsolete caretakers of the Temple that we now were. Gray. And where there was gray, we could not judge.

I couldn't be like that. But I also couldn't pick sides in this war. There was no clear right or wrong, but there had to be a better way to resolve this than watching Russell and the vampires battle it out until Baltimore was painted red with blood.

"Too many were injured tonight." Dario sighed. "I'm sorry about this, but I can't sneak you out of here with an open wound. We've got so many hurt and hungry upstairs. Every vampire in the house would come running if they scented fresh blood."

Dario's words filtered through my thoughts. I felt him let go of my arms and sit up, pivoting me so I was sitting on his lap, resting my shoulder against his chest. Hands gently turned my head and cradled my jaw as he ran his tongue across the gash on my head.

It felt far more sensual than someone licking my scalp should have. The pain vanished immediately, and a warmth trickled through my veins. I heard myself sigh and I snuggled closer, wiggling my rear end. His arms tightened for a brief second before he released me and helped me stand.

I was pretty turned on right now and judging from the response I'd felt under my ass he was, too. It wasn't anywhere near the blind lust I'd felt when he'd tried to enthrall me in the dragon bedroom. I felt happy and floating, like I'd just had a big glass of wine.

"Here." I felt something thrust into my arms and wrinkled my nose as I realized it was the nasty blanket from the corner. Dario chuckled. "I sealed your wound, so don't worry about germs. I just need you to cover your head with this and wrap it around you as best as you can to hide the smell of blood. We're going to duck out the back door to my car in the alley."

I'd worry about the fallout from this evening later. Right now I was just thrilled that Dario was helping me escape.

What price would he pay for his actions, though? Who was the vampire who'd locked me down in this cell as his midnight snack? I realized that I didn't really know Dario's position in the hierarchy of his *Balaj*. Yes, Leonora seemed to look to him as a senior member, but perhaps that was just due to his connection with me. Could he be punished for sneaking me out the back door? Would the other vampire lodge some kind of formal complaint against him? I reached out a hand to touch Dario's arm, tracing my fingers along the curve of his muscles. Once we were out of here, I needed to arrange for some kind of protection for him.

But where? Would he ever be accepted into another *Balaj*? Would he become one of the family-less rogues that wandered the perimeter of the city?

Ugh. Why was I worrying over a vampire like he was a lost puppy? Dario had survived hundreds of years wandering with his *Balaj*. He could certainly survive a disagreement with his family over what they probably saw as a midnight snack rather than a Templar consultant at this moment. Still, I worried.

Dario opened the cell door and I blinked at how bright the scant light in the basement seemed. I could barely see with the blanket like a shawl over my head and wrapped around under my chin and across my shoulders. It stank like sweat, mold, and urine, making me thankful I only needed to use it for a brief escape and not as regular bedding.

The house upstairs was silent as we crept out of the basement and through the back door. Dew from the grass soaked through my shoes and socks as we ran. I heard the sounds of my breathing echoed back from the blanket around my head, the faint noise of distant cars, the yowl of a tomcat, and then the crunch of my feet on the gravel. I slid the blanket back to see that we were in an alley, Dario's SUV ahead. Then I ditched the smelly thing on the ground.

The vehicle beeped and flashed its lights as the vampire unlocked it. He turned, letting go of my hand to help me in. That's when I first got a good look at him...and him at me.

We both gasped.

I had beaten the crap out of him. His shirt had holes streaked with reddish-black blood from where I'd tried to impale him with the chair leg. Crucifix-shaped burns dotted the fabric. But that wasn't the only damage his body had sustained tonight. Pores along his arms and neck were spotted with blood from the battle with the specters. Long gashes marred his face. I stared, wondering how long it would take him to heal—if he ever would heal from some of these wounds.

Dario turned his back to me and yanked the shirt over his head. My brain detoured to admire the well-defined muscles covered with dark brown skin. There were scars alongside the fresh wounds, but he was still a damned fine specimen of manhood…of vampirehood.

He walked to an alleyway garage, dunking his tattered shirt into a rain barrel poised under the downspout. That's when I saw the mark—a perfect impression of my chair-leg crucifix in raised pinkish flesh on his chest.

"Will that heal?"

He twisted the shirt in his hands, wringing it out before walking toward me. Under where I'd singed his shirt I'd seen additional, small pink marks—burn marks—across his shoulders and arms.

"I don't know. I've never been smited by a Templar before. Hold still." He brushed the wet shirt over my face and I shivered both with the touch of the cold wet fabric and the thought that I may have permanently marked his skin.

"It's not a smite, just a blessing to protect me." Technically it translated into a plea to be protected from unholy beings. My mixed feelings for Dario aside, I felt rather badly that the divine spell had lumped him into the "unholy" category.

Unaware of my guilty thoughts, Dario scrubbed at my face and neck with his damp shirt.

"What are you doing? I can take a shower when I get home."

"You look like an extra from a horror movie—the extra that gets killed off in scene one by the axe murderer. I've got to get this blood off your face and neck."

"Why don't you lick it off," I teased.

Yeah. He'd most likely been accessory to multiple murders. I'd decided not an hour ago to never speak to this vampire again. And now I was flirting with him. Conflicted? I think so.

Dario continued to scrub. "Dried blood doesn't taste all that great. Once it clots, it's kinda bland." He leaned in, licking my neck in a quick, smooth motion that made me shiver. "I might make an exception with you, though. You're pretty tasty."

And now I was speechless, continuing to hold still while he rubbed my face raw then tossed his shirt aside to land next to the nasty blanket in the alley. Reaching into the back seat of the car he pulled out a fresh shirt and yanked it over his head while I watched.

"Your sword is in here. Let me tell you, picking that thing up was one of the hardest things I've done in my life. That thing makes my skin crawl."

I'm sure that was less about the weapon and more about the considerable amount of spells and runes it held. And there was that whole holy weapon thing. If I could give him third degree burns with a chair-leg crucifix, I'm sure I could slice him like luncheon meat with my sword. No wonder none of them had wanted it in the house.

Then he reached into the SUV once more and handed me something.

"My purse!" I'd put it aside in the hallway as I'd prepared for the fight, then later dropped my key chain and knife. Glancing inside I saw everything had been put back inside. In the aftermath of a bloody battle, he'd not only tracked me down but remembered to retrieve my stuff.

"Yeah. I might be a vampire, but I remember how women are about their purses." His voice was teasing as he motioned toward the car. "Hurry up and get in. I'd really like to be out of here before one of my injured brothers or sisters heads out here in search of a snack."

Good idea. It wasn't until I was snug in his SUV, heading toward my apartment, that I realized there was a faint gray tinge to the skyline in the east, heralding the sunrise.

CHAPTER 19

Dario had insisted he walk me up to my apartment, which turned out to be a good decision on my part, probably not so good on his. Whatever pain-relieving, aphrodisiac had been in his saliva had started to wear off, and I'm not sure I could have made it up to the third floor without his assistance. I made a mental note to ask him later about this. Vampire bites held quite a punch drug-wise, and there was anywhere from a one to two week detox from just one encounter. There was either less of the chemical in the saliva than in their fangs, or I was somewhat immune.

And I was foolish even to consider the second explanation.

Once inside, the vampire left me sitting on the sofa to get me aspirin while I stared out the window at the lightening sky. "How long until dawn? I mean, how long until you're in trouble?"

"Twenty minutes, give or take a few."

He didn't sound overly concerned about this, but *my* heart sped up. If he left now and didn't hit any early traffic, he could be back at Leonora's house in time. But could he even go back there?

"Where can you shelter here and be safe?"

Dario didn't answer until he'd handed me two aspirin and a glass of water. "Maybe your bathroom. It doesn't have a window. There or the closet should be okay if you wedge a towel around under the door."

I couldn't make him sleep in the bathroom or in my closet! But there wasn't anywhere else in my apartment that would be light-proof. I guessed if I put some blankets and pillows in the tub it wouldn't be horribly uncomfortable. I could even close the shower curtain and drape my comforter over the rod, just in case some light leaked in around the door edges. I really needed to come up with something that would be more vampire-friendly for the future—like an enclosure in the bedroom. Not a coffin or anything crude like that. More like a light-safe bed.

What was I thinking? He was a vampire, quite possibly a murderer, and I was planning a guest room for him. He did save my life tonight, though. He'd protected me from one of his own blood brothers, snuck me out of the house. And he'd taken the time to pull me out of the middle of battle to send me to safety.

"Do you still think the gang is behind this?" My head was throbbing, my clothes and hair were sticky with blood, but I needed to know.

Dario sat next to me on the couch, his thigh brushing mine. I resisted the urge to lean against him as he placed his hand on my leg. "Well, it either wasn't the gang at all, or the warning we gave them wasn't sufficient."

"I want to help. I really think I can help, but I need to know how you guys got this symbol and specifically why you were so positive that it was the gang who attacked you."

He sighed. "I told you they'd employed magical methods

against us in the past? Ten years ago there was a tainted blood incident that we traced back to them. We cleaned house, but last week one of their blood donors roofied his vampire and proceeded to rob us. We tracked him down. Upon interrogation, he gave us a paper with the symbol on it and told us a man paid him to steal the items. The description fit one of the gang members, and they do have motive for revenge."

But it wasn't them—not unless Russell was somehow connected with the gang. And blood slaves as a front for a theft? How was all this tied together? What the heck was the necromancer doing? Stealing items from the vampires seemed a strange thing to do when he had the ability to summon murdering specters. Was the robbery a misdirection for something else he had planned?

I felt guilty letting the vampires continue to pin this all on the gang when I knew the true culprit, but I didn't want them killing Russell until I had a chance to make things right. They might continue to kill gang members in the meantime. It was enough for me to feel the need to hurry up and talk to Russell.

"So what's your next step?"

Dario glanced out the window at the gray sky. "Get in the dark before daylight. We have associates who will track this all down during the day. Depending on what they find, we'll take action right after nightfall."

Which gave me today. Not much time at all.

"Are you going to abandon Leonora's house?" It made sense. Now that Russell knew to attack there, he'd no doubt strike again tonight.

"That's up to Leonora." He sighed and rubbed his hand along my thigh. "I hate the thought of us running away like scared children each time they attack, but unless we can take out the person responsible or find a better way to kill these ghosts, we may not have a choice. And then there's the issue of Leonora herself. She's had some challenges to her authority lately, and she won't want to look weak by leaving the house."

I snorted. Yeah, like she hadn't looked weak having her personal bodyguards rush her while the members of her *Balaj* fought, and died, in her stead.

Before I could reply Dario turned to me. "But none of this is your problem. You've done what you were paid to do. Now it's up to us to take care of the problem."

There was my out, my chance to walk away. Russell had a right to want revenge. The vampires had a right to defend themselves. Any other Templar would turn their back on the whole thing.

But I wasn't any other Templar. And I wasn't about to tell Dario of my plans.

The vampire looked again at the window. "Sadly, taking care of things will need to wait until nightfall. Will you be okay? I need to take sanctuary."

I nodded, regretting the motion immediately, then rose. "I'll get you some blankets and pillows."

"No need." The vampire was already at my bathroom door. He faced me, a crooked smile on his handsome face. "I'll sleep like the dead."

I dozed on the sofa for a few hours, completely comfortable with the fact that there was a vampire in my apartment. It's not like he could do much during the daylight hours, and besides, I sort of trusted him. Who was I kidding, I did trust him. Murderer or not, Dario *was* my friend. And maybe a little bit more, if I was being completely honest with myself.

When I got up to get ready for my morning shift at the coffee shop I realized my dilemma. There was a vampire, for all intents and purposes a dead guy, in my bathroom, probably in my tub, and I was filthy with blood-streaked hair and breath that would fell a gargoyle. Even my go-bag was in there, in the cabinet under the sink. I couldn't even sneak in for fear that some stray beam of ambient light would filter through.

Which left me washing myself in the kitchen sink, shampooing with dishwashing liquid, and heading to work with a knotted mess of wet hair and no make-up. It wasn't until I'd punched in for the day that I remembered I hadn't checked my phone once I'd come out of the basement at Leonora's, and that I still had it off from last night.

My mother had called to remind me about the birthday party for Ajax at Roman and Hilda's place in Leesburg next month. Oh, and to ask me once again when I was going to take my Oath. The next message was the one I'd hoped for—Russell, responding to the note I'd left for him at the house. He wanted to meet, but at noon, at a pizza place in Mount Vernon.

I had no money for pizza, barely enough gas to make it through the week, and I was supposed to work until two this afternoon, but somehow I was going to make this meeting.

"You look like you haven't slept in weeks." Sean handed me a double-shot latte. One of the advantages of working at a coffee shop was drinking on the job.

"I've been running on two to three hours a night the past week," I confessed. My shoulder and head were also killing me. I was beginning to realize that vampire saliva might close open wounds but it didn't do anything for a concussion.

"You know, a little herb would clear that insomnia right up."

Sean smoked weed and didn't care who knew it. According to him it was the cure-all for everything from hangnails to hangovers. My problem wasn't insomnia though, it was a lack of time *to* sleep.

"You don't think I could get Anna to come in early do you? I'd be willing to take the last two hours of her Thursday shift." The more I thought about it, the more it sounded like a good idea. Thursday night was usually ladies' night, and Anna loved to soak up the cheap drinks, discounted food, and male attention. Not that it took a pub special for her to get dates with her red curls and mile-long legs. The girl needed a personal assistant just to keep her date nights organized.

"I'll call her." Sean looked around the coffee shop. "Morning crowd is gone. Why don't you go ahead and take off early. Get some sleep. I'll hold down the fort until Anna comes in."

I loved Sean. If he hadn't been twice my age and happily married, I would have kissed him. "Thanks, I owe you," I told him as I grabbed my bag from the back and headed for the door.

I didn't have time to get some sleep if I was going to make it to the pizza joint in time to meet Russell, but I did have time to swing by my apartment and grab my sword. And leave Dario a note.

I didn't know Russell, but Janice had mentioned he was "odd." It might be terrible manners, as well as possibly an illegal activity, to carry a sword into a pizzeria, but I wasn't going to take my chances at facing a necromancer unarmed. And just in case things went horribly wrong, Dario would know who to kill to avenge my death. If things went fine, I'd be back before nightfall—in plenty of time to destroy my note.

Taking one last look at my bathroom door with the towel tightly wedged under the bottom, I headed out.

The Mount Vernon neighborhood of Baltimore was just north of downtown and heralded as both a historic land-mark and the cultural hot-spot of the city. Mixed in with the parks, pubs, and trendy stores were galleries and restored brick homes. The area was out of my price range when it came to art, theater, and opera, but there was one place that had made Mount Vernon my go-to spot since the moment I'd moved to the city. The Walters Art Gallery was chock full of all the things that made my European History degree self sing. And it had a weapons collection to drool over.

But the museum wasn't my destination today. I parked and walked up to Jose's Pizzeria, scrunching my nose at the prices on the menu posted at the window. Yep. Way out of my price range even if it *had* been after payday.

The door chimed as I walked in. After a quick look around, I slid into a booth facing the door. The only picture I'd seen of Russell was from forty years ago. There were three African American guys in the place, every one of them staring at me. I figured if the necromancer was here, he'd approach me.

Someone did approach me, but it was the waiter. I could hardly take up space in a restaurant without ordering something. After digging around the floor of my car this morning, I'd managed to find a dollar bill and another buck fifty in change—just enough to order some fries and a glass of water and have a quarter left over for a tip. I felt like a vagrant telling the waiter what I wanted, but it was what it was. I couldn't dun the vampires for payment after what happened last night. They had greater priorities than paying me the rest of my fee. The coffee shop wouldn't have a check for me until Friday. That account my parents kept sticking money in was looking better and better each day, but for now I'd suck it up and eat my meal of French fries.

The waiter must have taken pity on me because the small order was ginormous and I also had a nice homemade pickle as a side. Six months in Baltimore had taught me the joys of dousing my fries with vinegar. I loved how the bitter snap meshed so well with the salty potatoes. Before I knew it, there was nothing in front of me but empty plates, and it was edging towards one o'clock.

That's when the waiter slid into the booth across from me. I blinked at him, remembering that Janice said Russell worked in warehousing. This couldn't be him. Was my server trying to pick me up? Was this a new method of delivering the bill? I put my crumpled dollar and change on the table and pushed it toward him, feeling my face heat up with shame. I really needed to get a second job, one that didn't involve vampires.

"It's on the house." The waiter's eyes darted around the restaurant, eyeing each patron with a wary suspicion. "I'm Russell Findal."

Heck, if I had known he was going to buy my meal, I would have ordered a pizza. I contemplated offering to shake his hand, but figured someone this paranoid probably was a germophobe, too. Instead I twisted my arm to show him the Templar tattoo on my wrist.

"Yeah. I figured that from the sword. Do you guys carry those things everywhere? You're going to get arrested."

I probably was. Eventually. "I figured with what's been happening in the past few days, the police were the least of my problems. I saw the spirits you raised at the cemetery last Wednesday, Russell, and I hear that isn't the only time they've been out of their graves."

I don't know what I expected, but the sad smile wasn't it. The man reached in his pocket and took out a photo, pushing it over to me. It was a smaller copy of the one that had been framed and in the plastic bin.

"I needed to talk to them, to confirm my suspicions. I'm a careful man and I don't want to act on hearsay and rumors, you understand?"

"Did your family confirm your suspicions?"

He nodded. "Knight Ainsworth, have you ever raised the dead?"

I winced at the title. "Aria. Please call me Aria. And no, Templar magic moves in a different direction, although I have read several texts on necromancy."

He leaned toward me, taking the photo and putting it safely in his shirt pocket. "They are never as they were when alive. Parts of their soul have forever moved on, and all that remains for us to call are the skeletons of spirit, burned with the emotions and experiences that weighed heaviest on them before they died."

As creeped out as this was, I'll admit I was intrigued. "What do you mean?"

His eyes met mine and I saw how haunted they were, as if all these encounters had burned him as well. "A woman who lost the man she loved may only talk about her feelings for him, her need to find him. As powerful as the spell is, I wouldn't be able to question her about anything else in her life. She'll always bring the conversation back to her lost love. She'll only be suited to performing tasks that deal with that emotion."

"So I'm assuming your family was angry and wanting revenge?"

"My parents, mostly, and Linc. The other two were young when they died. Hector didn't even really know what happened. He kept asking me if I knew where our cat had run off to."

Hector. His twin, forever trapped as an eight-year-old boy while Russell had lived, had grown up. Lord, this man had lost so much.

He sighed. "I let Kendra and Hector return to their eternal rest, but Linc, Mom, and Dad have a purpose here. I can't let them sleep again until they've avenged the wrongs done to our family."

Three spirits, but I'd seen at least four additional ones last night. Who were the other spirits? Had one of them been the dead sibling with the most reason to be angry? "Were you able to summon your eldest sister? Did you get to speak with Shay?"

He jerked backward, as if I'd struck him. "No. I have no idea what they did with her body after she was killed. I called her spirit, but she would have been raised at the site of her remains. Depending on where they are, it could be days before she makes her way in response to my summons."

My next question required some delicate wording. "What if there are no remains left? Would you be able to raise a spirit if she were cremated?"

The necromancer nodded. "Even in cases where no ashes remain, such as death by atomic blast, the spirit will return to the place they died. I'm assuming since Shay hasn't arrived yet, that her body was disposed of out of the city."

Atomic Blast? I really didn't want to know how necromancers figured that one out.

"When she arrives, she'll join the others. She'll be the angriest of all, killed right in front of her father. His spirit told me how she screamed, how she begged for him to save her."

My heart hurt thinking of it. No wonder they wanted revenge. Russell, too. I understood. I truly did. But there were still some loose ends in Russell's story. "Do you know *which* vampires killed your family?"

He tilted his head in surprise. "They all did. The man that took Shay never would have done so without the approval of their leader, and it was a group of them who killed her in front of my father. They are all to blame."

I thought of Dario, tried to imagine him participating in such a thing, and I couldn't. Maybe this was one of those kills from his past that he regretted, but I just couldn't see it. I refused to believe someone could change so much to have done this crime then become the vampire I knew.

"So what do you intend to do? When will you be satisfied that justice has been done?"

The necromancer's gaze dropped and he worried at the table top with a finger. "With the spell I used, these spirits have control over the physical realm. They can kill at will. Anything, anyone that they perceive as being involved. I leave justice in their hands."

I winced, doubting that risen spirits had much in the way of moral judgement when it came to guilt and innocence. It wasn't just all vampires they targeted, it was anyone in their way. They'd attacked me, and I honestly wasn't sure if it was because of my pathway of light or because I was guilty by association.

And from what Russell had said, a lot of their higher brain functioning was missing. Spirits who would attack all vampires, blood slaves, the pizza delivery guy—this wasn't justice, it was mass murder. And in the same category as what had been done to his family. I just needed him to see it that way.

"You and your family have suffered a horrible wrong, but how do you know those being killed are guilty? There are vampires in the *Balaj* who might not have even been turned when your family was killed, in addition to blood donors, or even innocent humans who just happen to be present at the time of the attack."

He shrugged, his eyes determined as he looked up from the table. "There is a possibility of collateral damage."

"Collateral damage." I tried to control my temper and failed. "How is what you're proposing any different from what was done to you and your family? How can you sit here and talk about justice when some housekeeper or Jehovah's Witness dude could be murdered by these spirits too?"

The necromancer snarled, a faint blue light snaking around the silver band on his left wrist.

"I am not like that group of murderous thugs who stole an innocent girl's life, tortured her in front of her parents, and then proceeded to kill a defenseless family."

"But what about the ones who aren't to blame for this? Or the humans? It's a slippery slope Russell."

"They are all to blame," he insisted. "The moment someone turns they are no longer human. Vampires are monsters. Every one of them is a killer, and the humans that serve them are no better."

It was no use continuing to argue with him like this. I needed to find another way of resolving what was quickly becoming Baltimore's most deadly feud.

"So three spirits, four if Shay shows up. Vampires aren't exactly easy to kill. How long are they going to go at it until they give up and return to rest?"

"They never will rest. Not until all the vampires are dead."

There was a flaw in that logic that only someone familiar with magic would likely see. "So you hinged their return on task completion? You must need to summon them each night anew as they wouldn't be able to remain here past sun up."

His eyes jerked to mine in surprise. "How do you know that?"

"I know something of magic, even if necromancy isn't a Templar art. You're summoning more than your dead family, aren't you? You'll need more than three or four vengeful specters to kill an entire *Balaj*."

A little smile quirked up the edge of his mouth. It was creepy. "My family weren't the only ones wronged by vampires. They leave a sort of calling card in their killings that make tracking their victims fairly easy. Even so, clearing Baltimore of these monsters will take time, but they will eventually die. Vampires will have no defense against the specters, not unless they are working with someone versed in magic."

He said the last with suspicion, looking up from the table.

I felt cold. Any chance I had at resolving this situation hinged on keeping my position neutral in Russell's eyes. I needed to somehow make him see that he wasn't in quite the superior position he thought he was. If Russell suffered a significant setback, he might be willing to compromise on his idea of justice. With luck and some research, I might be able to help the vampires provide that setback as long as Russell didn't know I was helping them.

I might not have much in the way of offensive skills when it came to necromancy, but one thing Templars could do was protect from undead. I wasn't sure whether my Templar protection would extend to the vampires or not. Technically they were undead too, and last night's blessing had burned the vampires it had touched. It would be gruesomely funny for me to cast a circle of protection, only to have the vampires excluded and forced to the outside along with the attacking spirits. No, whatever I did had to come from my extracurricular magical education as opposed to my Templar one.

"Templar Knights do not judge," I told Russell. It was true. Ever since the crusades where we'd slaughtered so many under the banner of faith, Templars made it a policy to not interfere. It sounded reasonable until our "only God has the right to judge" motto interfered with our mandate to protect Pilgrims on the Path. Protect from what? Didn't that involve making a judgment call about who was worthy of our protection?

But this wasn't the place for a philosophical debate. Russell seemed to know enough about Templars to be satisfied by my response that I was only an interested, informed onlooker.

"What happens if the vampires hire a mage? There's a huge *Haul Du* group in the northeast corridor, and they've been known to take contract work." I needed to give Russell a red herring to follow in case he sensed magic was interfering with the mission of the risen dead.

He smirked. "I've got a plan B."

Janice was right. Russell was creepy. More than creepy. I think he'd lost a few marbles in the course of his journey. Not that he didn't have valid reasons for being that way.

"What's plan B?"

"Top secret, that's what it is."

I figured he wasn't going to tell me, but I was nosy and not afraid to pry.

Russell shifted in the booth. "I'll admit I wasn't thrilled to find there was a Templar Knight in Baltimore, but I hoped that if I met with you, you'd come to realize that my actions don't interfere with any of your mandates."

I got it. He wanted to make sure an army of Knights weren't going to ride down on him and mess up his plans. He wasn't using a magical artifact that we needed to reclaim. Vampires would hardly be considered Pilgrims on the Path, so he wasn't crossing that line. Yes, he was a necromancer, but Templars don't judge.

Correction, Templar Knights don't judge. I wasn't a Knight.

I stood. "I'm so sorry for your loss. And thank you for the lunch."

The relief on his face made me feel even more conflicted. "You're welcome, Knight Aria. God be with you."

"And God be with you," I responded. Little did he know that my blessing held a very different supplication for divine intervention then the one I'm sure he hoped for.

I awoke in the dark, the sounds of evening traffic outside my window a soothing hum. My bed felt like a little slice of heaven. Eight hours of glorious sleep. I should have spent that time researching something to help the vampires tonight, but I'd found myself unable to make sense of a street sign, let alone a magical text. Now that I'd finally gotten some solid z's, I felt like I'd been reborn. Murmuring in contentment, I rolled under my sheets and stretched like a cat.

"I was going to offer you some coffee, but after that display I've got a very different offer in mind."

Dario. I bolted upright, clutching the sheet to my chest. I'd completely forgotten about the vampire in my bathroom. Now that it was dark, he was obviously up and about.

The vampire sat on the edge of my bed and extended a mug filled with the very elixir of life. I took it gratefully, eyeing him over the rim as I drank. He didn't look too worse for wear, beyond the faint scrapes on his face and arms from last night. I stared at the front of his shirt, wondering if the marks from my chair leg crucifix had healed.

"How's the burn?" Okay, I'll admit that my Florence Nightingale routine was more about an excuse to eye up his naked chest and back than any medical urges on my part.

He grimaced, crossing his arms and lifting his shirt up over his head. "Most of your smite-marks seem to be healing, but this one is going to leave a scar."

I caught my breath, a horrible wash of guilt running through me at the sight of the raised, cross-shaped mark on his chest. With my finger, I traced the mark, feeling the pattern of the wood grain perfectly reproduced in his skin. "I'm so sorry. I didn't know it was you. I thought it was that vampire coming back to attack me."

He shrugged and shifted on the bed, moving away from my touch. "You don't trust me. You don't trust any of us. Not that I blame you. We're vampires. You're a Templar. The uneasy truce we've had for the last century isn't exactly a good foundation for a working relationship, let alone any other kind of relationship."

His words stung, but they were true. I hadn't trusted him, wasn't completely sure I did now. I'd better decide fast because after my meeting with Russell it was clear that I needed to be on one side of this fight or the other.

"How's your head?" Dario asked. I noticed he didn't attempt to examine my wound in the way I'd done his.

"The gash is totally healed, thank you for that. Headache is currently being managed by aspirin and lots of caffeine."

His mouth twisted into a wry smile. "Guess we vampires are good for something after all. I take it you have no aftereffects from my saliva?"

He made it all sound so clinical. My mind flashed back to me curled up in his lap in the dark as he licked my wound, and everything south of my navel stirred in response. "Not really." I wasn't about to admit being more than a little horny. Besides, I wasn't sure that was due to his saliva or the fact that a gorgeous half-naked guy was sitting on the edge of my bed.

"Good. You asked last night about our next step? Whether we were going to abandon Leonora's house now that it had been attacked?" He waited until I nodded. "We've decided to hold fast and defend the house if it's attacked again. The gang members we killed the other night were involved with the robbery, and we found they were tangentially involved with the magician who is sending the spirits to attack us, but the rest of the gang is innocent. We're still trying to track down this magician and kill him, but in the meantime we're going to present a strong front and gather what information we can. I want you to know so you'll stay clear. I've got to get back there soon and help set up our defense, and I'll probably be out of contact for a while." He reached out a hand and ran his fingers through my tangled mess of hair. "I'll let you know as soon as this is resolved."

I felt sick. I knew who was doing this, what Russell had planned, and here I sat letting Dario drive away to a possible death. I couldn't. As much sympathy as I felt for Russell, a fellow human, I just couldn't.

"How badly did things go last night? I mean, how many died and how many were injured? Is this something you think you can defend against? Do you have any way to effectively fight these spirits?"

He twisted his mouth downward. "It was bad. We lost ten, and at least a dozen more are suffering wounds that will leave them immobile for several weeks. We can't continue to experience this level of damage every night, and we can't defend ourselves without upping our consumption levels. And no, we don't know how to fight these things. They appear to run out of energy after a few hours and leave, but nothing we do seems to hurt them. It's all a game of who can outlast who at this point."

I got the unspoken part of his statement. The vampires needed to find who was doing this and stop him, or they'd eventually all die. There was only so much damage a vampire could take before he'd succumb to his injuries, and only so much blood they could consume each night to help them heal. Upping their consumption levels would put them at risk of attracting human attention and jeopardizing their ability to hold this territory.

"I need to help. I'm…I'm worried about you."

He laughed. Laughed. This was the first time I'd heard that noise from him and it was in response to what I considered a very serious matter. "I'll be fine. I'm tough. I've survived worse than this in the last three and a half centuries. We just need to hold tight for a few days until we find the magic user."

I knew the truth he was trying to hide from me. I knew how bad this was going to get. I probably knew that more than he did. Russell had the ability to raise murdered humans from centuries ago as well as those outside the territory where the rogue bands of vampires didn't take such care to preserve human life. All those angry specters wouldn't care if the vampires they killed were involved in their murder or not. How long could Leonora and her *Balaj* hold tight against dozens? And how long would it take them to find Russell, a forgotten child from a family murdered decades ago?

I scooted closer to him. "Dario, I'm going to take a huge leap of faith here and trust you enough to tell you something. I need you to be absolutely honest with me in return. Do I have your word?"

Ever since the fiasco over Linguini Alfredo, he'd been remarkably open with me when I questioned him about vampire matters, about personal topics. I just needed to make sure he'd continue to be, that I knew the truth before I decided what to do tonight.

"You have my word," he replied solemnly.

I turned to face him on the bed, folding my legs into a half-lotus position. "Forty years ago a fourteen-year-old girl was preyed upon by a vampire, not once, but multiple times. He eventually took her and made her a blood slave."

He nodded. "We try to enforce a minimum age of our prey now, but this was not always the way things were. I know it sounds horrible, but many older vampires came from a time when fourteen was considered well into adulthood. Marriage, sexual relations, and pregnancy were common in young teens not too long ago, and some vampires find it difficult to adapt to modern ideas regarding the age of consent."

I'd read enough history to know he was right, but it still made me rather sick to think about. "We can argue about that later. This particular girl was killed."

He looked at me blankly. "I would assume so. As much as we try to prolong the life of blood slaves, average life expectancy can be anywhere from a few weeks to a few months. Only the strongest of us are able to keep our blood slaves alive for over a year."

And that was the life he'd offered me, admittedly in the heat of the moment and in blood lust. My heart sank.

"She was killed right in front of her father. He didn't even get to keep her body. Months later the whole family was killed in their home by vampires, their throats slit to cover it up."

Something flickered in his eyes. Shame? Or perhaps just regret that this dark secret had been discovered. "I'll be honest with you, Aria. These things happened and more than once. We don't do that anymore. I know you're not a fan, but Leonora isn't the sort of Mistress who would allow that to happen in her *Balaj*."

His reassurances went right over my head. All I could

focus on was that these things happened. And more than once. A child was taken as a blood slave, murdered in front of her family, and this had occurred more than once. An entire family was slaughtered, more than once.

I jumped to my feet. "Did you recognize the spirits that attacked last night? Did their faces mean anything to you, or has every person you've killed become blurred together by this point? Are there so many you can't even count them, or remember who they are?"

I pushed past him and marched into the living room. He followed me; I knew he did, even though his footsteps were silent on the carpet.

"Shay. Does that name ring a bell? The Robertsons?"

I felt his hands on my shoulders as he turned me to face him. "I was *honest* with you. If you really want stories of blood and violence, then I'll tell you what happened during the centuries we spent making our way north to Baltimore. I'm not proud of the things my *Balaj* has done, but that is the past. We don't do those things today."

I thought of babies preyed upon, bodies blood-raped by multiple vampires until there was no liquid left in them to spill. And then I thought of our Order's past—of babies murdered, of old men, women, non-combatants killed so the Templars could claim their lands and treasures for their own. All in the name of God. We didn't do that today, and I would hate to be judged for the actions of my ancestors.

But this wasn't Dario's ancestors, it was him and his contemporaries. And forty years ago wasn't the same as nine hundred.

I pulled from his grasp and opened my laptop, clicking on the obituary photos. "The Robertsons. Surely you must remember them. Please tell me you remember them."

I was practically pleading, because worse than murder was the thought that their deaths had meant nothing, hadn't even left a lasting impression upon him. I didn't want the Robertsons to be yet another in a too-many-to-remember string of violence.

He shook his head, swiping through the various photos without recognition until he came to one of Shay—the picture her parents had given the police for the missing persons folder. "Her. She was Jean-Marc's blood slave."

I let out a breath I hadn't realized I'd been holding. "I know who is summoning the specters. If I can arrange for Jean-Marc to be handed over to justice, then I may be able to end this now."

Dario had me against the wall so fast I hardly had time to register he'd even moved. "You lied. You lied to me and to Leonora. I trusted you, told you things no Templar has ever been privy to, slept vulnerable here in your apartment. I trusted you and you lied to me. Did it not bother you that my family *died* Saturday night? Last night?" He pushed me against the wall, his eyes dark with anger. "I'd thought you were different, that maybe you'd actually care about vampire lives."

"I didn't know then," I protested. "I suspected who it might be, but I didn't know for sure. You were positive Saturday night's attack was gang related and…"

He was right. I had known, but how could I have told them and stood by as they slaughtered Russell? *Did* I put the necromancer's life before that of the vampires? If I was totally honest with myself, I had.

Dario's knuckles whitened as he gripped my shoulders. "How long have you known who this magician is?"

My heart thumped in my chest. "Since last night, right before I went to see Leonora. You killed his elder sister, his entire family. Doesn't he have a right to justice? If I *had* told Leonora, she would have hunted him down and killed him.

You *know* she would have murdered him in cold blood. I couldn't allow that."

The vampires would have killed him in cold blood, so instead I kept silent and let Russell kill *them* in cold blood. Suddenly I didn't feel so righteous.

Dario let me go and took a step back. "But you couldn't trust *me*? No, of course you couldn't trust me. Stupid of me to think otherwise."

I bit my lip. No, I hadn't trusted him. I'd immediately thought him guilty, and tonight didn't seem to be proving those initial assumptions wrong. He hadn't even flinched when I'd shown him the photos of the slain Robertsons, had said murders like these had been common. Didn't he feel even the slightest bit of guilt over what his family had done?

Dario gave a bitter laugh at my silence and turned away, running a hand over the top of his close-cropped hair. "Brothers and sisters of mine *died* last night. They died Saturday night. You knew who was behind this and you just let my family die." Walking casually over to my kitchen table, he shut the laptop. "Well, your necromancer friend is thirty years too late. Jean-Marc is already dead."

Thirty years. That clicked in my brain and spurred a memory from the conversation we'd had at Sesarios. "He died with your previous Master?"

"Yes. Aubin was our master, my sire. He turned me in Haiti. I as well as his other children and several of his blood siblings followed him when we were exiled."

My mind whirred trying to figure out a way to resolve this thing without being able to deliver his sister's killer to Russell. "So I can assure the necromancer that all the vampires who participated in the murder of his family are dead?"

"Hell if I know," Dario huffed. "Jean-Marc is dead. Aubin

is dead along with his siblings and eight of his offspring. Still, over two thirds of the current *Balaj* were turned at the time."

I frowned in confusion. "But did any of them participate in the Robertson murders? If I can turn over those at fault to the necromancer, then I might be able to resolve this without further bloodshed."

He turned to me, his eyes cold. "No. We are a family. There will be no turning over of anyone. Jean-Marc is dead. The master of the *Balaj* at the time of the murders is dead. If that doesn't satisfy this necromancer of yours then we will hunt him down ourselves and kill him."

I had a feeling just the knowledge of Aubin and Jean Marc's deaths wouldn't be enough. Although maybe there was some way I could spin this. "How did they die? Rogue vampires outside the city? A savvy human? Drank bad blood?"

"We killed them."

That, I did not expect.

"It was decades in the planning. Some of us didn't like where Aubin had been heading with the *Balaj*, but as his blood-children, we were sworn to obey him. I won't go into details, but suffice it to say there was a coup."

I was already thinking about how I could relay this information to gain Russell's buy-in for a peaceful resolution. Could I claim that the current members of the *Balaj* not been involved in the murder of his family, had ousted those who were and killed them?

"I'll help resolve this without bloodshed, and come to a solution that works for both your family and this necromancer."

"Like hell you will." The vampire snarled, and I felt a return of that fear I'd felt when I'd been locked in the basement last night. "There has already been bloodshed. This human has attacked my family, murdered my brothers and sisters. For that, he'll die."

It sounded eerily like what Russell had said. "How about nobody else dies? This guy lost his entire family to your *Balaj*. He's got reasons for what he's doing."

Dario turned so all I could see was his back. "That was forty years ago. What's happening right now is my concern. I won't let any more of my family die at this man's hands. And as much as I respect your abilities as a Templar, I can't put my faith in your reassurances that you can 'handle this.'"

Everything was falling apart right in front of my face. No wonder Templars just stood back and let God sort it all out.

"What if I help you defend against the spirits? I'll neutralize them each night until I can manage to come to a peaceable solution."

The vampire's laugh held three hundred years of bitterness. "Oh, like you did last night? Your pathway-of-light spell severely burned two of us. Any vampire who falls into that light is going to wind up cooked, and there'll be no coming back for them the next night like there is for the spirits."

He was right, but I had a few other ideas up my sleeve. "I can banish. It won't create a holy area like the pathway blessing, it will just return the dead to their graves."

Dario turned to face me. "Us too? Because we're technically dead, in case you haven't noticed."

"But not really," I argued. "Your spirit selves haven't been released from your bodies. If I can come up with something that—"

"No." He slammed a hand down on my table, cracking the wood. "You've done enough. Stay out of it. Just…just stay out of it."

I wasn't sure if he was worried I'd do more harm than good, if he didn't want me to interfere with the massacre that was about to commence, or if he just wanted me gone from his life.

"Please." I had no reason to ask him this, but still I did. "Please let me try first. Stay out of Leonora's house tonight so the necromancer has to search for you. Give me twenty-four hours."

Dario's eyes met mine. "There are reasons why we can't abandon Leonora's house, reasons that have nothing to do with this. And a lot of my brothers and sisters could die in twenty-four hours. More if he finds our daytime resting spots."

"Please." I let the word hang between us and held my breath.

"No. This is an internal matter between us and this necromancer. Your services are no longer needed."

Ouch. I needed to do something to buy time. I needed to help fix this, to redeem myself in his eyes.

"Let me help. There will be repercussions if you do this your way. You've already killed a whole bunch of people who may have had nothing to do with this. What if you get the wrong guy? Or what if you get the right one? Continuing to kill in retaliation is going to set up a chain of events that might not end with his death."

"What, if the Templars get involved, you mean?" Dario's voice was soft. "Are you threatening me, Aria? Be very careful where you're going with this. I doubt even your own family is going to care about a *Balaj* and a practitioner of the dark arts duking it out, and you are only one Templar. One. How much can you do against so many of us?"

I winced, knowing full well I didn't have the strength to take them on solo, and that there would be no Knights to back me up in this. Still, I wasn't the only human who would take exception to a series of murders. "What if your gang partners join forces to take your *Balaj* down? What if they partner with some of the rogue vampires outside the city? What if the feds get involved?"

He raised an eyebrow. "You think we can't handle that? I can't say either of those scenarios would be pleasant but neither would damage us more than letting this necromancer live."

Threats were clearly the wrong angle. "Give me two nights, Dario. Tonight and tomorrow night and I'll make this right." I wracked my brain, trying to think of something I could propose in exchange. An alliance with the *Balaj* seemed a paltry offering given I wasn't even a Knight. Plus I wasn't convinced I *could* partner with them long-term and keep my sense of morality, as shaky as it might be.

He laughed. "Oh yes. Please go ahead and take a few nights to work something out while I lose a dozen or so brothers and sisters. No problem, we'll just sit back and accept our losses. It's a small price to pay to save the life of *one* necromancer."

I had nothing. "Please, Dario. I don't want things to end like this, with you hating me and blaming me for the deaths last night. Evacuate Leonora's place. The necromancer will need another day or two to find another one of your houses to attack. I'll try to get him to call things off, and I'll work on a spell that will banish the spirits without harming any of your family." I blinked, ignoring the sting of tears in my eyes. "Please. Give me a chance to redeem myself, to make this right."

A muscle in his jaw twitched. "Twenty-four hours. I'll give you until tomorrow night to get him to back down, otherwise we're going after him. I can't guarantee what we'll do with Leonora's house. Just be aware that if things go bad tonight, I might not be able to hold them back."

I let out the breath, knowing this was the best I could hope for.

"I know you need to head out to feed and to safeguard the *Balaj*, but can you stay just a few more minutes? I want to try something. Are you up for being my guinea pig?"

Yeah, like that was going to happen. I needed a vampire to see how these spells might possibly affect them, though. Dario was the only vampire I was somewhat friendly with, although after tonight I wasn't sure how friendly we were going to be going forward.

He hesitated, looking at the sword at the end of my table before he replied. "No."

I bit back a smile, realizing humor wasn't really appropriate at this moment. "Not that. I want to try a non-Templar spell, one that deals with banishment of the dead but is more specific and without the religious slant to it."

His eyes narrowed. "Make it fast. And I'm going to be really pissed if you kill me."

Yeah, that would upset me, too. "I'm not going to hit you with it full force. I just want to see if you're excluded from the area of effect or not. Worst case scenario is you have some minor pain."

I hated to do this, but needed to know if this spell was going to work or not. And if it was going to wind up putting vampires in their graves as well as the spirits.

Dario folded his arms across his chest, still looking unconvinced. "Okay. But if I say 'stop', you need to end the spell. Got it?"

"Got it."

I left my sword on the table, and motioned Dario to follow me over next to the window. Mindful of his impatience to get out of here, I gathered my supplies and set them up around the room.

"Stand as close to the bookcases as you can," I instructed, lighting the candles and tracing a symbol in salt around each one. "The incense is going to burn out fast. Let me know if you feel any discomfort or…anything."

Dario raised an eyebrow, watching as I lit the tiny button of incense.

"*Durmir unha vez.*" To my eye, nothing happened. But since there wasn't a ghost or spectral being within the confines of the candlelit circle, that wasn't surprising. "Can you feel it?"

"Yes," Dario squinted. "It hurts my chest. It's a sort of pressure, and sharp prickling feeling combined."

That wasn't good. If he felt the pull of the spell from the outside, then vampires would most definitely be affected by it. Somehow I'd need to keep the vampires on the outside and the spirits on the inside as I lit the incense. Not easy given that the spirits would be attacking the vampires, and thus right on top of them.

"Can you enter the circle? Cross the line of salt?"

Dario raised a hand to shield his eyes. "You're kidding, right? I can feel it from here. There's no way I'm going to come any closer."

He had a point. I sighed. "This will banish the spirits. Bam. Gone for the night. The only hitch is that you all can't be in the house when I'm doing it."

The incense fizzled into ash, and I began to extinguish the candle flames.

Dario frowned. "Just give it up, Aria. We'll take care of this."

I wasn't about to give this up. "No. I'll spend the night researching this. Is there someone from your *Balaj* that you can send over to help? I promise nothing will happen to him. I just need someone to tell me how the spells are working from a vampire perspective."

"Fine. Just make sure he can get home before sunup."

I watched Dario leave. He was angry and rightly so. There

was a chance that even if I made this work he'd never trust me again.

But that was something I could cry over another day. I had to hurry. If Leonora refused to abandon her house and more vampires died tonight, there was a good chance tomorrow evening would start with Russell's murder. Vampires had humans who assisted them—and not just gangs they partnered with. Blood slaves could assist the *Balaj* until the point in their service where they got too weak. And there were Renfields.

Far from the bug-eyed sycophants of films, Renfields were vampire wannabes who acted in the interests of the *Balaj* during daylight hours. No exchange of blood took place until they received their ultimate reward—being turned and taking their place in the hierarchy of the vampire family. While vampires slept, Renfields guarded, did research, and broke whatever legs needed breaking. I had no doubt that if Dario didn't convince Leonora to give me this twenty-four hours, she'd know Russell's name by sundown, and he'd be dead shortly after.

Yanking books back off the shelves I sorted through them. Three grimoires in Greek, Latin, and Armenian. Mercer's *All Things Undead*. Van Petersen's *Grave Tidings*. Lawrence and Singtha's *Beyond the Veil*. It was a good start in my search for a spell that would send the dead to their graves without killing the very beings I wanted to protect.

This was going to require more than research, though. I was going to need to make a phone call. And scrounge up some food, I thought as my stomach grumbled. Those French fries and the pickle seemed days ago, and I'd left my dollar and spare change as a tip for Russell. Which left me facing a night of research with a cup of Ramen noodles.

If only I still had my Emergency Beer.

"How about this one?"

"Nah. Thanks, though." I didn't have to look at the book the vampire was holding out. In the last hour she'd suggested a Woodsman spell, a Siren protection amulet, and a scroll of blue fire, no doubt because she couldn't read the Latin and was mainly going off the engraved, woodcut illustrations.

Dario had sent me a female vampire named Opal. Her ebony skin gleamed in the light of my apartment, her natural hair a poof of wooly black. I'll admit I'd had some envy of her long legs and thin figure. As pretty as she was, I was sure she had no problem at all finding blood donors.

"Are you sure? This one says care-ooolea-um Ignatius."

"*Caeruleum ignis.*" I glanced over at the book to confirm. "Blue fire. It has to do with dragons."

"Dragons? No shit, there are really dragons?"

So asks a vampire. I glanced up at Opal before turning back to my own text, one that actually dealt with undead instead of giant reptilian beings. "Yes, there are dragons. And put your fangs away."

"Sorry." The fangs disappeared with a *snick.* "I've got a thing for dragons. Say, you don't know any, do you? Would they be interested in a kinky vampire girl?"

"No, they'd steal all of your stuff then eat you." I glanced at her again. Opal was a bit of a pain, but she'd proven herself to be very eager to help in all my various magical experiments tonight. I looked over at my clock, wondering how much longer I had until Opal had to return.

"I'm good for another hour," she announced, carefully placing the book back on the shelf. "Do you wanna try that smoke thing again?"

The one that nearly combusted my vampire helper? I don't think so.

"The protective radius one showed promise. Let's try it with a modification of the End Times spell."

She grimaced. "If you weren't the boss's blood slave, I'd never have signed up for this."

That very liquid in my veins ran cold. Blood slave? Not in this lifetime. "Leonora hired me to do some research for her. I'm not her blood slave."

Opal laughed. "I know. You're hardly her type. She likes the soft, cuddly blond ones. I mean Dario. He asked for volunteers and we all practically staked each other for the privilege."

I sat the *Undead in the New World* aside, and turned my attention to the leggy vampire, not sure what shocked me most—that the vampires wanted to work with me, or that she'd assumed I was already Dario's blood slave. I went with the latter revelation first.

"What makes you think I'd ever allow Dario to feed from me, let alone start a short and deadly relationship with him?"

The vampire folded her arms across her chest, fangs peeking out once more as her eyes roamed down my form. "Are you kidding me? He's smokin' hot. Everyone says that you can't keep your eyes off him, and he practically beat Federico to death last night when he smelled your blood on his breath."

Somehow it was very gratifying that Dario had whupped my assailant. But it wasn't so gratifying that because of it, everyone assumed I belonged to him.

"Dario told everyone hands-off you last week. Federico is lucky he isn't dead. Poaching blood slaves, even ones who haven't been marked yet, is a cardinal sin."

Nice to know, although I was hoping to make it through this life without ever becoming anyone's blood slave.

"And you called him boss?"

Her gaze jerked to the window, muscles tightening. "I didn't…Leonora's our Mistress. Dario is kind of a second-in-command. I shouldn't have called him that. Some of the blood slaves do because he interacts more with them and the newer vampires than the Mistress does. And he helped me after my maker was killed."

I took a more careful look at Opal, her dress, easy use of modern slang, and ever-appearing fangs. "When were you turned?"

"Seventy-two. Nineteen seventy-two, that is. I was Chantal's blood slave for two months. We got a little carried away one night and she honored me with immortality."

From what I'd read it was a rarity. Turning a human required approval, and it took a terrible toll on the maker. "When did Chantal die?"

Opal's youthful exuberance faded, her smile sad. "Three decades ago, when Leonora became Mistress. Chantal had been Master Aubin's blood sister, and she stood with him in the battle."

"And you didn't?" I should have been working on spells, not wasting precious night hours digging up this vampire's past, but I was curious.

"I was too young and weak to fight. Normally I would have been culled. No vampire wants to take on the burden of a newly turned child, especially one that was the offspring of an opponent. I'm grateful to Dario for letting me live."

Okay, the guy was beginning to sound like a saint, at least in the eyes of these vampires. Which made me wonder why he hadn't taken over the *Balaj* after the coup. I was no judge of vampire power, but I got the feeling he wasn't far behind Leonora when it came to mojo.

"Why didn't Leonora shelter you? I'd assume that would have been one of her first deeds as Mistress." I know it would have been mine. Conquering a group of people didn't end well unless you could get them to see you less as a violent ruler, and more as a benevolent one. And yeah, we Templars had learned that one the hard way.

Opal laughed, reaching out a finger to caress the spine of an ancient grimoire. "Leonora is old world, she's…French old world. I don't think it ever crossed her mind to consider what might happen to the young or the weak. The *Balaj* was in a bad state back then, too. There were external threats to our territory as well as divisions within the family. Her first priority was to show herself as a strong leader—one who could fight off rogue bands from outside the city and force our human partners into compliance."

"How do you pick your leader? Leonora didn't sire most of you. What makes her Mistress as opposed to someone else?"

"Age, power, leadership ability, charisma." Opal shrugged. "I don't really know much more than that, just that after the coup Leonora came out on top and she's stayed that way without any internal challenges since."

Which spurred my next question. "What would happen if there was an internal challenge?"

The vampire's hand stilled, her voice tight as she replied.

"Someone would die. No one gives up leadership. None of us would respect a fallen leader. It's kill or be killed."

"Or exile?" It seemed like a viable alternative.

Her head lifted, brown eyes serious as they met mine. "That's death. The rogue bands outside the territory would be merciless. An exiled vampire lives in constant readiness for attack."

Well hopefully Dario wouldn't get any ideas. And I needed to get back to work and stop pumping this young vampire for information. Time was ticking away. That sort of research could wait until later.

"Protective Radius with modified End Times."

Opal sighed and got to her feet. "I heal fast, but my hair doesn't. Just be careful because bald isn't a good look for me and I'm young enough that I need every feminine wile I've got to attract prey."

This time Opal felt no adverse effects. Finally I'd found a spell that worked...sort of. End Times wasn't a simple or quick spell, I'd altered an old Templar blessing that sent restless spirits back to the grave to await the day of reckoning. The only problem was each restless spirit had to be banished by name. This fact meant none of the vampires would be harmed, but it also meant I needed to know the name of every specter or they'd remain.

I knew three. Maybe four if Shay had finally shown up. Which left six or more spirits remaining.

"I've got to get going." I looked over to see Opal sling her huge bag over one shoulder. "It was fun, girlfriend. Give me a shout if you need any more help." She winked, her hand on the doorknob. "Or if you've got any friends looking for a fun night with a vampire. Male, female, I'm not picky."

That was so not going to happen, but Opal had been a big help and an entertaining, if rather exhausting, companion tonight. I waved her out and turned back to my spell. I had something to use. And I had enough time to grab a two hour catnap.

Tonight, once the vampires arose, I was going to fight this thing head on. Although this time I was going to need human assistance. Namely Janice and Rob.

CHAPTER 22

I'd sent a quick e-mail to Janice before going to sleep, figuring her job at the paper would afford her greater research avenues than my generic internet searches. Since I didn't have Rob's number, I'd need to hope he was working tomorrow and swing by the records office after work.

It was a lot to squeeze into one day. Work, Rob, Janice, and then preparation for tonight's spell. I also needed to try to meet Russell and make every effort to convince him that justice had been served. The fact that I was doing all this research and spell prep was a big clue as to how I thought the meeting with the necromancer was going to go.

If all that wasn't enough to make me toss and turn for my two precious hours of sleep, I was worried about the vampires—well, one vampire in particular. I hadn't heard from Dario, and Opal had refused to contact him saying they'd been told to only call in case of emergency. I assumed someone would have clued her in if a massacre had occurred and she had no safe home to return to. Or maybe not. Who would call if they'd all been killed or severely injured? Had they stayed away from Leonora's house or stubbornly decided to make a stand? Had the vengeful spirits attacked again? How much damage had they caused? How many vampires had been killed this time? Was Dario okay?

And how was I going to fare tonight when I didn't get any sleep at all and had a day, and night, full of activities? I was going to find out.

I grabbed a quick shower, breakfasted on a stale piece of bread with the scrapings of margarine that remained in the tub, then loaded my sword in the car. One of my tasks after Opal left had been to put enough enchantments on my weapon that I could feel safe leaving it in my car without worrying that someone would break in and steal it. Let's just say anyone trying it would get a severe burn, and nightmares about hydras for weeks.

Trusty also had a modified version of my "yucky face" spell. I needed to be able to carry the big-ass sword around in public without getting arrested, but didn't want people feeling like they were going to throw up every time they saw it. I had no luck in getting dates now, I'd have even less of a chance with the equivalent of a dead groundhog covered in barf strapped to my back.

I wasn't about to try out the sword's spell at work where failure would cost me my job, so Trusty stayed in the car while I brewed coffee and stirred up fancy lattes for the good citizens on their way to work. Wednesday. Payday was Friday, and I had nothing but a dozen packs of Ramen in my house. My situation had become so dire that I was eyeing the pastries in the cabinet, wondering if any of them were destined for the garbage can today.

I had no hope of getting payment from the vampires, although if I managed to take care of their necromancer problem, I was going to have a serious talk with Dario about collecting what I'd been promised. Seriously. As I frothed milk, I was busy thinking of what hexes I might threaten the vampires with if they didn't pay up. It's not like I could garnish their wages, or attach a lien to their assets or anything. No, my debt collection efforts would need to be of the magical kind.

I raced out of the coffee shop at eleven-thirty and headed toward the Inner Harbor, where I was pleased to see that no one batted an eye at the sword on my back. The day was heating up to be a scorcher. Hot waves shimmered off the blacktop. Tourists down midweek for a summer day off were glowing with sweat. Children danced about in lawn sprinklers, sheltering under store awnings and canopies to avoid the sun.

The sword on my back, even in its leather sheath, felt like it had just been brought out of the forge. Once again I lamented that Templars hadn't updated to the use of handguns. Sure, we trained in all modern weaponry, but our lives were linked to the sword. Of course, I'm not sure how I could use a pistol to aid in a blessing or in establishing a protective area. The thought of me in chain mail, kneeling to place a gun muzzle downward before making the sign of the cross was amusing.

And it was all about the cross. Our swords mirrored that shape, complementing the theme of our holy mission. That fateful Christmas Day so long ago the pope had granted us our charter, but a higher authority had been the one who bestowed us with our skills. In return, we pledged our lives in service.

Nearly a thousand years later, what had that vow become? We kept the Temple safe, kept dangerous magical objects from use. I'm sure that wasn't what God intended when His messenger gave us our holy mission. Security guards. Research that no one ever came to us for. No more pilgrims. Why were we still here? Why hadn't we all been killed that Friday the thirteenth when pope and king turned on us? What use were Templars in a modern world?

There was a line to get into the aquarium, people milling about aboard the Constellation, admiring the rigging and weaponry of the old sailing ship. I walked past to the water's edge and sat down, sliding the sword from my back and pulling it from the sheath.

So far so good. No one was screaming and running. I hadn't been arrested as a suspected terrorist. People went about their business as if I wasn't sitting on the dock of the bay holding a thirty inch blade in my hands.

The sun reached its zenith and I began, scribing the runes on the blade as I chanted. When they covered both sides, I raised the sword to the noonday sun.

"Tocar e virar espirito para corpus."

The runes glowed red then vanished, leaving me holding a sword that looked no different from what it had this morning. If this worked, it would be worth every sleepless hour.

I strapped Trusty to my back and made my way to my car, eyeing the foodstands along the way. I'd scored a blueberry scone that was past the good-by date, but wouldn't be able to put anything else in my belly until much later.

Rob was out on his lunch break at the records office, so I left him a message to call me and crossed my fingers that the suspicious woman behind the counter would actually give it to him. Then I swung by to meet Janice. At a deli, where I would try hard not to stare at the food as we spoke.

The reporter was an angel—an angel who slid a bulging folder toward me then offered to share her giant plate of fried pickles. I tried not to look like a starving vagrant as I stuffed my mouth and opened the folder.

Holy crap. I was in for a very long day. In fact, I wasn't sure I was going to be able to prep for this spell quite as thoroughly as I'd wanted to.

"These are all the murders?" I'd asked Janice if she could get me everyone in Baltimore city who had died in the last forty years by having their throat slit.

"The first paper-clipped set are murders. The second are assaults. I figured that if this was a gang signature, there may have been some that survived and were too afraid to identify their attackers."

I pushed that stack aside for later. It was intriguing enough that I wanted to go through it, but for tonight's purposes I was only interested in those who had actually died during the attack.

"There must be sixty names in here," I commented. I'd need to write each of those names on individual pieces of paper in the ceremony, then recite the spell for each one of them to banish. The task was beginning to seem overwhelming. I had visions of vampires dying around me as I slowly went through each piece of paper. Add to that the very real danger that one of the specters might attack me while I was casting, and the whole thing added up to disaster.

Janice nodded. "I tried to sort out the ones where there had been a reasonable amount of blood at the crime scene, but couldn't. Some had been murdered outside where rain and the elements played a part. Other bodies were moved after death. I ended up just including them all, figuring it would be better to start with a broad range and narrow it as we researched."

Except we had no time to research. I thumbed through the stack, wondering if it was worth it for me to prioritize the names in case I ran out of time tonight—a triage of sorts.

"So...what's the deal?" Janice squirmed, her eyes gleaming. "Did you find the link? Is it a rival gang? Some kind of seventies mob scene carry-over?"

"Vampires," I announced, stealing another handful of fried pickles.

"Right." She laughed. "The Nosferatu kind of vampire, or the sparkly kind. Ooo, please let it be the Wesley Snipes one, because if I'm going to get my throat ripped out I want it to be him."

"I'm completely serious. They're very secretive but not as in-the-closet as you think. There's a sizable *Balaj* in Baltimore and under their Master forty years ago, they did some horrible things."

I didn't mention that there were some borderline horrible things going on in this decade, too. Ethics were a personal thing, and I was well aware that even non-lethal blood drinking probably fell into the first degree assault category.

Janice's eyes strayed to my Templar mark. I think it was the only thing that was keeping her from writing me off as a complete nut-job. "Vampires. In Baltimore. And they're cutting throats instead of biting them. What, are they all defanged?"

What an intriguing idea. I'd need to ask Dario if vampire fangs grew back, or if such a handicap would result in starvation.

"The throat cutting is to cover up the bite wounds. They drink the blood, but don't want law enforcement to start sharpening stakes or anything, so they make it look like a murder with a knife."

"A murder with a knife except there isn't enough blood and the victims didn't struggle," Janice mused. "And who the heck would kill four notorious gang members by slitting their throats? That's just suicide."

"Unless you're a vampire. People have varying degrees of vulnerability to their entrancements, but it's not just that. Vampires are strong." I remembered my encounter with Federico. "Very strong."

The reporter shook her head and looked at the open

folder in front of me. "Should I worry? Should I carry around a crucifix or a jar of garlic?"

I didn't have the heart to tell her that neither of those would do her any good. The only reason my keychain worked was that it was sanctified and I was a Templar.

"Normally if you encountered one you'd think you had an awesome and slightly kinky one-night stand, and feel a bit hungover the next day." I gestured toward the folder. "Most of these are probably just normal human-on-human murders."

Her hand went to her neck. "Shit. I've probably already been preyed upon a few times in my life by that description."

Maybe. Maybe not. I stood up, needing to get going and not wanting to scare her further. "I know this isn't exactly something you can print in your paper. Let me get through the weekend, and we can get together to come up with a story you *can* write. Something about knife murders versus shooting ones maybe."

She stood and nodded. "I'll work on it, too. Although the vampire story would be pretty amazing."

And probably result in her being the next on this list of names in the folder. "Too bad you don't work for that sort of newspaper."

She grinned. "Yeah. Too bad."

CHAPTER 23

I needed to get back to my apartment and start prepping for tonight's spell—all sixty names of it. But not until after I'd spoken to Russell. It was a long shot, but if I could just convince him to call off his attack, then I wouldn't need to do all the spell prep. Actually I wouldn't need to do anything but get a message to Dario and sleep until morning.

First stop was at the pizzeria, where I'd learned Russell was off for the day. The next stop was at the abandoned house, where no one answered my shouts. I'd texted the necromancer before leaving the Inner Harbor, but called and left a voice mail message before heading to the next place on my list.

Leonora's house looked completely different in the daylight. The trees still shielded it from view, but the oaks and maples seemed less like sentries and more like stately accents to the huge home. Wrought iron gates and fencing were lined with dense hedges. Hanging baskets of flowers ornamented the wraparound porch and blocked the windows. One man carefully trimmed an already perfect rosebush. Another mowed the same strip of grass over and over. Renfields. I'm sure there were more inside, along with an elaborate security system to raise the alert if anyone—or anything—threatened the vampires during their slumber.

Of course, the security might be more for the dwelling than the occupants. They may have temporarily abandoned this house in light of the attack. Also, I wasn't completely sure that Leonora and her vampires actually *slept* here. I know if I had such a vulnerability, I'd have a red herring. I'm sure the vampires were just as, if not more paranoid than I was.

Still I sat and waited in my car, watching for anything out of place, something that would let me know if Russell was around. My phone buzzed, and I looked down at the text from an unfamiliar number, instructing me to go to a nearby gas station. It was then I noticed the tiny globes attached to the poles of street lights and signs, blinking an occasional blue light. Video cameras. Russell wasn't just relying on his necromancy skills to enact his revenge, he was using technology. I frowned, thinking he most likely wouldn't be dissuaded from a plan this elaborate.

The gas station was at the cross section of two major streets, with a convenience store attached. A steady stream of customers came and went, meaning no one paid the slightest bit of attention to my Toyota blocking access to the air pump. The necromancer approached, his eyes straying to the sword hilt protruding from the scabbard that I'd slipped over my shoulder the moment I got out of the car. I didn't see any amulet, but Russell must have some charm that blocked my look-away spell.

"You guys should really start using a stealthier weapon." He gestured at my sword.

I shrugged. "Tradition. I wanted to meet with you because

I've discovered some information about the vampires that murdered your family forty years ago."

His eyes gleamed. "Do you know where they rest during the day?"

It bothered me that Russell knew they weren't in Leonora's house as much as it reassured me that he *didn't* know where they slept.

"No, but the vampire that took your sister was named Jean Marc. He, as well as the Master of the vampires who attacked your family were killed in a coup decades ago."

"How many of them are left alive? By my reckoning there are at least two thousand vampires in the city."

Two thousand? I blinked in astonishment at the number. Leonora's *Balaj* was much larger than I'd ever imagined. That was something I'd need to deal with later. Right now I had to focus on Russell. The guy was like a dog with a bone.

"Russell, the ones who killed your family are dead. The other vampires haven't done anything to you. Let this go."

He recoiled. "They're vampires. They prey on humans. You wouldn't allow a rapist to wander the city just because he hadn't killed anyone lately, would you?"

I winced. Ah, the slippery slope of morality and ethics. "We're food for them. I know you see it as a deviant and evil practice, but for them it's dinner. No different from us picking up a package of boneless chicken breasts from the market."

The necromancer shook his head. "I don't believe I'm hearing this. Would you let one of them babysit your children? Spend the night with your parents?"

Ouch. I remembered the inhuman, predatory look in Dario's eyes the night he'd pinned me to the bed. My parents were well equipped to deal with a hungry vampire, but others? "We can't deliver preemptive justice, Russell. These vampires haven't done anything wrong."

I was well aware than in general society's view, they had done wrong. Their feedings lacked informed consent, and I doubted those four gang members were the only ones killed over the last forty years. Add in all the blood slaves who, somewhat willingly, had gone to their deaths and that was a whole lot of wrong.

"You Templars take this no-judging thing a bit too far. Would you really stand by while these monsters feed on us? Watch while one of them feeds from a young girl and shrug it off with an 'it's their nature' excuse?"

I opened my mouth, only to shut it with a snap. What would I do? Nine hundred years ago it was humans first. Actually it was Christians first, which was only a sliver of what the religion encompassed today. We couldn't go back to that. *I* couldn't go back to that. My faith wasn't strong enough to believe God would turn my sword from the righteous. Too many innocents had died back then because we took our holy mission to an extreme.

But to do nothing was a cop-out. An entire race, a whole *Balaj* wasn't responsible for the actions of a few, even if the current members did have a lot of answer for.

"You're right. I won't stand by and do nothing when I see an injustice. If you continue to target the vampires, you will find me blocking your path."

His eyes shot to my sword, then narrowed.

"Let it go, Russell. Justice has already been served by the very hands of the people you are trying to kill. Let it go."

The necromancer spun around and crossed the street, climbing into an old pickup truck as I watched. He wouldn't give up, which put me in the odd position of helping to defend a group of murderous undead.

Vampires had just become my Pilgrims on the Path—at least for now.

CHAPTER 24

Dad picked up on the second ring. After the usual pleasantries, I got right down to business. "I'm looking for a blessing that will return restless spirits to the grave and keep them there but not harm the vampires. I've come up with a hybrid spell, but it requires individual names and I don't have time to pinpoint every attacking spirit. And it only is a temporary banishment. I need something that puts them to rest until Judgement Day and shields them from being raised again by necromantic means."

I heard him make a hum noise, heard the snip of gardening shears in the background. "Come on down, sweetie. I've got a few books in the study we can look through."

I didn't have time for that either. Although his words sent a wave of nostalgia through me, reinforced by last weekend with my family. I remembered the smell of boxwoods as Mom and I sparred, the aroma of old books and fresh-baked gingersnap cookies as my father and I pored over manuscripts, our heads so close they almost touched. Athena smuggling a dozen kittens into the house, Roman magically locking us all out of the bathroom.

"I can't Dad. These specters are attacking every night, and I need to work fast. People are dying."

I didn't mention it was vampires that were dying. Dad wasn't a bigot, but I doubted he'd have quite the sympathy for dead vampires. It was just as well if he assumed the dead were humans.

There was a pause. The Order had insisted on face-to-face meetings when it came to exchanging information from the date of its inception. The excuse in a modern world was that it was tradition, but I think it kept us from becoming an impersonal hotline, a faceless wiki of the supernatural. And in Dad's case, it ensured his children, his siblings, and his colleagues spent time with him. Human contact—something that seemed to be slipping away in a digital age.

But I didn't have time to drive to Middleburg. "I've got the LARP this weekend, but I'll come down the next. I promise."

The clipping sound faded, and I heard the close of a door. "Aria, shouldn't you concentrate on the cause of these attacking spirits? That might be a better use of your energies. For every specter you put to rest, this necromancer is likely to raise another. You can't spend your life sending restless spirits to the grave every night."

I remembered what Russell said about the nature of spirits, and how difficult they were to direct. I'm sure there were plenty of humans Jean Marc and Aubin had killed over the decades. He'd eventually run out of dead who were willing to kill vampires, but Dad was right. There could be a whole lot more than the sixty names Janice had come up with, especially if Russell decided to raise the dead outside the city limits. I could be at this for a long, long time.

"I tried to stop the Necromancer. I found out who he is

and confronted him. He knows that the vampires who killed his family are dead, but he's set on vengeance against the rest. Nothing I say seems to be able to dissuade him."

"Genesis 25."

"What, like dead Abraham, Genesis 25?"

"No. Verse 19 onward."

"Esau? So you're saying that someone stole the necromancer's birthright?" I hated it when Dad threw scripture at me. I was a literal kinda girl, these homilies went right over my head.

"Esau repudiated his birthright long before Jacob gave him the stew or put on the animal hide to gain their father's blessing. Our destiny cannot be stolen without our desire to give it away."

"Isn't that blaming the victim? Russell was a little boy. These vampires stole his family from him—stole what should have been a wonderful childhood. I really doubt he was complicit in that."

"He wasn't complicit then, but he is now. It's your necromancer that has the restless spirit, it's him that needs to be given eternal peace."

There's no way I was hearing this right. "So you're telling me to *kill* Russell?"

Dad gave a very audible sigh. "No, Aria. His spirit needs to settle. He needs to recognize the blessings he has in this moment and stop giving his precious gifts away."

Oh, good Lord. I should have just driven down there. Or spoken to Mom. At least she wouldn't have counselled me to sit Russell down for a therapy/life coaching session. "Right. Got it. I'll soothe his soul just as soon as I take care of the malignant spirits he's summoning to *kill* the vampires."

I heard something muttered that sounded similar to "just like her mother".

"The permanent method of banishing spirits involves

salting their graves and burning their bones in a ritual such as Rigby or DeSantos. That's the only way you're going to get them to stay put until the Second Coming. For a temporary measure, you can setup a protective area, and use incense plus the chant in Campbell. That way you don't need to call them out by name."

"But Dad," I protested. "The vampires. I've done a few test runs with the Campbell chant and I think it's going to put the vampires in their graves as well as the spirits."

"Then you're back to using the individual names. I'm sorry, Aria. Vampires are undead beings. Very few spells are going to exclude them from the area of effect."

Crap. I'd really hoped there would be something else. It was evident from my father's tone that this was all I was going to get out of him. If I didn't get back to writing these names, I wouldn't be ready come sundown.

Write names. Gather all my materials. Drive to Leonora's and spend another sleepless night hoping I could concentrate enough to pull off this spell. Once again I thought of boxwoods and hyacinths, of the smell of horse sweat and leather in the August afternoon, the sound of cicadas from the porch as we sipped port in the evening. What was I doing here in this hot, ungrateful city?

I was helping Pilgrims on the Path, that's what I was doing.

"Thank you, Dad. I love you." My whole heart was in the goodbye. I missed my family. I missed my old life, the legacy I'd been raised to accept. And still I walked toward a future that was all my own.

"Love you, too. Text me pictures of this LARP thing, okay?"

I smiled, thinking of how Dad would laugh to see me in my plastic armor. "Absolutely."

Obviously there was no time to be digging up graves

tonight, so I concentrated on writing down sixty names while memorizing the chant. That done, I ransacked my apartment to find enough of the specific mixture of resin and herbs that made up what I was now calling ghost-smoke. Shadows lengthened across my floor as I put the finishing touches on the runes acid-etched into the butter knife that had been converted into a weapon. I was ready. And I had just enough time to load all of this into the car and drive north to Leonora's house.

There was a knock on my door and I watched it, expecting it to just swing open when I realized that Dario wouldn't be visiting while the sun still shined above the horizon. Was it one of the LARP people, here to go over armor or battle plans for this weekend? If so, I'd need to get rid of them fast.

I didn't recognize the guy at my door. He was big and burly, like a club bouncer, with tribal tattoos down his arms. In spite of his size and the obvious intimidation factor, he was the one shifting nervously from side to side as he eyed the sword I'd grabbed on my way to the door.

"What are you cooking?" He sniffed.

I stood aside to let him in. "Magic." Actually it was the incense. I'd burned a bit to make sure I had the mixture correct. God love Campbell; he was one of the few authors thorough enough to detail exactly what the incense should smell like when lit, as well as the changes in fragrance when it encountered a spirit.

He hesitated at the "m" word before taking a tentative step over my threshold. "I'm Sarge. Dario sent me to bring you."

It was then that I noticed the puncture marks on his neck. Vampires had a clotting and healing enzyme in their saliva that left their victims with nothing more noticeable than bug bites. Repeated or particularly enthusiastic bites didn't heal as fast, and I'd heard that a quick wipe with a soapy cloth after being bitten would ensure the kind of marks this man had on his neck. They were a deliberate sign of ownership, worn as proudly as any engagement ring. And they usually meant the victim was a blood slave who could count his remaining life in months at best.

"You're Leonora's?" I asked while gathering my equipment together for tonight's activities. Probably not. I remembered Opal said the Mistress liked her blood slaves blond and soft. Sarge was bald and as far from soft as a brick from a feather pillow.

He flushed. "I'd be honored if I was. No, I belong to Geraldo."

It was none of my business, but I had to know. "How often does he take you?"

Sarge smirked. "Not nearly as often as I'd like him to."

Oh my. I could have gone the rest of my life without the visual now running rampant through my head.

"He sips daily, just to keep my mark fresh, but he actually feeds from me once every six to eight weeks."

That surprised me right out of imagining this man naked and sweaty with a vampire. This Geraldo had enough control to hold back his hunger. Six weeks was a long time for a vampire to restrain himself from a beloved blood slave. "How long have you been together?"

This time Sarge's smile was downright sappy. "Six months."

Wow. He looked pretty good for six months. Huh. Whoever Geraldo was, I tipped my hat to him. If he could keep it under control, Sarge was liable to live another few years. *If* he could keep it under control.

"I assume you're here to escort me? I know where Leonora's is, but I appreciate this. I'm still kinda new to the city and I don't want to get lost."

Yeah. It would really suck to arrive late to this particular party. Sarge nodded and eyeing my sword once more, gingerly picked up the bag holding my spell supplies.

"Okay, let's go." I grabbed the rest of my stuff, locked the door behind me and led the way downstairs to my car. I bit my lip when I saw it, hesitating.

"Is this it?" Sarge waved a hand at my Corolla, clearly perplexed as to why we weren't getting in.

"Did you bring your car?" I walked around my vehicle, eyeing the fenders. It wasn't as I'd left it hours ago. Someone had been messing with my car. And given that I'd put a protection spell on it, I had a good idea who the vandal was.

"Yeah, it's down the block. Dario said you'd want to drive yourself."

I did want to drive myself, but not with a magical tracking device on my car. "Got a napkin? A tissue, or something?"

He shook his head. It wasn't hard to find a used one balled up in the weeds beside the building doorway. Trying not to think about what kind of germs and old food were on the paper, I unfolded it and carefully removed the tiny cloth bag from just inside my wheel well. It had been attached with a magnet. Pretty clever, although a few days of driving probably would have dislodged it. Not that Russell needed it to work forever—just long enough for me to lead him to where the vampires rested during the day.

The joke was that I really didn't know. The not funny part was that Russell no longer saw me as impartial, but in league with the enemy. I'd need to tread carefully.

I attached the magical tracker to the VW Bug parked next to me. "Let's take your car, just in case I missed something." If I hadn't thrown together the spell now attached to the little dolphin charm around my neck, I would never have noticed the tracker. Who knows what other items Russell had put on my car? I'd need to check it thoroughly tomorrow, just in case it was rigged to explode or something, but right now I had a *Balaj* to protect.

Sarge was driving one of the big, black SUVs the vampires seemed to have bought in bulk. I was actually glad he was driving, because in this neighborhood he'd be lucky if he only found the side dented in when he returned. Twelve hours tucked away in a little side alley pretty much guaranteed the car would be without wheels and an airbag by morning.

"Dario wants me to take you somewhere to meet someone before we go to Leonora's."

Okay. I wasn't uneasy about climbing into a big SUV with a bouncer-sized guy partially because of all the magical gear I was toting, but also because he'd clearly shown himself to be afraid of said magical gear. I *was* uneasy about him taking me to some unknown place to meet an unknown person. After what had happened with Federico, I was more than a bit wary of these vampires.

Trusty was comforting in my lap, and the charged runes sparked along my skin as I stroked the sheathed blade. Even if there were hundreds of them, I knew I could kill enough vampires to clear a path. Besides, the sun hadn't quite set. I should be okay.

The sun *had* set by the time we pulled up to a battered row house only three blocks from the ruin of the Robertsons' family home. An elderly lady rocked on the porch, the handle of a pistol visible at the edge of her denim skirt.

"Elaine." Sarge nodded at the woman, and she lifted her nose in reply, dark eyes dissecting me as she jerked her head toward the doorway. I gripped Trusty tight, wondering how much of a faux pas it would be for me to remove the sword from its scabbard.

Inside the house was like a time capsule from the sixties.

Rose upholstered chairs were decorated with lace doilies on the arms and headrests. Mauve shag carpeting matched the paisley drapes. Glass candy dishes filled with mints accented the side tables. Sarge led me through the avocado and burnt orange kitchen and down a set of basement stairs to a room with a sofa, a television, and a stereo console. And a woman.

She was sitting on the carpet, drawing in a notebook. Her long hair hung in a snarl of tight black curls.

"Has she fed?" At Sarge's question, a pale woman stepped from the shadows. She had a comb in one hand and what looked to be a bottle of olive oil in the other.

"Yes. First thing upon waking. It's not a good day for her."

The woman on the carpet looked up, her pencil pausing. Dark eyes shined in a golden-brown face whose soft roundness hinted at childhood. She was beautiful in an otherworldly way, a girl caught between youth and womanhood. Even with the tangled hair and sharp fangs, I recognized Shay.

"But, they killed her," I sputtered. "Right in front of her father, they killed her."

The woman looked over to Shay with obvious affection. "Yes, they did. Tore her throat out and left her dead on the cold ground."

Sarge growled. "Shitty way to treat your blood slave. I'm glad I wasn't alive back then."

Wait. I was so confused. "Someone turned her? Did Jean Marc come back later and turn her? Or Aubin, your former Master?"

The woman clenched her teeth, taking a moment before answering me. "No. That scum Jean-Marc left her for dead and Aubin didn't care. That wasn't uncommon for a blood slave back then, but Jean-Marc took particular pleasure in making her death as painful as possible—for the girl as well as for her family."

I walked slowly toward Shay. The girl watched me with intent eyes. Something was wrong with her. "Does she speak?"

"Not more than a few words here and there. She understands quite a lot, but hasn't spoken much since her rebirth. We call her Bella."

Vampires took new names when turned, another way to shed their old lives and embrace the new. Still, it was hard for me to look at this girl as anything but Shay Robertson.

"Who does she feed from?" I couldn't see her trolling the pubs and nightclubs like Dario did. Beautiful as she was, there was something eerily off about the intensity of her stare.

"Donors. She's not gentle, so we assist her and give the donor a little something to help with the pain."

I winced. "Hi Bella." The girl tilted her head as I spoke, her tongue darting out to touch the tip of a fang. It was disturbingly erotic. "What are you drawing?"

She turned the notepad so I could see. Lots of scribbles. Something that looked like a stick figure with a hat.

"Who is that?" I pointed to the stick figure.

She stared at me, her eyes blank.

"Time to do your hair, Bella." The woman walked forward, extending the comb. "Let's make you pretty, then we'll put on some records and dance."

I watched as the woman smoothed the snarled curls, humming under her breath. Bella tilted her head and continued to draw.

"What happened to her? Is this sort of thing common when humans are turned?"

Sarge shook his head. "They figured she was dead about an hour beforehand. The process is supposed to start immediately—drained then given new life with the sire's blood."

I knew so little about it and was surprised that Sarge, a

blood slave, knew. "How do they drink their sire's blood if they are drained?"

He hesitated a moment. "They don't drink it, they bathe in it. It's ceremonial, and I'm not privy to the details, but the sire needs to come close to exsanguination to bring on a rebirth. It takes a lot out of him and leaves him vulnerable, which is why the support and approval of the *Balaj* is needed. A rebirth means there are two vampires that require care or they'll both die."

It was clear from the longing on his face that Sarge hoped he'd be offered the opportunity. But wouldn't that change the nature of his relationship with Geraldo? I assumed vampires had meaningful relationships with each other, but I couldn't imagine they'd have the same all-encompassing passion as what was between a vampire and a blood slave.

"We need to get going." Sarge checked his phone. "It's long enough past sundown that everyone should be awake and fed sufficiently. We're to all meet at Leonora's."

I remembered Dario saying there were donors that came by the house. So it sounded like tonight they'd all had an appetizer, so to speak. It would be enough to hold the vampires off until they could find a fresh victim to drink deeply from—and do other things.

All these revelations made me wonder if feeding always involved sex, or if there was some personal preference in the combination of the two activities. Dario had indicated that sex usually wasn't a stand-alone practice, but surely feeding didn't *always* include intimacy. Well, intimacy beyond biting someone's neck and drinking from their circulatory system.

I wasn't sure that this was something I felt comfortable asking Sarge about. He'd made clear his feelings for Geraldo, and the fact that he didn't give any significant amount of blood more than once every six weeks. His vampire obviously was getting his needs met elsewhere in between those times, and I didn't want to rub it in Sarge's face if those encounters included sex. I could ask Dario later, but the thought of discussing sexual practices with him made my breath quicken. Besides, I wasn't sure I'd be discussing anything with him after last night.

I followed the man back out of the house to the SUV and climbed in, placing my sword on my lap. Sarge had been very forthcoming to me, a complete stranger. It was obvious he'd been given permission to share these things with me, which seemed unusual for such a secretive race of beings.

"Why are you telling me all this? Why did you take me to see Shay, I mean Bella?" I turned to watch the blood slave as he pulled the car away from the curb.

"Dario said you were to know. He said to answer every question of yours that I could and not hold anything back." Sarge shot a quick glance at me as he stopped for a light. He had that smirk on his face once again. "Think you've got an admirer, Templar."

Admirer? Not anymore. Although maybe Dario was as eager to make things right between us as I was? Maybe he wanted to give me a reason to trust him as much as I wanted to regain his trust in me. Because he had trusted me—enough to sleep in my bathroom, enough to tell me, a Templar, so much of his history.

I thought about Shay. Bella, now. She seemed to have a peaceful life, surrounded by those who protected her. The vampire woman combing her hair clearly loved her. I wondered if it would make any difference to Russell to know his eldest sister was alive. Probably not. It would probably do more harm to the situation if he knew the vampires had turned Shay into one of them. Which made me wonder.

"Who turned her?"

"Dario."

I blinked in surprise. "Dario?"

"Yes, Dario. Geraldo told me that it started the war that nearly destroyed our *Balaj*. Jean Marc was furious. Aubin threw Dario out of the family, cast him into the unclaimed suburbs to roam alone. For nearly a decade Dario was an exile."

An exile. Him and a newly turned, clearly disabled, vampire. How had he survived? Clearly others in the *Balaj* had helped him against the Master's orders.

And how had Leonora wound up on top in all of this? Dario's exile was the spark that fanned an already fractious *Balaj* into a flame of rebellion, and somehow in the end Leonora wound up Mistress?

"Do you know why Leonora became Mistress? I mean, I know she's older, but I would have thought Dario would have taken over after Aubin was killed."

Sarge shrugged. "Geraldo said that Dario didn't want the job. Leonora did. She's a good leader, but many vampires turn to Dario for guidance before her. I'm no expert, but I think they're one disagreement away from another rebellion."

Vampires didn't co-rule, and Dario's loyal followers had to threaten Leonora's sense of security in her leadership status. One disagreement away from a war. I only hoped this issue with Russell wouldn't be the straw that broke this camel's back.

CHAPTER 25

There was a tenseness at Leonora's house. Both humans and vampires came and went with deceptive casualness, but their eyes darted at each shadow. Every vampire showed a hint of fangs, betraying their readiness to defend. Sarge led me into what I was now calling the throne room where Leonora waited—alone and pacing.

"Can we cut the formality, just for tonight? I've got a lot to do." Russell had probably begun summoning right at sundown, which meant I had about a half hour to get all my stuff set up and ready to go.

"Watch your tone," she snarled, reminding me an awful lot of Dario when he'd snapped at me at Sesarios last week. Unlike that incident, I didn't curse the vampire Mistress and storm out. Instead I took a calming breath and waited, hoping that she'd hurry up and say her piece so I could get to work.

"You have tonight." She pointed a red-nailed finger at me. "If you can't resolve this by dawn, we will hunt down this magic user and kill him. We have his name. We know who he is. One night, and that's it."

I nodded, well aware that this wouldn't end well for Russell if I failed. The vampires would find him. They had enough manpower for day and night searches, and the necromancer had to sleep sometime.

The woman stalked toward me, her leather bustier creaking as she moved. "And if you fail, you're mine. And I mean mine. I don't care if you're a Templar. I don't care if Dario has put a claim on you. If there's so much as a scratch on any of my family tonight, I'm going to chain you in the basement and make you breakfast."

Opal had called Dario "boss". He'd beat the snot out of Federico for what he'd done to me. He'd been the vampire to step up to the plate and turn Shay, to face exile rather than see a young girl die. He was the one with a Templar in his pocket, the one who fought last night while Leonora had run to safety. I remembered what Sarge had said, that they were one disagreement away from rebellion.

This wasn't about me. And it really wasn't about Russell either.

"Don't you forget that *I* am the Mistress here." She towered over me, her boobs practically in my face. "You are to do as I say, or you'll find yourself back in that basement cell before you can so much as light a candle."

I shivered, then remembered something Dario had said to me. "I don't give a shit about your internal politics. The deal was that I had one night to resolve this peacefully. You presented Dario as someone with the authority to speak on your behalf, and thus my deal with him is binding on the entire *Balaj*. You got a problem with that, take it up with him."

Leonora sucked in a breath, but I continued. "You might not personally care about me being a Templar, but know that if you lock me in a cell and feed from me, and you'll find yourself with a war on your hands. This necromancer thing may have divided your *Balaj* and put your fitness to rule in question, but imagine how you'll fare once everyone knows that you brought down the wrath of an entire family of Templars on their heads."

Her eyes flickered to my sword, then she drew herself up to her full height. "Templars haven't done more than study and guard the Temple in over a hundred years. They won't risk themselves to find a foolish girl, one who has spurned her birthright and turned away from the Oath of Knighthood."

True, but there was a loyalty besides that toward the Order. "A father will always come for his daughter. That's what got you all into this mess to begin with. Jean Marc took someone's daughter, tried to intimidate an entire family, and thought that he could do anything he wanted without reper-cussion."

"And they all died. We slaughtered that whole family of humans," she interrupted.

We. I got the feeling that wasn't the royal we she was using. Leonora had been there, had participated. She'd prob-ably watched carefully as the *Balaj* split in two, choosing the side that would work to her best advantage.

"And now they all haunt you and kill you. Their remaining son won't rest until he sees every last vampire dead. See how this snowballs? Continue to threaten me and play the heavy; we'll see how you fare against a more powerful family than the Robertsons. Templar Knights have stared into the eyes of Satan himself; we won't tremble before a *Balaj* of vampires."

"Enough." Leonora and I both froze at the one word from Dario. He tossed a bag at me and I caught it from reflex. "Eat. You're grumpy. And you," he pointed at Leonora, "you have no reason to threaten her. Back off before you alienate the only Templar who would even think of coming to our aid."

I wasn't sure how this was going to go down tonight with such an obvious fracture in the vampire management. What happened to Dario not wanting to lead? He was totally confrontational with his Mistress tonight and in front of a human witness, too. I looked inside the bag. Smoked ribs and cornbread. After my betrayal of his family, the guy bought me dinner. As if my feelings for Dario weren't conflicted enough.

"We should just kill this magic user," Leonora snarled. I wasn't sure whether she meant me or Russell at this point. "We don't have time for this nonsense. Every night we're attacked we lose credibility among our human partners and present a weak front to those who lurk outside our territory waiting for a chance to take over."

"I'm all for killing the magic user, but what happens when his aunt or cousin avenges *his* death? Or the local paper investigates? Or the police decide to stop turning a blind eye to our activities? Already your neighbors are noticing the amount of traffic in and out of your house. A drug task force stakeout is going to really put a cramp in your lifestyle, Leonora."

I shoved a piece of cornbread in my mouth and watched the two argue, amazed that I was being allowed to witness the disagreement. I'd learned so much about vampires in the last week. Dad would be impressed. I should write a book. I'll bet it would become the equivalent of a Templar bestseller.

There was a loud, vocal battle of wills between the two vampires, then Leonora broke eye contact with Dario, waving a dismissive hand at him as she turned to me with a huff. "So what's your plan, Templar?"

I swallowed the cornbread. "If you're done with me then I need to hustle and get set up for when the specters come. Once they arrive, I'll need your vampires to hold them off while I light candles and incense then chant them back into the grave." It would take me a bit of time to run around the house, lighting candles and incense to contain the spirits, and even more time for me to recite the banishment spell on sixty names. Well, hopefully not all sixty. I was optimistic that I'd manage to banish all of them within the first twenty or so. Of course, that would all depend on how many Russell summoned. Last night there had been ten. After our confrontation today, I had a feeling he might up that as much as possible. Still, the prospect of me in a magical battle against a house full of violent spirits kinda turned me on. I'd learned so much in the last seven days. This experience would help me in the future, the next time I went head to head with a necromancer.

Wait. I wasn't a Knight, I was a part-time barista at a coffee shop. How was it that I felt it my duty to fight supernatural baddies in Baltimore? The idea had an odd appeal, though. I had a sudden urge to get a cape.

"And that will rid us of them permanently? This spell that you and Opal worked on last night should end these attacks?"

I squirmed at Leonora's question. "No. Once I find out which spirits he's summoning, I can salt their graves and lay them to rest for all eternity. But even with that, the best way for me to stop the attacks is by delivering a whole lot of whoop-ass on the necromancer. If he fails miserably tonight, then I'll be in a better position tomorrow when I try to convince him to give this up."

The vampire Mistress snorted, shaking her head in disbelief. "Whatever. Tomorrow he dies."

"More than a necromancer is going to die if I don't get going on this spell."

They both ignored me, once again doing the vampire version of a Mexican standoff.

"So you banish the attacking spirits, salt a bunch of

graves," Leonora commented, her eyes on Dario the whole time. "What if this necromancer is the stubborn type? What if he just summons more spirits the next evening? There are thousands of dead in the city of Baltimore. That's a whole lot of grave salting."

It was. And she was totally right. This all hinged on me delivering a giant throwdown to Russell. Enough so that he gave this all up and decided to settle his restless Esau spirit and take up his birthright once again.

Although none of this was going to happen if these two didn't stop their pissing contest and let me get to work.

"Have a little faith in her, Leonora." Dario lifted an eyebrow. I noticed his unusual reference to faith, as well as his addressing the Mistress so informally.

"Can I get started? Guys, I don't want to break up this power struggle happening right before my eyes, but killer ghosts could arrive at any moment and I'm not ready for them."

Dario folded his arms across his chest, still facing Leonora. "Aria has said that revenge is a very personal thing for this necromancer. The point of these attacks are that his own family's ghosts are the ones here each night enacting revenge for their deaths. Lay them to rest, and I think it will be easier to convince him to cease his attacks."

Dario was right, although who was to say random spirits that Russell raised would be motivated toward killing, or killing these vampires. I remembered my conversation with Russell and thought how funny it would be for him to raise a spirit, only to have them go haunt a cheating lover or cry over a spouse's grave each night.

And then there was the focus item. Getting a focus item for summoning an unknown spirit would require a lot of work. Yes, if I hit Russell hard tonight, I would be in a prime negotiating position tomorrow.

Leonora snorted, clearly not pleased with Dario's explanation. "Tonight, Templar. You have tonight to prove your worth. Then we kill him."

I opened my mouth to respond and heard a huge crash. And a scream. Dario snatched the bag of ribs from me. "Hurry."

CHAPTER 26

I knew this was going to happen, and I suspected that Leonora had been intentionally stalling me to set me up for failure.

It wasn't even an hour past sunset and they were starting. What happened to midnight? I knew Russell would probably start right up at sundown, but spirits took a while to get going. Midnight was the usual hour of action for them. These specters didn't waste time, and I couldn't either. I dumped my backpack on the floor, frantically yanking candles and Ziploc baggies of incense out. I shoved a lighter in my pocket, and slung Trusty over my shoulder. The sword was still in its scabbard since I didn't have enough hands to light incense and candles, plus carry a sword. As an afterthought, I stuck the butter knife through a belt-loop. It hadn't been effective last night, and I hadn't had time to switch the spell on it. It might not help against the specters, but if Leonora got any ideas, or Federico tried to grab me again, I'd be prepared.

"Try to herd them toward the center of the house," I told

Dario and Leonora before running out of the room, my arms full.

I wished I'd paid more attention to the layout of the house while Federico was marching me to the basement the other day. I made a few wrong turns before hitting the kitchen pantry in the far back of the house. The specters seemed to always start at the front of the house, so I figured I'd set up where there was no fighting first, then deal with trying to light candles and incense in the middle of a battle last.

There wasn't much time for planning, but I did have enough concerns about open flame in a house full of vampires that I stuck the candle in a dusty stock pot before lighting it. An old saucer served to hold the incense. I grabbed a few more cups and plates, all probably unused for a decade, before dashing out. I had thirty minutes before the incense burned out and four more sets to light. With sixty names I'd be cutting it close, and that's if I didn't have any issues getting the other candles lit.

The dining room was to the west, and the throne room to the east. I headed to the front door and found my way blocked. I'd need to get through the scene of a battle to light the north candle, and I had less than thirty minutes to do it in.

"Move. Out of my way!"

Probably not the best way to address a group of vampires, but I was in a hurry. They paid no attention to me, but one shout from Dario had them all luring the spirits away from the door.

I had no idea where Leonora was. Probably hiding somewhere. It irritated me more than usual, feminist that I was. I *wanted* her to be a strong kick-ass leader. I wanted her to be someone I could support fully. But the thought that she'd stood by while Jean-Marc had killed Shay and then her family, that she'd hedged her bets while Dario took a stand…it bothered me. Dario was willing to put his life on the line for what was right. He'd do the dirty work when it came to what the *Balaj* and his blood-siblings needed to survive. As much as I wanted to see a female break through the vampire glass ceiling, Leonora wasn't it. She was self-centered, weak. I was pissed at her for that, and I was equally pissed at Dario for not taking the reins of power thirty years ago instead of letting her rise to the top.

Although now was not the time to think about politics within the Baltimore *Balaj*.

My hands shook as I lit the candle and incense. Twenty minutes. Maybe less. I didn't have a second to spare checking my phone, and honestly I was dreading what it might tell me. I hadn't counted on this when I was devising the timing for the spell, and had come to the horrible realization that I might fail. The chanting didn't have instantaneous results, and if any of the incense in the four quarters ran out before I'd begun the banishment ritual, the specters would escape my reach.

Done. I ran through the icy cold in the foyer, and found my way blocked by a wall of vampires in combat.

"Move!"

My shout didn't do squat. I wasn't even sure they heard it with all the chaos going on. I had to get by and fast. Time was running out while I stood here, waiting for a space to squeeze through. I couldn't use my tunnel of light blessing without killing the vampires I was trying to defend, so I did the only other thing I could. I drew my sword.

I elbowed the nearest vampire in the ribs, putting all my weight into it before jumping back. That did nothing. It was time for drastic measures. Using a half-sword grip, I used Trusty as a wedge to squeeze between two fighting vampires.

That worked. I'd never seen vampires move so fast.

Trusty flared with a white light, and the pair yelped, jumping to the side. Others did the same and I instantly found myself in a room with vampires pressed frantically against the walls as they ran for the exits, leaving me to face six non-corporeal figures.

They advanced and I swung, thrilled to see my blade do what hands and fangs could not. The spirits howled in pain and rage, trying to edge around me just out of range to my back. I spun, holding them at bay and giving the vampires a chance to exit the room. When I was sure the last was out, I dropped to my knee, placing my sword tip-down with my forehead resting on the blade. I waited.

And I felt them, digging into me, pulling at my soul. Blood beaded on my pores, and I forced myself to concentrate. Just one second more.

Jesu, luys im chanaparhy.

The tunnel blasted from me to the doorway, instantly frying every spirit. I took a breath to steady myself, well aware that time was ticking away. Then I dismissed the tunnel of light and ran.

I'd killed six specters with one blessing, but Russell had gone all out and summoned at least two dozen for tonight. The hallway was a battleground, but I didn't have the time to do my trick twice. Fighting my way past the bloody vampires that crawled with broken limbs in the hallway, I ran up the stairs. Ten minutes? Less? Crap, I didn't have enough time! Not wanting to waste a moment longer to find the best spot, I dropped my supplies down on the carpet at the top of the stairs and melted the bottom of the candle, jamming it onto the carpet. Pulling my sword I knelt once more.

"Souls without form, restless spirits, I command you to return to the grave and await the trumpet call of the Lord's messenger. Sleep until Judgement Day, then rise to await your measure at the gates."

I repeated the chant over and over, sprinkling the incense on the candle flame where it sparked and spiraled upward in a ring of white smoke. I called and ordered the spirits to rest in peace as I burned the slip of paper with the name of the dead. My breath became visible, sudden chill raising the exposed flesh of my arms. They were searching for me, trying to climb the stairs as the vampires struggled to hold them at bay.

"Await the trumpet. Await the call of the Lord's messenger. Sleep. Sleep."

One by one I felt the specters blur and fade, their spirits reluctantly making the journey between this world and the next. I also felt the vampires nearby, their presence sparking like static along my skin. Funny how I'd gotten used to it with Dario, but not with the others. The spirits that remained quickly seemed to realize what was going on, and the noise of battle approached. The incense for the perimeter was now gone, and all that was keeping me going was the steady chant, the dying incense before me, and the sulfur smell of paper on the fire.

Eight down. I'd gone through thirty names, and there still had to be at least ten spirits working their way up the staircase toward me. I chanted faster, worrying that Janice's list wasn't all inclusive, and that even after I'd recited and burned the last name, there still might be spirits to battle. Worse was the blood that decorated the hallway. Dario, or perhaps Leonora, had called out all the stops on this one, and the house was full of vampires. Some of them were screaming in pain, injured at the bottom of the stairs. Others were motionless, their eyes blank in faces coated in blood.

I remembered Leonora's threat, but it wasn't nearly as horrifying as looking at those dead vampires and knowing I'd failed them.

There was something else raising the hair along the back

of my neck. It wasn't just the chill of the specters and the electric feel of the vampires I was sensing. Something else was there, growing in strength, something that smelled like a dead possum in the summer's heat and felt like sticky fur as it pressed on my mind. My concentration slipped, and I redoubled my efforts, straining to focus against the foul presence as I recited names, commanding them to the grave as I burned the slips of paper.

One by one, the spirits flickered in and out of this plane. I leaned heavily on my sword, well aware that my incense only had a few minutes left tops. I pushed, holding nothing back. The dead possum smell filled my nose and mouth, and suddenly there was nothing. The air around me echoed with its silence and I toppled forward with the vacuum of sensation, my sword clattering against the ground.

"You okay?"

I looked up to see Dario at the top of the stairway, five other vampires crowding behind him to get a look. "Yeah. They're gone, and shouldn't be back. I'll get to salting graves first thing in the morning."

He nodded, cool and distant toward me. I struggled to my feet, legs shaking, and picked up my sword.

"Are all your people okay?" I thought about the blood in the hallway, the dead I'd seen as I'd chanted my spell, about the arterial red sprayed against the walls.

"We lost six, and there are a lot of injured that aren't healing as quickly as they should. It's too soon to know if they'll make it."

Damn. I'd done my best and still felt like I'd failed. If the mass banishment didn't convince Russell to stop this attack, I really *would* have no choice but stand by and let the vampires defend themselves. Six. Plus those that had died last night and Saturday night. Plus all the injured who would need a massive level of blood consumption to heal. The loss of vampire life was devastating, but the risk of discovery once they had to increase their feeding was also worrisome.

"Do you need anything?" Dario half turned, as if he wasn't sure whether to come closer or leave. "I need to go help with the injured downstairs, but if there's anything…"

A thank-you would have been nice. Although I felt like a total selfish jerk for even allowing that thought to cross my mind after he'd just witnessed the death of his brothers and sisters. "That bag of ribs would be great about now." I tried to laugh. "And a beer if you all have any. I just need a few moments to re-group, and then I'll be out of your hair."

He nodded, his expression remote. "I'll send someone up with them."

And then I was alone at the top of the stairs with my sword, a gutted candle, and a little pile of ash. It seemed so anticlimactic. There was still work to do. I needed to confront Russell again and try to dissuade him from continuing with his revenge. I needed to salt the graves. Just some loose ends to tidy up. Why, then, did I feel like I was missing something?

I jerked my head around at the sound of scuffing feet right next to me. A vampire stood there holding the bag of ribs in one hand and a bottle of beer in another. He'd managed to climb the stair and come right up to me without my even hearing him. On the street, I might have picked up his presence, but here where a house full of vampires constantly plucked at my senses, his approach hadn't been noted.

"You need to leave the house," he announced.

Were they throwing me out? What the heck? I'd come here, risked myself, used my own personal supply of incense materials and candles, and they gave me a bag of ribs and tossed me out on my ass?

I gripped my sword tight. The vampire's eyes darted to it

and he took a step back. "I'm not threatening you or anything. It's just that Leonora doesn't wish you any good, and injured vampires need to feed to heal. You're not safe right now."

That was the explanation I'd been looking for. So much better than *you must leave this house*. "Sarge drove me here. Is there someone available to drive me home? Is there somewhere safe I can wait for a taxi?"

Taxi. Crap, I couldn't take a taxi. I had no way to pay for one. Hopefully Sarge was still around, or another vampire's...companion. I didn't want to ask for a 'blood slave' to give me a lift. I was coming to hate the term and didn't want to use it.

The vampire frowned. "We evacuated the humans when the attack began and can't spare someone to drive you right now."

Which left me walking, or locked in the basement room. I think I'd rather walk.

"I'll stay with her, Marcus. You go back downstairs and help."

Dario. Relief flooded me. I hadn't realized how tense I was. A house full of injured and hungry vampires and the prospect of a midnight walk through the city carrying a sword weren't all that had me on edge. I was worried about what would happen between Dario and Leonora. Vampires had been injured and killed tonight, and the spirits were only temporarily banished until I managed to salt the graves. It was a night of success and failure—mostly failure. I'm sure the death toll would have been far worse had I not helped, but perhaps if I'd let the vampires find and kill Russell, none of them would have died at all. One life in exchange for many. I wasn't convinced I'd done the right thing. As much as I didn't want Russell executed, was his life worth any more than the six who had died this evening?

Marcus handed me the ribs and silently vanished down the stairs, leaving me holding a bag and a sword, and staring at Dario. "Can I borrow your SUV? I'll get out of here. I know you've got injured to take care of."

He shook his head. "I'd prefer you stay here. This necromancer knows who you are, right? Sarge said there was a magical tracking device on your car tonight. This guy has to know you were involved tonight, and he's going to be pissed. I don't want you home alone, and I can't spare anyone go with you right now. You'll need to stay."

He still cared. He didn't want me home alone. I clung to those words.

"Here? You want me to stay at the top of the staircase?" It wasn't the windowless cell in the basement that Leonora had threatened me with, but I still felt uncomfortable being somewhere with no secondary exit beyond a long drop from a second story window.

Dario shrugged. "Yes, here. Or the back garden, if you prefer. We've moved the injured out of the hallway. If we're quick, your presence shouldn't upset them."

"They need blood? Who is supplying them with blood?"

Of course they needed blood. The real question was how were they going to get it if they were injured and dangerous? I thought about Shay. Perhaps there were some donors who would accept some pain and violence for an appropriate recompense.

"I won't lie to you, Aria. We have humans who are willing to help for drugs and money. There is considerable risk to them in donating blood to vampires so severely injured."

I caught my breath. This was their nature. Dario's *Balaj* seemed to be far more careful and concerned about human lives than other vampire families I'd read about. Templars should never judge. There was no evil here, just the circle of life. I shouldn't judge. But I couldn't help it.

Dario reached out and took my arm. "We do everything we can to ensure our donors survive, but family comes first. I'm sorry, but it's true."

Would I sacrifice a chicken to save my sister? A cow? One of the puppies in the barn? I understood the moral dilemma, but wasn't sure I could ever make that call. When did one life become more important than another?

"I promise you, we will restrain the injured. We will do everything within our ability to ensure the human isn't killed. We don't want to lose any of our regular blood donors. They're who we can call upon in emergencies when hunting for a meal isn't possible."

I knew all this. My mind accepted it, but my heart thought of the injured desperately biting and drinking from a human too high to know the danger they were in. My heart was conflicted.

So I transferred the bag of ribs to my other hand and gripped my sword tight. "I think I'll wait in the back garden."

I practically had to run to keep up with Dario as we dashed down the stairs and out the back door. The yard wasn't large compared to my family estate in Middleburg, but the landscaping made it seem a little paradise. Stone pathways meandered through wildflower gardens. Tall trees shaded cushioned benches. Hedges blocked the view of neighboring houses and provided a maze of private corners and secluded spots. We wandered into their dark depths and sat in an alcove where I dug into the ribs like a woman starved.

"Better?" It was dark, but I could see Dario's shape beside me. "Sure you don't want to eat the bones too?"

Was he teasing? Humor, after all we'd been through? Maybe there was hope for our friendship after all.

"I was saving the bones for you." I laughed the joke off,

too embarrassed to admit that this was the first decent food I'd had in days.

It reminded me of something, though. "Have you eaten?"

He turned his head from me. "We're rationing donors to ensure they're available for the injured."

Which didn't answer my question, at least not directly. He'd have no time to go out and hunt either, not with the entire *Balaj* on high alert for any follow-up attack. "When will you be able to feed again? I mean *really* feed?"

"Depends on if this is over or not. Is it over?"

I winced. "I don't know. Those spirits won't be back tonight. I'm not sure if the necromancer will have enough power to summon more until tomorrow. I'm hoping I can have a sit down with him come morning and show him this is a war he can't win."

Dario sighed. "I'm sorry, Aria. I can't hold back any longer. Leonora has put out a kill order on this necromancer, and I agree with her."

I couldn't argue with him. Honestly, I didn't even have faith in myself to bring an end to this. I couldn't fault Dario for the same.

"You didn't answer my question, though. When will you be able to feed again?"

"Until we kill the necromancer, we're on lock-down. We'll probably let the younger ones out tomorrow night in rotation, but the older vampires will need to wait a few more days." He shrugged. "I've gone weeks before. I'll be okay."

I remembered the dragon room in Middleburg and shivered. "The longer you go, the weaker you'll be?" I waited for his nod. "So how can you defend your family if you aren't full strength and there's an attack?"

"You'd be surprised the resources that are left to draw upon when you're fighting for your family's, or your own, life."

Still…I sat and listed to the music of the night as I thought. "I can be your donor. Just for tonight, you know, and that's it."

He laughed, and I winced at the bitter edge to the sound. "No. Because it wouldn't just be tonight, and you could never be just a one-time blood donor to me. That's a very slippery slope, Aria. Make sure you want to ride it all the way, or step away from the edge."

I was truly a coward, because I did step away from the edge, desperately trying to find another topic of conversation.

"Thank you for letting Sarge take me to see Bella."

"I wanted you to know that we take care of our own, and that there are vampires in our *Balaj* with a sense of honor." He glanced over toward me as if he wanted to say something else, but then turned away once more.

I *was* beginning to trust him, was beginning to hope that maybe the impossible could become possible. But in spite of my optimism, we both had prior loyalties. "I know you're not a bunch of blood-thirsty killers, Dario. I know that, but I still don't agree with your casual attitude toward the death of humans. I want to trust you, and I want you to trust me, but there will be times when we can't be honest with each other, when we'll need to keep secrets."

His back still faced me, and it was a few moments before he spoke. "Of course, but I hope that will be the exception and that we can manage to overcome centuries of distrust and violence. I had hoped that maybe if a Templar finally understood us, this tentative truce between our people could endure."

Endure what? The cynic in me had always assumed the truce had been because we Templars wanted to stop hunting down vampires and focus more on research and the artifacts in the Temple. And polo, and gin, and perfecting their golf swings. No Templars wanted to end the truce. Did the vampires not realize that?

But that was something I didn't have time to contemplate right now, not with a war going on right in my own city. They'd kill Russell, and I wasn't sure tonight's defeat would stop him. What would?

I stared at Dario's back, trying to will him to face me. "Do you think it would help if the necromancer knew Shay lived on, even though she is undead and…disabled?" Crap, I wasn't sure how to refer to her condition. "I don't know if it will do any good or just make the situation worse."

He slowly shook his head. "I don't know either. You've met him. You would have a better opinion on that than I would."

"Do you think they would be allowed to meet? Shay and her only surviving brother?"

"No." The word was a sharp, quick utterance. "Bella is barely verbal and I don't know how much she remembers of her human life. Also, there is the fact that she can be quite violent when hungry or upset. If he attacked her, if he even tried to hug her, I couldn't guarantee she wouldn't kill him before we could intervene."

And Russell wouldn't like to see his sister restrained for his protection. Heck, he probably wouldn't even want to see his sister as a vampire. He might consider her already dead and lost to him, just another monster to kill.

"You're right. It's probably best if he doesn't know, if he still believes her to be dead." I wasn't sure if I was right or not, but I didn't want to be the one to upset Shay's calm and peaceful life. Or hurt Russell, who had been hurt so much already.

"I'm just glad we can provide for a vampire like Bella. A hundred years ago, we would have been forced to put her down. Of course, a hundred years ago no one would have ever attempted to raise her."

I remembered what Sarge had told me, how Shay had been dead for so long and how Dario had been the one to sneak back and risk himself to try to right a horrible wrong. I felt a surge of admiration, and affection, for the vampire.

Dario and Leonora. What was up with the strange game of chess going on in this *Balaj*'s leadership? That was the question I really wanted to ask, but I didn't want to start this newfound trust, this tentative thing between us with a question he couldn't answer. So I asked the other question on my mind instead.

"Why did you go back to Shay and turn her? After she'd been dead for so long, why condemn yourself to exile by trying?"

He shifted his weight and turned enough that I could see his profile in the dim light. "So many had died, and I remembered...I remembered a time when friends, family, people I cared about were used and tossed aside like garbage. I remembered the fear, the anger, the sense of helplessness. We were trapped back when I was a human, owned by another and not given even the same consideration as cattle or dogs. I couldn't do the same thing to these humans as had been done to me. I couldn't stand by and let my family treat them this way."

Dario looked out at the little pathway lights that led to a quiet koi pond. "She'd been dead for nearly an hour but I had to try. I didn't expect her to awaken, but I had to try."

But she had awakened, and he couldn't euthanize her once he realized she'd never be fully functional. Suddenly it made sense, our earlier conversation about not abandoning family, about working around their special needs and making every attempt to keep them in the fold.

And something inside me ached as I realized how I'd

misjudged Dario. I'd taken everything I'd learned in our Templar archives about vampires to be gospel. If he was different, if his *Balaj* was different, then there was a good chance others were, too. Yes, their blood slaves died. Yes, they killed with the ruthlessness of a mafia when crossed. But there was an odd honor about them.

"Sarge says he's been Geraldo's blood slave for six months."

I didn't know where that came from. Okay, I did. It had been on my mind from the moment Sarge had mentioned it.

"Yes, but Geraldo is struggling. It doesn't help that Sarge constantly tempts him to up the frequency of their significant encounters. He'll need to break things off soon or risk killing his lover."

My eyes focused on the pond, too, the lights blurring a bit as the breeze stirred the surface. Six months. They might have one more "encounter" left to them, then Sarge would face heartbreak and withdrawal. And from the look on Dario's face as he'd spoken, so would Geraldo.

"Dario?" It was Marcus, and again I was startled that I hadn't even noticed him approaching. "Bridget…there's something wrong with her and Leonora needs you."

Dario looked my way and I patted my sword. "I'll be fine. Go."

They vanished in a blur of speed and I sat alone in the dimly lit garden, feeling anything but fine. Behind me was a house full of injured vampires—vampires who needed blood. And here I sat, safe in a backyard. I had clean, healthy blood, and I was hiding while my Pilgrims on the Path suffered.

My actions caused this. They died because I'd refused to give Russell up. Screw it. If they hurt me…well, I'd been stabbed, burned, and sliced. I'd had more concussions than a football player, been kicked by horses, as well as fallen down a few flights of stairs. Things happened when you're a knight in training, and those things were probably a whole lot more painful than a desperate vampire savaging my wrist with his or her fangs. It would hurt. I'd probably have some minor withdrawal over the next few weeks. I'd survive, Dario would make sure of it. And if I could save one vampire, it would all be worth it.

I stood, putting the sword back into its scabbard and slinging it over my shoulder as I strode toward the house. Inside, there was an eerie silence. Dario said they'd moved the injured from the foyer, but to where? Where would be a safe place to put a hurt vampire in case of another attack?

CHAPTER 27

I didn't have to guess for long. A piercing scream rent the air, followed by the sound of something thumping on the floor. I ran past the stairs and down a narrow hallway into what appeared to be a study or a library.

It was like a scene from a disaster movie, or one of those emergency room dramas. Blood was everywhere, thick and dark. Dismembered bodies lay on the floor and I wasn't sure if they were alive or dead, vampire or human. The row of disheveled people with bandaged arms and heavily dilated pupils were definitely human—the blood donors.

"Get them out," Leonora shouted. Her black leather didn't show the smears of blood that stained her pale skin. She and the others were holding someone down with difficulty. I saw thrashing feet, heard another scream.

Two vampires broke from the crowd and grabbed the blood donors by their elbows, pushing past me in their rush to get them out of the building. For a brief second I wondered what the neighbors must be thinking about all of this. Junkies coming and going late at night, screams and crashing noises. Why the police weren't here, I didn't know.

One of the bodies on the floor suddenly began convulsing. I jumped aside to avoid his kicking feet. What should I do? There was no way I had the strength to hold him down. Vampires were strong and it was taking at least five of them to hold the other one.

"Guys? Guys, there's another one here that needs help."

Dario jerked his head around at my voice. "What are you doing here? Get out!"

"I'm helping." I illustrated the limited scope of my helpfulness by moving a small table and a lamp away from the convulsing vampire. He was already hurt. The best I could do was move items out of reach so he wouldn't be injured further.

Dario and another vampire left Bridget to hold the man on the floor. He jumped and kicked, making a series of moans and short screams as the other two vampires spoke to him soothingly.

I felt like a complete idiot, useless and in the way. "What does he need? Blood? He can have my blood."

"It's not that." Dario adjusted his grip on the man's shoulders, leaning his weight into him. Red began to leak from the wounds that had been closed seconds ago. "I don't know what's wrong with him. I've never seen this before."

I took a few steps backward, unwilling to go hide in the garden while they were all in crisis mode. What could I do beyond watch like some morbid voyeur?

And then I felt it. Smelled it. Sticky fur and long dead possum. I yanked the sword from its scabbard and whirled about, searching. Necromancy. But where were the specters? Had Russell summoned others? Was this his plan B? If so, I'd completely misread the man.

"Put that damned thing away," Leonora shouted.

I ignored her. "Uh, Dario? I think—"

"Bella was like this," he interrupted. "That night I left you and had to rush back. I've never seen that happen to a vampire before."

I frowned, thinking. Bella seemed okay now, but she hadn't been injured before having the seizure. I could only hope these guys could ride this out because there was a necromantic spell or summoning coming our way.

Then it hit me. Bella. Shay. That was the night Dario had ditched me on the curb and I'd needed to walk home, the night the Robertson family had been summoned from their graves. The first night Russell had performed his magic on his family.

And Shay hadn't risen, hadn't come to him, not because she was buried far away but because she wasn't dead. Well, sort of not dead.

I lowered my sword and gaped at the vampire convulsing on the floor, new wounds opening beside the old and adding their dark blood to the soaked carpet. Summoning the spirit of a living human would do nothing. Outside of demonic action, our spirits remained solidly in our bodies until we died. But vampires weren't truly alive, and thus their spirits were in a sort of transition zone between this life and the next.

The seizures suddenly made sense. Russell was summoning the souls out of the vampires. Shay had survived it, but these vampires were weak from their injuries. Plus I was sure the necromancer was putting considerably more force into this spell than one meant to awaken a beloved sibling.

They were going to die—this vampire and probably the others, too. And I still had no idea what to do to help them. Think. Think. I had nothing handy to anchor vampire souls in their bodies, no research to fall back on. I had only one idea, and it wasn't going to be pleasant for anyone in this room.

I placed the sword tip-down on the floor and grasped it low. Touching my heart, I went down on one knee and made the sign of the cross with my other hand.

"Jesu, luys im chanaparhy."

A tunnel of light shot from me across the room, creating a wall in front of the injured vampires. I spun around and did another. And another until there was a ring of light surrounding them all. It wouldn't last, but it didn't need to. It only needed to be enough to disrupt the summoning.

It seemed to be working although my blessing was giving them all a heart attack. Instead of two vampires screaming, I now had eight. Arms and hands shot up to shield their eyes. I saw Leonora paw at her skin, faint blisters forming on the pale flesh. It wasn't touching them, but the presence of the holy light wasn't without effect.

"Turn it off! It burns. Turn it off!" she shouted, waving a hand in front of her as if she could push the light away.

I couldn't turn it off. Not yet. Because while my light was causing everyone pain, the two injured vampires had stopped convulsing. A few burns were better than having one's soul ripped out, at least in my opinion.

A spell takes seconds to disrupt, but I wasn't going to take any chances. I counted down from twenty then dismissed the passageways. Holding my breath, I watched the vampires on the floor, praying they wouldn't begin convulsing again.

"What the hell was that?" Leonora spat. Her teeth were dark with blood, and her eyes pale, as if she had cataracts. "If you ever do that again, I'll rip your throat out."

I took a step closer to Dario. He was examining the injured vampire. The others seemed to have suffered no worse than blistered skin after proximity to my blessed pathway. "I had to break the spell. The necromancer. He's using his spirit-summoning ritual to pull the souls from vampires and kill them."

"How can he do that?" Leonora asked.

"Technically you're dead. The spell works on the dead."

"I get that." The Mistress stood and gestured toward the vampire on the floor. He wasn't breathing, and with vampires I wasn't sure if that was a good thing or not. "But how? And why weren't all of us affected? How can he target just the injured ones?"

He couldn't. It was a different sort of targeting all together. "He needs a focus item in order to call forth a spirit. In theory, if he were powerful enough, he wouldn't need a focus and he could do a blanket summoning. If he did that, then all of you would have been affected. He's not that powerful. Somehow he managed to get a focus item from the vampires that had seizures."

"A focus item?" Leonora's eyes were beginning to lose their cloudy film, and her mouth was no longer bloody. "What, like hair or fingernail clippings?"

"That's not the foundational path of this spell. It needs an item of significance." I thought back to the collection I'd seen in the ruins of the Robertson family home. "A beloved stuffed animal, a favored piece of jewelry. There needs to be a significance on the part of both the caster and the spirit. Something the mage clearly identifies with the intended recipient of the spell, as well as something that the victim recognizes as their own."

The stronger the emotional tie to the victim, the better, but any ownership tie would do for a focus.

"The stolen items." Dario walked over to me. "Last week when that blood donor poisoned his vampires and we first found the symbol, there were items stolen from the house. For the most part they weren't items of value, so we thought it was just an annoyance act."

"Can you put together a list of everything stolen and which vampire the objects belong to?"

Dario exchanged a glance with Leonora. She nodded. "There might be one or two items that we miss. I don't always inventory my belongings every night, and I'm sure others don't either."

"That donor wasn't here long that night, so I'm thinking it would be items in plain sight—ones that would be noticed missing. And certainly a vampire would remember if a human physically assaulted him and took something from his pocket."

"Bridget's ring was taken," one of the other vampires spoke up. "She was really upset about it since it was the only item she had left from her human life."

Again, Dario and Leonora did some kind of wordless exchange. What the heck were they "talking" about?

"And him?" I motioned toward the vampire on the floor, the one who still wasn't breathing.

The woman still hovering over him looked up, her face strained. "A scrap of cloth. His shirt was torn in the fight that night. And Marcus said he lost an earring. We didn't think anything about it at the time, figuring it must have fallen out earlier when he was out hunting."

"We've all had something taken," Leonora spoke up, her face whiter than usual. "Every one of us."

"We need to tell her." Dario's eyes were fixed on Leonora. "She needs to know."

Know what? I had the feeling whatever I needed to know wasn't going to be something I was happy about.

The vampire Mistress glared at me. "That human stole the scepter. It was Aubin's from when he was turned a thousand years ago in France. We tortured the thief, killed him, but all he gave us was a copy of the symbol we asked you to research and information that some man had paid him to steal it as well as anything he could get his hands on. We weren't as worried about the other stuff. The scepter is the symbol of our *Balaj*. It signifies our family, our territory, and our leadership."

Scepter. Why couldn't they just use articles of incorporation like everyone else? "Please tell me it's just a pretty stick with a ball of glass on top of it."

Dario shook his head. "It's more than symbolic. Remember when you said there was an artifact in the Temple that would allow a necromancer to command an army of the undead? Well, this does the same."

"Let me get this straight, Aubin had an object that controls and commands an army of undead. He lugs this thing around Europe and across the ocean. Then your family, headed by Aubin, was cast out of your territory in Haiti and spent nearly a century roaming up the east coast of the U.S., trying to find a new spot to establish your *Balaj*. The whole time you had this scepter and didn't use it? How exactly does this particular artifact even work? Do you wave it at the other vampires and command them to get out? Do you bonk the other Master over the head with it?"

Leonora didn't seem to appreciate the dark humor I was trying to bring into the situation. "We can't use it without a magic user with enough strength to power it up. Aubin had seen it used once when he was young, and recognized the value of such an item. We're immortal, and with that comes patience. An object such as the scepter is worth holding onto, even if we only have the chance to use it once in a thousand years."

"But you did use it," I said.

Dario nodded. "When we came to Baltimore. There was a

magic user in Virginia who agreed to activate it and help us seize this territory."

I got where this was going. "In return for what? I doubt this magic user would have agreed to use a scepter to control undead without sizable payment."

Leonora sneered. "Of course. He wanted us to kill a rival, pay him a sum of cash."

"And he wanted the scepter," Dario added.

Of course he did. No magician worth his salt would walk on by an artifact like that. Heck, I wanted the scepter, too. Although as a Templar, it was kind of in my job description to collect items like this and take them to the Temple.

"He *didn't* get the scepter, obviously."

Leonora made a grunt sound that I took for a laugh. "We got our territory, then killed the mage."

I winced. I understood, though. A magic user wouldn't have given up trying to get the artifact, even if the scepter hadn't been part of the deal.

Dario glared at his Mistress, then turned to me. "We were starving, exhausted, we'd lost over half of our family members and were giving up hope."

All of that was history. What now mattered was that a powerful magical device was in the hands of a necromancer. "So why hasn't he used it before now?" I mused.

Leonora shrugged. "I don't know. Maybe he'd rather kill us than order us out of Baltimore."

I blinked realizing she was probably right. Russell wanted his family to have their revenge. Stealing the scepter was probably a way of ensuring that Leonora couldn't control the specters he summoned. Not only would that throw a huge monkey wrench into his plan, but he'd hate the thought that vampires once again controlled his family. But now?

"Exactly how does the scepter work?"

Russell had called forth murdered dead to attack the

vampires, and now he was using focus items to rip their spirits from their bodies. What was plan C? Because there had to be a plan C.

Leonora took a deep breath and looked around. "Dario, you stay here. This sort of thing needs to be discussed in private."

I didn't like the idea of being alone with a vampire that had threatened my life not two hours earlier, but Dario nodded and turned to attend to an injured vampire, leaving me few choices. If I wanted answers, I'd need to trust Leonora.

It was much easier to trust her on a full stomach with my sword in hand.

I followed her out of the room, through a maze of hallways and up a narrow set of stairs to a dark room. She flicked a match against the wall and lit a series of candles that lined the room. "This is my room. It was Aubin's before, and now it's mine."

"You sleep here?" It seemed odd that she would, given the public nature of this house and her vulnerable position during the daytime hours.

"On occasion. There was a time when we dared not rest above ground, when the killing rays of the sun weren't the only thing we feared."

The vampire walked around the room, the elaborate silver candelabras. The room was huge, windowless with brocade wallpaper in brown and gold. A giant four-poster bed sat against the far wall, fur pelts draped across the gold satin comforter. The room was rich, opulent and reminded me of Opal's comment about how Old World Leonora was—French Old World.

"Templars. I was Aubin's first offspring, turned over six hundred years ago. Usually over half the vampires in a *Balaj* are the children or direct descendants of the Master. Such a blood bond creates a tie of loyalty and ensures obedience. It's important, you see, for the *Balaj* to act as one. To be 'on the same page' as humans now say."

"What does this have to do with Templars? Or the scepter?" I didn't have the patience for this monologue while vampires downstairs died and a potentially dangerous magical artifact lay in the hands of a necromancer.

Leonora waved a hand at me.

"During your crusades, vampires were slaughtered by the thousands. It didn't matter if we broke the ridiculous human laws that shouldn't apply to us or not. Death came to any vampire who crossed paths with a Templar. In later centuries, heretics were less of a priority for the Templars and they began to hunt supernatural creatures with the purpose of ridding the world of them. Of us."

"Not all," I argued. "We no longer kill heretics, and we no longer blindly kill sentient beings simply because humans are part of their food chain."

She laughed, the sound musical and appealing. I suddenly saw Leonora without the leather, as the human she would have been in France six hundred years ago. "No, now you are the kingmakers. Don't deny it. You hold the knowledge and items of power that would let Templars rule the world if they so chose. Instead they choose to watch, picking who would suit their needs best, and ensuring those individuals rise to leadership positions."

I wondered what the hell she was talking about, and I asked her.

"Do not think to unseat me, Solaria Angelique Ainsworth. I know you favor Dario, that you tease him with the idea that you might someday consent to be his blood slave. If it comes to a battle of power between the two of us, he will die. I hold the loyalty of a majority in this *Balaj*. I am the eldest, the one with greater power."

"But you don't have the scepter." It was a stretch, but I figured these topics were somehow connected.

She swung around to face me, tendrils of black hair flying around her creamy shoulders.

"I can hold power even without the scepter. Do not think I will be so easily replaced by another of your choosing."

Oh good Lord. She thought *I* was some kind of king-maker. The idea was just as funny as me being the vigilante paladin of Baltimore.

"So the scepter makes the *Balaj* loyal to you? It enforces their obedience?"

There was a hint of fangs between her blood-red lips. She had to be upset if she was losing control like this. "I'd always been told that the scepter was for commanding armies of the undead. I never realized until a century ago that the undead it commanded weren't zombie humans or ghosts."

Leonora sat carefully in one of the wing-back leather chairs opposite the bed and motioned for me to take the other one. I did, careful to keep my sword at the ready. The room was romantic in a strange, Gothic kind of way and I wasn't sure that Leonora didn't have ideas beyond a private chat in mind, her preferences for soft blondes aside.

"None of us realized the power the scepter granted just through possession. We can't use it. No one can without magical powers and skill. Still, the one who owns it commands the loyalty and obedience of the *Balaj*."

"No one knew this?" It seemed inconceivable that they hadn't realized such a thing. How could they not know that their loyalty was magically enforced?

The Mistress shook her head. "No. We normally owe fealty to our sire. Vampires want a leader to follow, and automatically look toward the eldest and strongest. We thrive in groups with definitive lines of hierarchy. Lone vampires are vicious and quickly fall to human law enforcement or to other vampires. There was nothing to indicate that Aubin wasn't just an especially charismatic leader."

"But what happened? When did you realize otherwise?"

Leonora steepled her fingers under her chin. "Richmond. In order to secure the assistance of the magic user, Aubin had to leave the scepter with him. A few days later dissention began. Older members of the *Balaj* began to question Aubin's judgement and leadership. I was by no means the eldest among us at that point, but as Aubin's offspring, I knew him best. I also was the only one who knew about the scepter and that he'd needed to loan it out to a magic user."

"But Dario knows. And given that you were discussing it downstairs, others in the *Balaj* know, too."

She nodded. "Yes. When we defeated Aubin in the coup, we needed to steal the scepter from him. That gave us the strength to rebel—even those of us who were his offspring."

And now it was gone, and Leonora was facing a division in her ranks. She must be desperate to get it back, but that didn't explain the danger of such an item in Russell's hands.

"You said that Aubin made a deal with a mage to use the scepter in order to gain the Baltimore territory. What happened? What does the scepter do when a mage with the knowledge and power uses it?"

A smile flickered at the edge of Leonora's lips. "It commands armies of undead—vampire undead included. They'll fight for you, die for you, vacate a territory and kill each other for you. Whatever the magic user commands. We could all rise from our sleep and walk into the noonday sun if a mage holding the scepter commands it."

She stood and paced as I watched her and digested all this. They'd known the theft of the scepter and the magical symbol were related. No doubt that had been what they feared, not a group of spirits rising from their graves for vengeance. And that's why Dario had been so cagey about how they'd come across the symbol. I was a Templar, and if I knew about the scepter, I'd be duty bound to find it and haul it away to the Temple—far away from vampire hands. But how had Russell found out about the scepter, and why had he waited this long to use it?

"Tell me about this guy in Richmond. Do you know anything about his magical specialty? His training and abilities? What exactly happened to the *Balaj* that used to call Baltimore home?"

She sighed, her shoulders dropping as she exhaled. "I believe he was involved in demonology, but beyond that I'm not sure. Aubin was not specific about what happened to the vampires in Baltimore. We made our deal, then arrived to find the city cleared and ready for our occupancy. Later a group of Renfields were sent to Richmond to dispatch the magic user."

So Russell might turn the vampires upon themselves, cause them to commit mass suicide, or something else. No doubt it would take him some time to learn how to use the scepter. How long, was anyone's guess. I'd need to research further, as I assumed Russell had been researching. The difference was that I had the advantage of an entire Templar library at my disposal, and I wasn't up every night summoning the dead.

No, I was up every night protecting vampires, then working during the day at the coffee shop. Russell was probably fresh as a daisy compared to me right now. I'd proven his summoned spirits could be conquered. I'd proven I could block his attempts to rip the souls from living vampires. I'd given him no choice but to turn his attention toward the scepter now. All my efforts to block the necromancer and corner him into a compromise may have led us into an even worse position.

"I'll need to do some research, then see if I can't come to a peaceable solution to the issue between you both."

Leonora stood. "Research all you want, but this magic user will be dead by next sundown. And mark my words, even if I do not recover the scepter, I won't yield my position as Mistress of this *Balaj*. If you want to live, stay out of our affairs. And stay away from Dario."

CHAPTER 29

J'd half hoped that Dario would drive me back to my apartment, but it was Sarge that dropped me off in the early morning hours.

Leonora had warned me off, but I didn't take threats lightly. Actually I pretty much ignored threats. I'd like to blame it on the Templar heritage, but in truth I was just really stubborn. I was going to see this whole thing out, although I was going to try my darnedest to stay out of their internal power struggles. As for staying away from Dario…I got the feeling he'd be staying away from me.

Which was probably for the best, given my somewhat obsessive thoughts lately when it came to the vampire. I had fledgling friendships. I needed to start dating, to get out there with human men and take my mind off this unsuitable vampire one.

But in the meantime, I had a scepter to recover and a necromancer to stop. Or possibly kill. I winced at the thought. I'd never killed anyone before, which was odd given the militaristic nature of our order. We used to kill, to protect the Temple, to guard the Pilgrims on the Path. Wasn't this the same? If I considered the Vampires to be somewhat innocent Pilgrims, then Russell was a threat whose death was justified.

Then why did I feel so sick about it? I envisioned my sword, tearing through flesh and bone and shuddered. He was a human being. Someone who had been wronged and who truly believed he was doing the right thing. He wasn't a monster, even if his actions were murderous and his mission misguided.

Wasn't he my Pilgrim too? Just one on the wrong path?

I picked up my phone and stared at it a moment, remembering my last conversation with my father. Something about Jacob and Esau. I needed to speak to someone, but I was reluctant to get another obscure biblical lesson in return. Mom was out of the question, so that left me with Roman or Athena. Or Essie.

I dialed, thinking again how odd it was that my century-old great grandmother had a cell phone.

"Hello? Aria, is that you?" she screamed into the phone.

"Yes, Gran. It's me. I need some advice."

Her laugh roared through the phone line and I couldn't help but smile. "So you call me? Your old witch of a granny? I hope it's about that gorgeous vampire boy, because you know what my advice is going to be."

Yeah. Bring him home for Essie to play with. Poor Dario. "No, it's about a necromancer." I told her the story as succinctly as I could, amazed that she remained silent and attentive through the whole tale.

"Quite a pickle you're in, my girl," Essie said at the end. I was relieved that she *had* in fact been listening and not dozing off in the middle of my story as I'd feared. "If I were in your shoes, I'd lop off that Russell-man's head and ride off into the sunset with the smoking-hot vampire."

I rolled my eyes. That was Essie. But once you got past her shocking statements, she usually had some good ideas. And they weren't couched in biblical stories, or lectures about how I needed to take my Oath. "Thanks, Gran, but what would Tarquin do?"

Essie snorted at the mention of her husband, the renowned Templar and my great-grandfather. "Tarquin would cut his head off, too. Then he'd decapitate all the vampires after he killed the necromancer. Much as I loved the man, he was known to use extreme violence as a solution to any problem."

Great. "I don't want to kill Russell. He's not really a bad man, he just is misdirected. He's on the wrong path."

"And there you have your answer, my girl." Essie's voice was softer, lower. It rang through me. "You're not me, and you're not Tarquin. And much to your mother's dismay, you're not the rest of your family either. You're Aria, and you need to come up with a solution that lets you sleep at night. Put the man on the right path so he's no longer a threat to your other Pilgrims."

"He won't go. I've tried to talk to him. I've told him these vampires are blameless in the deaths of his family. He still sees them as monsters that he needs to get rid of."

"Sometimes words don't work, Aria. Sometimes to change a man's mind, you need to smack him upside the head—preferably with a hard, blunt object. When men have their emotions involved, they won't see reason until you drive it through their thick skulls."

I'd had an idea nudging at the back of my mind for a while, but it was so risky and the price of failure so high that I didn't want to consider it. But if it came to a choice between Risky Idea and Killing the Necromancer, Risky Idea won.

"Thanks, Gran. I love you."

"I love you too, Aria."

I stared at my cell phone a moment after hanging up. I had a lot to do. In order to make this work, I had to remove all of Russell's other options, to herd him down a path like a cow in a chute. And as suspicious as he was, I knew I was going to need help.

After a quick nap I began researching the scepter and what I found wasn't comforting. In addition to controlling vampire undead, it also held dominion over ghouls, zombies, ghosts and more. Grimoires that detailed the spells and ceremonies needed to activate the scepter were under tight magical security at the Temple, but that didn't mean other documents weren't out in the public. I read the brief overviews of the rituals and they weren't simple by any means. If this thing was what I thought, it held great power—but it was only as powerful as the mage who held it.

If it were just in my possession I'd have an affinity toward, an appeal to the dead. Those specters wouldn't harm me and would be open to suggestions I made. Vampires would feel an urge to protect me and not want to harm me. Other than that, nada. With the correct spells, I could raise and command armies, and rule the world. With shitty partial spells…who knows? Russell might be using it to enhance his command of the undead he raised—which meant he'd be able to bring up thousands of spirits and direct them to kill. I'm not sure he had the mojo or the knowledge to be able to command and kill the vampires. Although I wasn't sure.

The guy in Richmond had the knowledge and power. It wasn't a terrible stretch to imagine Russell might, too.

I closed the books and packed up my supplies, swinging by three fast food restaurants on my way to the cemetery so I could decimate their supplies of salt packets. With my pockets loaded and my sword in hand, I once again walked through the big metal gates and across the neat rows of headstones toward the Robertsons' graves. They stood out, rectangles of dirt in a field of thick green. Little shoots of grass were beginning to sprout through burlap and straw covering the dirt.

With the tip of my sword, I slashed a narrow line across the symbol on the grave markers. It glowed red then faded, leaving the stone unmarked. Any further magical marks would slide right off the granite.

But that wasn't enough. There were other ways to raise the dead. I needed to make sure that didn't happen. One by one I circled the graves with salt, blessing the dead as I went. Then I kneeled at the foot of each grave, my sword hilt like a cross against my bent head.

"Yeraz minch'yey shep'vori zangeri."

The salt sizzled like acid. The brown rectangles of disturbed dirt smoked, singing the sprouts of new grass. I felt a moment of guilt that I'd set the growth back a few months, that grass would be unlikely to cover these graves again until spring. But at least these souls would be at rest.

These five graves were the most important of all. I'd just blocked Russell in a way that would hurt his heart. Yes, he could raise other victims of vampires to do his revenge or use other spirits with the aid of the scepter, but nothing would give him a sense of satisfaction, of closure like having his own family deliver justice.

I'd taken that from him. He'd be even more pissed. Which would mean more spirits, a doubling up of efforts on his part. I was squeezing him into a corner and I wasn't sure how this was going to end. A cornered fox needs an out. I just needed to make sure the out I gave him lead in the direction I wanted him to go.

Pulling the sheets of paper out of my pocket I looked at

the fifty-five other names. I could salt graves all day and not finish by nightfall, and with the scepter it wouldn't really matter. I'd need to bless and salt every damned grave in the city. And ones outside the city. This was insane. I couldn't spend all my time trying to stay one step ahead of Russell, especially when the vampires planned to kill him tonight.

I'd laid his family to rest. It was time to skip the others and go straight to the finish. My meeting with Janice wasn't until noon, so I went by the Robertson family house. It was a long shot that Russell would still be storing his memorabilia there after our last discussion, but I thought I'd try anyway. If I could grab the focus items, somehow manage to luck out and find the scepter, I'd be ecstatic.

The old house looked the same, but I could tell something was very different from the last time I'd been here. Sure enough, the magical wards were down on the stairway, but there was one in place in the master bedroom—a trap. It was crude and loud. If I had been blind enough to trip it, it would have hurt me but not killed me. And I would have had to have been truly blind not to notice the pattern painted on the floor or the airsoft pellets poised to explode out of a bag when tripped.

Russell was warning me off, and it gave me some hopes as to his salvation that he didn't want to kill me either.

I disabled the trap, and searched the room, just in case he'd left some sort of clue behind about where he'd moved his base of operations to. Another former family home? Where he was currently living or working? I had a few more hours to check between my meeting with Janice and my late shift tonight.

Trying to be as stealthy as I could with a sword strapped to my back, I headed back to the pizza shop, asking about Russell's schedule. He'd quit, and the manager was reluctant to give out any personal information on the necromancer. Luckily for me, his coworkers weren't so circumspect.

"Here." The waitress handed me a slip of paper with two addresses written on it. "He also worked at the Citgo part-time and may still be there. This is the address he gave for his tax papers."

I smiled up at her, reading her name tag. Tania was about my mother's age, with a maternal figure and a liberal amount of gray in her black hair. Lines creased her cheeks when she smiled.

"If I see him, I'll let him know you've got news about his family. I hope it's good news." The creases remained as her smile turned into a worried frown. "He was always talking about them, how they died when he was young. I hope what you have to tell him will let him live the rest of his life in peace, cause he sure hasn't had much of that to date."

I hoped so, too. The Citgo was close enough to hit up before my meeting with Janice, but the other house would have to wait. This time when I drove there, I left my sword in the car. Russell could see past the look-away spell, even if the other humans couldn't, and I didn't want him thinking this was an attack. It wasn't. It was a sneaky, herd the necromancer where you want him, meeting.

Russell stiffened when he saw me, his hand going to a talisman around his neck. I raised my hands, showing him that I was free of both physical and magical weapons. "I just want to talk," I told him.

"I have nothing to say to you." His eyes narrowed. "You protected them. They're monsters. How could you do that?"

"They're no more monsters than you or I. I told you, the ones who did this to your family are dead. By continuing your attacks, you're proving yourself to be no better than they were. How can you think that killing an entire *Balaj* makes you any different than the vampires who massacred your family in their home?"

"They prey on people. They kill people."

"We kill for food, too." I had a sudden vision of a cattle uprising—cows storming the city and killing every human in their path. Even the vegetarians.

"Animals don't have the same emotional capacity that we do. You know what they did to me, how can you even think of defending them?"

This was going nowhere. Time to bash Russell over the head. "You will either cease your attacks on the vampires, or I will be forced to kill you. Your choice."

He sneered. "You? A Templar? You're going to kill another human to protect a bunch of bloodsuckers who prey on humanity without remorse?"

"They are Pilgrims on the Path. You are interfering with their progress. Therefore, their plea for help is more righteous than yours."

He threw up his hands, obviously just as frustrated with my stance as I was with his. "You won't kill me. I've been studying since I was ten. I've dedicated my life to the magical arts, where you've spent yours drinking martinis by the pool and studying Latin."

I winced, because his words struck close to the mark. All the military training and the practice with weapons had all been somewhat academic. It was like rich guys who took fencing to spar with other rich guys, and never saw combat. At twenty-six, enlisted soldiers had already experienced war up close and personal, where I was still sparring and slicing up practice dummies.

And honestly, who fought with Bastard Swords anymore? Or rode a charger in full plate with a lance at the ready? Yeah, I knew how to use modern weaponry, but my lifetime of practice had been geared toward a fighting style long out of date. We were relics. We were rich, entitled, aloof snobs drinking martinis by the pool, confident that no one would attack the Temple, that we no longer had Pilgrims on the Path to guard.

It was an obscene life, and I was embarrassed by it. Which was the reason I was here in Baltimore, working a minimum wage job. It was why I was a Templar but not a Knight. It was why I'd refused to take my Oath—an Oath that was a mockery of the holy mission we'd once been charged to uphold and defend with our lives.

But Russell was wrong if he thought I was without skills. And he was dead wrong if he thought I wouldn't put away my reluctance to kill another being and end his life. He might be a Pilgrim, but he most definitely was on the path to hell.

"I will continue to guard them every night, while you waste your precious resources attacking the impenetrable defense my faith provides. And I *will* ensure that those I return to the grave are only awakened by the trumpet of Judgement Day."

He narrowed his eyes. "There are a lot of dead in this city—more dead than you can possibly counter in your lifetime. And as for the vampires, you can't protect them all. They eventually have to go out to feed, to be away from you, and I'll have them. I've got focus items from nearly half of them, and I'll keep at it until they die. One by one I'll rip the souls from their rotted corpses."

"And your backup plan? You told your thief to steal the scepter. You knew exactly what the vampires had in their possession."

He smirked. "Just taking it is revenge enough. They'll turn on each other soon enough. If not, I'll make them kill each other."

I sensed his bluff. He was skilled, but not that skilled.

"The best you can do with that scepter is make them fight over the television remote."

"I think I can do more than that. It's a three pronged attack. I'm not going to give up until they're all dead, every last one of them.

This had to stop. Now.

"You won't live long enough to manage a prolonged attack. I found you today. I'm sure the vampires have people who are tracking your every move. They plan on killing you at sundown, and if they don't I will. Give this up or you'll be seeing the inside of a coffin by the time the sun rises."

Doubt flickered in his eyes. I leaned forward to press my advantage home. "I found the tracker you put on my car, Russell. You're not the only one with skills. I'm more than a Templar, and if you think I can't find you or that I'll hesitate to end your life, you're mistaken."

"You wouldn't." There was a tremble underneath the strength of his voice that betrayed his fear. "Kill me and the police will have you on death row. I'm not the only one who notices the sword you carry around."

I smiled, watching him take a step backward. "I wouldn't kill you Templar-style. No, when you least expect it, a car will fly around a corner and flatten you. Or a freak wind-storm will blow a tree on your head. Maybe a chicken bone will stick in your throat, or an unknown food allergy will take you out." I leaned closer. "Who knows? Ebola. Avian flu. Anthrax. Small pox. Maybe I'll send a demon after you."

"You're a Templar," he stuttered, his face ashen.

"I'm not a Knight," I replied smoothly. "I haven't taken my Oath, and I dealt with a very nasty demon last week that would love nothing more than to tear a human apart and take his soul. End your attacks and leave this city right now, or you'll die."

I turned around to leave, hoping my bluff worked. Yes, I

would kill him if I had to, but I was hoping that wouldn't be necessary. And if it was, I certainly wasn't going to mess with that demon who'd shown up in Vine's place ever again.

I had one more card to play if my threats didn't dissuade him. And if that didn't work, it was time to scare the living crap out of him with a horrible case of magical food poisoning.

And if that didn't work…well then, Russell really left me no other choice.

CHAPTER 30

Janice bought me lunch again. I was beginning to really like this reporter woman. I scarfed down my burger and fries like the starving woman that I was, grateful that I wouldn't need to start my shift at the coffee shop with an achy, growling stomach.

"This is a pretty fantastic tale you're telling me." The reporter shook her head. "I can't exactly report that the surviving member of a murdered family is into the occult and siccing his dead family on the family of the vampires who killed his loved ones, or that he has a scepter that might allow him to command an army of zombies."

I was just grateful that she didn't have me locked up in the loony bin as soon as I began telling her of necromancers and vampires, and that she was still willing to pay for my lunch. "Maybe if you say it's the family of the gang that killed his loved ones forty years ago?"

It made me wonder if the vampires were tax-paying citizens in the eyes of the U.S. government. Not that it mattered. Janice would want to hide the identity of the "gang family" to protect them from other retaliation and harassment. To the vampires, remaining out of the public eye was important. The fewer who knew about them, the safer they'd be while they rested, vulnerable, during the day.

She tapped a French fry against her bottom lip. "That would work, but what Russell is doing is a crime. He's killing people…well, sort-of people. The police are going to want to get involved, and being jailed for contempt of court because I refuse to reveal my sources isn't in my long-term career plans."

"You'll need to push it more as a human interest piece. Survivor tracks down the family of the people that killed his family."

"Don't get me wrong, that sort of thing is golden. People love these kind of follow-up stories that deal with karma and grief. I'm just worried that I won't have much of a story without the unbelievable supernatural angle."

"Trust me, there will be one hell of a story either way."

She slapped two twenties down on the table. "Then I'm in. I'm trusting you on this one, because I'm hoping you'll come to me with other information in the future."

"Absolutely. It might be weird stuff, and you'll need to figure out how to spin it, but I'll give you the heads up."

Janice checked her phone. "Then I better get going. It seems Russell Robertson, a.k.a. Findal, is eager to meet with me in regards to information I have regarding the murder of his family."

My heart raced. This was all coming together, but it seemed too easy. I knew better. The big risk was in what was going to go down tonight. I wasn't sure how Russell was going to react. Heck, I wasn't sure how Dario was going to react. Screw the other vampires, it was him I was worried about. If he hated me for this, if things went horribly wrong, I'd have made myself an enemy instead of repairing a friendship.

"I'll see you tonight," I told Janice as she rose from the table.

"I wouldn't miss it for the world," she replied.

* * *

MY SHIFT at the coffee shop seemed to crawl along. Every few minutes I was checking the windows, watching the sun slowly creep toward the horizon.

"Think I can get out of here right at nine?" I asked Petie. "Or earlier?"

He smirked. "Got a hot date?"

"Yeah." It was easier to let him think I was running off to meet an eager boyfriend. In reality I was worried about my ability to get to the north end of Baltimore before sundown. Nine would cut it close—too close. And my arriving late would spell disaster. I'd texted Dario giving him the heads-up, but he wouldn't get the message until nightfall.

"I don't know, Aria. You've switched shifts and come in late a bunch of times this past week."

I had. It was totally not like me. How did superheroes do this? Somehow they managed to juggle their secret-identity jobs and crime fighting. Yeah, Spidey got chewed-out a lot at the newsroom, but his boss was a total ball buster. Did others have this problem? Did Superman have to call in to change shifts because Lex Luthor was bombing the city?

Batman. Now that guy had it good. Wealthy, with a butler to take care of all the loose ends. That could be me if I took my Oath, if I accepted the money my parents had been sticking in my other checking account. But then I wouldn't be *me*, I'd be a martini-by-the-pool Templar, not one who would face down a necromancer to protect a group of vampires. And hopefully protect the necromancer, too.

Leonora would be thrilled to see him dead, and she would no doubt accomplish that if she had a few more hours.

Hopefully I could avoid that scenario. Hopefully I could ensure the vampires were left in peace, and Russell lived the rest of his natural life with a soul at rest. Somehow that meant a lot to me. Russell locked in a jail cell, or with anger festering inside him for another forty years wasn't the solution I wanted.

Because he was a Pilgrim, too. He just needed a course redirection.

Petie waved a hand to the door. "Fifteen early, girl. But only because I'm a fan of true love."

I smiled. I loved my coworkers, really I did. "Thanks. You're the best."

"Huh. Just remember that when it's Secret Santa time. And I like cognac, classic vinyl, and wool socks."

I winked. "Got it."

Quarter of nine I busted out the door and revved the engine of my little Toyota, hoping there weren't any cops as I sped through the city. I didn't encounter any delays, and pulled up outside the neat brownstone row house as the sun tinted the sky pink and lavender. The same woman rocked on the porch. I took the steps two at a time, and paused to greet her.

"Whatcha want, hon?"

I got a feeling that her "hon" was more local speech than any kind of endearment. "I need to talk to Bella's guardian."

She lifted an eyebrow and shook her head. "The girl ain't fed yet. Won't be safe for you to enter until she's got a full belly, if you know what I mean."

Crap, I'd totally forgotten Bella's lack of control. Dario should be arriving as soon as the sun went down, but I was hoping to move things along before then, just in case he thought my idea was horrible, or too dangerous. Which it probably was.

"When does her donor for the evening arrive?"

The woman nodded, and I turned, watching as a young man sauntered toward us, grinning as he joined us on the porch.

"I'm Mario, here to meet with Bella?"

Elaine shot me a quick glance. "Can you take Mario in and entertain him until Bella is ready? There's wine and other refreshments in the parlor."

I went in, feeling a bit like a Madam in a whorehouse. Mario followed, his swagger indicating his complete ease with the whole process. The table did hold wine with several glasses, as well as…other things.

"Help yourself," I told Mario as I uncorked the wine. He did help himself—to a jalapeno popper and a line of what looked like cocaine to me. My only experience with drugs beyond Tylenol was what I'd seen on television, so I wasn't sure what the white powder was. I remembered Sarge and Dario mentioning that donors were provided with drugs, and that with the less restrained vampires, like Bella, they helped numb the pain of the experience.

"You done this before?" I asked the man as I handed him a glass of wine. Was it okay to drink wine with a line of coke? I assumed so since the guy practically downed the contents of the glass in one gulp. If he died tonight, I wasn't sure whether to blame Bella or his careless disregard when it came to mixing chemical substances.

"Screwed some handicapped woman? Yeah. I mean, they got needs and I need the money. No different than anyone else, except it's usually wrapped up in under an hour."

I held back from a massive eye roll. This guy was an arrogant asshole, but even a cocky gigolo didn't deserve to walk into a situation like this blindly. "You know she can get a little over excited?"

Mario snorted. I wasn't sure if he was laughing or it was from the drugs. "Yeah, sure. Guy did her last night. She weighs all of ninety pounds, and is a real looker. A little rough stuff doesn't bother me, especially with what they pay. Plus there's a woman that watches and makes sure nothing gets out of hand. They pay extra for the audience, ya know?"

Oh God. What an idiot. "She bites."

This time he did laugh. "I've been tied up, spanked, got it in the backdoor with all sorts of stuff. Trust me, some hot young thing's love bites are nothing compared to deep-throating an eighty-year-old guy in the back of a minivan."

He had a point.

"True. Just making sure you know."

Mario tilted his head, taking another drink of wine. "What, you her sister or something? I promise I'll show her a good time. I've got a reputation to protect, you know. Plus with this kind of money, I'd like to make sure they call me back."

In six weeks, once he was medically cleared to donate another pint of blood. This was all on the up-and-up, just as Dario had said, just as Sarge had said. Mario got what he wanted. Bella got what she needed. And someone stood by to make sure nothing got out of hand. The fact that it was kind of icky for a vampire trapped in a fourteen-year-old body to be getting nightly services from a male prostitute bothered me. So did the fact that Bella mentally was far younger than fourteen with the brain damage that had occurred between her death and rebirth. Whatever. Her body had needs, and Mario seemed happy to provide for the compensation offered.

"She should be up soon." I eyed the fading light outside

the window. The sun was down, the sky a million shades of grey in that twilight space between day and night.

"Cool." Mario did another line and poured himself a second glass of wine, popping a pill with the beverage. Good grief, that guy was going to be freaking comatose by the time the vampire was awake—unless that little blue pill was for something else.

A woman walked into the room, starting in surprise as she saw me. "Aria? What are you doing here? Is Sarge with you?"

"No." I smiled, trying to look relaxed in this very awkward situation. "I texted Dario to let him know I was coming, so he'll probably be here soon. I need to speak to Bella as soon as she's finished…ummm, with Mario here."

The man in question grinned, puffing his chest out. "My girl ready?"

"Should I just hang here?" I asked. Not that they were expecting me to watch. Although I'm sure Mario wouldn't mind tacking on extra for the viewing.

But should I watch? It would be a rare opportunity for me to see a vampire feed, especially one who had very little control. Would there be a risk to me? Would I be able to watch the process objectively? And more to the point, was there actual sex involved, as Mario seemed to think there was? I know vampire victims always got an orgasmic rush from the process of giving blood. I'd assumed that for many vampires, sexual intercourse was part of the feeding ritual. Watching Bella take blood would be instructional, watching her hump a male prostitute was beyond what I wanted to experience.

Actually it was all beyond what I wanted to experience. Nope. Sitting this one out.

Mario left and I was grateful for either the silence of the participants or the excellent sound proofing of the house. I assume it was the latter. I was just finishing up my glass of wine when Dario slammed through the door

"No. Just no. I won't have you endanger her, or upset her that way."

I'd prepared for this conversation. "I'll be there to protect her, as will you. And you don't know that she'll be upset. She might not even recognize him. She might not remember anything about her human life. Actually if she does, it would help. Did you ever think that she might be glad to see someone she recognizes from her past? She's been surrounded by vampires for the last forty years."

"Then what about him? It's going to rub salt in the wound to see his older sister like this. It was Jean Marc's taking her as a blood slave that started the whole feud."

That was a strong possibility, but this was my last chance to try and get Russell onto a better path. "If so, then we'll have no other choice but to kill him. I'm hoping he'll see that you're not all like Jean Marc and Aubin. You tried to save his sister the only way you knew how. Your family has lovingly cared for her all these decades. That's got to make you humane in his eyes. If he can see just one of you as redeemable, then we might be able to salvage this situation without further bloodshed."

Dario rubbed a hand over his face. "He'll see her as a monster like the rest of us. He'll think we made his sister into a monster. Bringing her to meet him will be the same in his mind as Jean Marc killing her right in front of her father."

He might be right, but this was my chance to change Russell's mind. I glanced out the window. "We don't have time to argue. How long does it take Bella to feed?"

"Another ten maybe. It depends on if she wants to play first. She's hungry, but she's not always focused on getting the job done."

Great. I didn't need that visual. And I was worried about

the vampires back at Leonora's house. "Did everyone vacate Leonora's house?"

He nodded. "Not because Leonora is evacuating the place, but because they're off to hunt down your necromancer."

I caught my breath, wondering if everything I was doing tonight was for nothing. If the vampires had tracked down Russell, he could be dead before Bella finished her dinner. "Have they…do they know where he is?"

Dario shrugged, his eyes cold as they met mine. "Our humans interrogated the gang connections until we discovered where he worked and lived. Then we worked those angles. He might be dead, he might not. If he isn't, he soon will be."

Interrogated. I knew what that meant, knew very well that there had been a message sent about the price of betrayal. The vampires had cleaned house when they'd caught the blood donor/thief, but now that vampires had died…

"Please tell me you didn't kill the coworkers or neighbors."

Dario turned away from me. "Helpful and cooperative humans don't need to be killed."

I didn't like that answer, but I didn't have time to question the vampire further as Mario staggered through the room, pupils dilated and a smile fixed on his face. I could barely see the tiny marks on his arms and neck. It was time to go—and to pray that we'd get to Russell before Leonora did.

Bella's caregiver, a vampire I was finally introduced to as Suzette, sat with her in the back seat of Dario's SUV. The young vampire was fascinated by the car ride, making soft noises and pointing out the window as we passed buildings and parks. Her interest and animation gave me hope that this might actually work.

When we drove up to the block where the Robertsons had lived, she grew quiet, her hand touching the glass of the window. Dario pulled around to a side street and parked, and we made our way through the weed-choked back yards to the back entrance. Bella walked slowly, silently taking it all in. She went to a large oak, its mid-section rotted where a storm must have torn the tree in two. Looking up into the dead, bare branches, she made a rocking motion with her hand.

Swing? If she could remember her human life then maybe she could make a connection with Russell. She wouldn't be a monster to him if he saw that something remained in her of his sister, Shay.

We went inside and waited. Bella seemed disturbed by the presence of the vampires even though she knew them. She kept shooing them with her hands.

"Do you remember it here, Bella?" Suzette soothed the girl, rubbing her hands. "Did you eat breakfast at the kitchen table? Braid your doll's hair?"

Again the girl flicked her hands at the other vampire, scowling a bit. The two vampires obliged and watched Bella explore the room. She touched the shreds of wallpaper, moving room to room and making surprised noises as she ran her hands over everything. Her hands and clothing were filthy with dust by the time she plopped down on the kitchen floor. Hair falling forward over her shoulders, she dumped a handful of crayons from her pockets, wiped the dirt clear from the chipped linoleum and began to draw.

Suzette let out a breath. "She seems okay so far. Excited, maybe a little anxious, but okay."

Dario folded his arms across his chest. "I still don't like it."

I knew he was worried about Bella's emotional and physical wellbeing. Crossing my fingers, I sent up a quick prayer that all would be well.

And then a voice came out of the darkness. "Where is she?" I felt the creep of necromantic magic, sweet with the smell of rot. "Where is my sister? Give her to me and I will leave you in peace. You have my word."

Janice had come through. She'd told Russell that she'd found Shay, that all these years a gang had been holding her hostage, but that she was still alive. The hope and fear in the necromancer's voice gave me faith that this would all work out. He'd do anything to have a member of his family back, even give up his revenge. That was the first positive step toward compromise that he'd ever made.

"We can't give her back," Dario spoke up. "Her home is here. It's all she's known for the last forty years. She's happy here with those who love her and can take care of her special needs."

"Special needs?" Russell snarled. He still wasn't anywhere close enough for us to see, or close enough to see his sister who sat drawing on the floor. "She's an addict. Get her away from you vampires so she can detox and she'll be just fine."

"She's no longer a blood slave." I called out. "Russell, come meet your sister. I vow on the Order of the Templar Knights that this is a neutral space. No one will attack you."

There was a curl of smoke that rose into a wall of fog. The necromancer stepped from it and I blinked, amazed at how skilled he truly was.

"Shay?" His voice trembled, his eyes desperate as they looked down at the girl.

The young vampire continued to draw on the floor as if she didn't even hear him.

"Bella," Suzette said softly. "Bella, someone is here to see you. Someone from long ago."

The girl looked up at the vampire, then her gaze slid around the room, halting on Russell. She tilted her head, wrinkling her brow in confusion.

"Shay," the necromancer choked out. "What have they done to you? You look the same as you did forty years ago. And your hair..."

I guess Shay hadn't worn her hair in long tangled ringlets. The girl reached up a hand to pat her hair and smiled.

Smiled. With vampire fangs fully exposed.

I didn't wait for Russell to react. *"Argelap'akel Satani dzer-rk'y."* At my words a shimmering wall rose between him and the vampires, just in time to deflect a surge of flame and heat. Broken bits of cabinets caught fire, raining sparks onto the dry floor as they burned.

Bella screamed, scooting backward away from the fire, her eyes wild. Suzette knelt to comfort her, Dario snarled and stepped forward. Russell shot again. Fire bounced off my barrier, lighting up exposed bits of flooring. I gritted my teeth trying to hold my protective wall. Of course the wall wouldn't do us any good if the house burned down on top of us.

"Shay," Russell thundered. "You bastards turned her. You made her a monster."

I'll give Dario credit, he didn't even give me a side-eye I-told-you-so look. The vampire moved quickly to Bella's side. The girl rose, side-stepping Dario and flinging out a hand at her brother.

"No, Daddy. I love him."

We all froze. A chill ran up my arms. Her voice was husky and rough from disuse, but there was no mistaking her words.

"It's okay, Bella." Dario's voice was full of affection, love even. "No one is going to hurt you. And no one will take you away."

"Where is Jean Marc?" The young vampire swung her head from side to side, looking for the long dead vampire. "He loves me. Where is he?"

Did she not remember that he'd murdered her in front of her father? He hadn't loved her at all.

Dario shot me a look full of warning and shook his head. "He'll be here soon, Bella. I'll take care of you until he comes."

Shay turned to Dario, wrapping her arms around his waist before facing Russell once more. Tears filled her eyes, and began to spill down her cheeks. "I love him, Daddy. I'm waiting for him. He's going to come for me."

A forty-eight-year-old Russell probably did look a lot like his father had back when Bella had been Shay, a young girl sneaking out at night to meet a much older vampire lover.

She had loved Jean Marc. It was the foolish love of a fourteen-year-old girl for a man who would eventually kill her and toss her aside. The real tragedy wasn't Russell, it was Shay who had paid dearly for a mistake so many teenage girls make.

The fire died and I saw Russell staring, not at the girl, but at the picture she'd drawn in the dust. A family of six, all holding hands. On the outskirts stood a teenager with braids, removed from the rest of her family. The crudely drawn girl had a pair of fangs.

"Shay, it's me, Russell. I've grown up, but it's me."

She smiled, mouth full of sharp teeth, and pointed a foot at two identical little boys in her drawing. "Russy and Hector. Linc and Kendy. Mommy and Daddy." She pointed to the girl outside the group and added sadly, "And Shay."

She knew. Bella might not remember everything, might have a terribly reduced mental capacity, but she *knew* she was different from the human she'd been. And that difference made her no longer part of her family—a family she thought lived on without her.

All those years, had she waited for them to come see her, to find her? Had she assumed they hated her? That they considered her a monster just as Russell had called her?

"Shay," she said again, letting go of Dario's waist to rub the image of the vampire girl out with her shoe.

"No," Russell's voice was choked. "You're not gone. I thought you were dead. I didn't know, or I would have looked for you. I didn't know."

The girl looked sadly at him then placed her head on Suzette's shoulder. "Home. I want to go home."

The other woman stroked her hair. "Of course, dear."

I dismissed the protective wall and stared at Russell as he watched the vampires leave the house one at a time, Suzette and Bella with Dario guarding the rear. We stood in silence until I heard the cars start and was certain they'd left.

"That last vampire? The one she had her arms around? He's the one who turned her. He went back after Shay's lover had killed her. Dario is the one who tried to save her. She'd been dead so long that she's had brain damage, which evidently vampirism doesn't cure. The man who did this to your family, Jean Marc, is dead. There is no need for revenge."

"So for forty years they took care of her," Russell said, his voice shaky. "She was a stranger to them, a lowly blood slave, but they tried to save her and have spent decades making sure she's safe and healthy."

"More than that," I added. "She's happy. The woman with her, Suzette, is her caregiver. She makes sure Shay, now Bella, has regular meals and doesn't harm her human donors. They watch movies, color, make brownies, paint each other's nails. That vampire has dedicated her life to taking care of Shay. Do you see how not all of them are monsters? By killing them, you'd be killing Shay once again, and killing the woman who has become like a mother to her as well as the man who defied his Master to save her."

His shoulders slumped. I know this was all so much for

him to process, but finally Russell Robertson was a Pilgrim on the Path.

"The vampires have agreed not to retaliate, even though you have killed dozens of their family. In return, I need to collect all of their focus items. And the scepter."

Especially the scepter. It was more than a pretty ball on a stick, and it shouldn't be in the hands of a necromancer, even a reformed one.

"Okay. I'll take you to where I have them stored." Russell looked once again at the picture drawn in the dust. "Do you think she…?"

"I think she would love pictures and letters from you, even supervised visits."

He nodded and I saw the tears gather in his eyes. "Maybe I will. Do you think they *would* allow visits? She's all I have left, my only sister, even if she is different, she's still my sister."

I wasn't sure after tonight what I'd be able to talk Dario into, but I'd try. "I'll ask." I looked at Russell, a grown man crying as he stared at a picture in the dust, No matter what, I'd make it happen for him, and for Bella, who needed to keep a piece of her lost humanity in memory if she was ever going to remain sane as a vampire.

CHAPTER 31

Ibarely made it down to Middleburg without slipping into unconsciousness. Yeah, I could have slept through the night and made this trip the next day fully rested, but I hadn't wanted to spend any more time with the scepter in my presence than necessary.

There had been negotiations, all conducted at the neutral territory of a multi-story parking garage. Leonora had been unwilling to budge both on the scepter and lack of punishment for Russell. I'd needed to wave my sword around a bit to convince her to play ball. Actually I think it was less my sword waving and more the fact that the game was up. Once Templars are aware of an artifact, they are relentless in their efforts to retrieve it and secure it in the Temple. Even if she had walked away with it tonight, she wouldn't have held it for long.

Not that any of them had a chance. I'd already made a phone call. If I didn't seize the artifact, a whole group of Templars would mount up and trample all over Baltimore to retrieve it. The Order might not give two cents about vampires, necromancers, or foolish non-Knights flirting with the idea of becoming a blood slave, but they took the artifact-in-The-Temple part of their oath very seriously.

And both Leonora and Russell knew it. Now that the scepter was out of the closet, so to speak, the Knights wouldn't rest until it was secured with all the other magical booty.

The scepter itself wasn't quite what I'd expected. It was long, with an S-shaped handle and a head that looked like a fist. A Ruyi, a ceremonial object in Chinese folklore that symbolized power and luck. I'd not asked Leonora for a description of the scepter, and had just assumed it was of Egyptian origin.

Would the *Balaj* fall apart without the unifying effect of the scepter? Time would tell.

I pulled down the tree-lined driveway to our family home, unsurprised to see the lights still on. Even at two in the morning, Mom was awake and doing crossword puzzles in the kitchen. I lurched in and smacked the boxed scepter down on the island's marble counter. My mother didn't even flinch at the loud crack noise.

"Here it is," I slurred, trying to form the words through my exhaustion. "Please secure this and ensure it arrives safely at the Temple."

I expected a snarky comment about how if I was a Knight, I could take it to the Temple myself, instead Mom tapped the pencil against her lip. "What's a four letter word with the clue 'Celeste Aida'?"

I smiled. In spite of her mighty sword arm, Mom was a bit of a puzzle addict. I think it's one of the things that initially drew her and Dad together.

"Aria." Celeste Aida was a romanza from the first act of the opera Aida.

She nodded, her pencil scraped against the paper. "Are

you planning on finally taking your Oath, Solaria Angelique Ainsworth?"

She knew the answer to that one. "No."

Again, she tapped the pencil against her lip, not quite hiding their upward curve. "Then you'd best be going. I believe your shift at the coffee shop starts in six hours."

Yes, it did. I turned to leave and halted as Mom called my name.

"Good job, my daughter." That was all she said. It was all she needed to say. I left the house, got into my car and drove north, smiling the whole way.

* * *

NEVER MISS A NEW RELEASE. Sign up for e-mail alerts at http://debradunbar.com/subscribe-to-release-announcements/

<u>IMP WORLD NOVELS</u>

<u>The Imp Series</u>
A Demon Bound

Satan's Sword

Elven Blood

Devil's Paw

Imp Forsaken

Angel of Chaos

Kingdom of Lies

Exodus

Queen of the Damned

The Morning Star

With This Ring

* * *

<u>Half-breed Series</u>
Demons of Desire

Sins of the Flesh

Cornucopia

Unholy Pleasures

City of Lust

* * *

<u>Imp World Novels</u>
No Man's Land

Stolen Souls

Three Wishes

Northern Lights

Far From Center

Penance

* * *

<u>Northern Wolves</u>

Juneau to Kenai

Rogue

Winter Fae

Bad Seed

ACKNOWLEDGMENTS

A huge thanks to my copyeditors Kimberly Cannon and Jennifer Cosham whose eagle eyes catch all my typos and keep my comma problem in line, to Meredith Bond at Anessa Books for her formatting expertise, and to my brother, Frank, for lending me his Photoshop brilliance in cover and ad design.

Most of all, thanks to my children, who have suffered many nights of microwaved chicken nuggets and take-out pizza so that Mommy can follow her dream.